TOUCH-ME-NOT

———

TOUCH-ME-NOT

A MARTHA'S VINEYARD MYSTERY

CYNTHIA RIGGS

MINOTAUR BOOKS

A THOMAS DUNNE BOOK

NEW YORK

A THOMAS DUNNE BOOK FOR MINOTAUR BOOKS.
An imprint of St. Martin's Publishing Group.

TOUCH-ME-NOT. Copyright © 2010 by Cynthia Riggs. All rights reserved. Printed in the United States of America. For information, address St. Martin's Press, 175 Fifth Avenue, New York, N.Y. 10010.

www.thomasdunnebooks.com
www.minotaurbooks.com

Library of Congress Cataloging-in-Publication Data

Riggs, Cynthia
   Touch me not : a Martha's Vineyard mystery / Cynthia Riggs.—1st. ed.
      p. cm.
   ISBN 978-0-312-64871-8
   1. Martha's Vineyard (Mass.)—Fiction.   I. Title.
   PG3610.I394T60 2010
   813'.6—dc22

2010022127

First Edition: September 2010

10 9 8 7 6 5 4 3 2 1

FOR
DIONIS COFFIN RIGGS
POET
1898–1997

ACKNOWLEDGMENTS

One of an author's challenges is to think up original names for her characters. Fortunately, there are six names I didn't have to conjure up. Six real people bid at various auctions to have characters in my book named for them. Casper Martin won at the Vermont College of Fine Arts auction. Jim Weiss, Superintendent of Schools for Martha's Vineyard, won his prize at an auction held to fund the Edgartown School's class trip. Lucinda Chandler, famous on the Island for riding her recumbent tricycle cross-country from California to Florida, won at an auction to benefit Windermere, the Island's nursing and rehabilitation center, and at a second Windermere auction, Diana and Whit Manter bid and won. Hugo A. Blinckmann was not yet born when his grandmother bid at an auction for Sail Martha's Vineyard, which provides free sailing lessons to Island kids. Thanks to all from the organizations they helped and from me.

Thanks, too, to the members of my three writers' groups. I rely on every one of them to keep my writing coherent. Here they are, in alphabetical order: Lisa Belcastro, Charles Blank, Judy Campbell, Gerry Jackman Dean, Mike Ditchfield, Catherine Finch, Jeanne Hewett, Les Holcomb, Ed Housman, Elissa Lash, Paul Magid, Shirley W. Mayhew, Barbara Moment, Carolyn O'Daly, Nelson Potter, Amy Reese, Ethel Sherman, Sarah Smith, Valerie Sonnenthal, Susanna Sturgis, Ernie Weiss, Bonna Whitten-Stovall, Sally Williams. I hope I haven't forgotten any of you.

Thanks to Alvida and Ralph Jones who've gone over every one of my manuscripts, not once, but three times.

Most of all, thanks to Nancy Love, my agent; and Ruth Cavin, Editor, and Toni Plummer, Associate Editor, who work long and patient hours at Thomas Dunne Books, St. Martin's Press.

Thank you all.

TOUCH-ME-NOT

———

CHAPTER 1

From the bottom of the stairway, Victoria Trumbull called up to her houseguest, who'd dashed upstairs to her room after her shower, a towel wrapped around her, her hair still dripping.

"Don't plug your hair dryer into the guest room outlet, Nancy, the wiring is—"

At that point there was a blue flash from the bedroom, a loud *snap* and the smell of singed wires.

Nancy popped out of her room, towel askew. "I'm so sorry, Mrs. Trumbull."

"You don't need hair dryers on Martha's Vineyard," said Victoria with some asperity. "There's a good west wind. We don't waste electricity."

"I'm so sorry," Nancy said again. "What can I do?"

"Get dressed so I can check the damage," said Victoria, who, at ninety-two, was one-third the age of her ancient house and not quite twice the age of its electrical wiring. She looked at her watch. "It's almost five. I'll try to get the electrician before he leaves."

LeRoy Watts was finishing up his paperwork in his shop on Circuit Avenue in Oak Bluffs when the phone rang. Maureen, his office manager, had left for the day.

"Watts Electrical Supply. How can I help you?"

Victoria explained what had happened.

"Sure, I know that outlet under the window," said LeRoy,

tapping his pen on the side of his coffee mug. "You and I talked about replacing that old wiring."

"The outlet is partially melted, there's a foot-long plume of smoke on the wall above it, and the fuse blew."

"You've got circuit breakers, Mrs. Trumbull. Jerry Sparks replaced your fuse box last fall."

"Circuit breaker, then," said Victoria. "Would you please ask him to repair my guest's damage? I fail to understand why people use hair dryers on the Vineyard."

LeRoy paused. "I had to let Jerry Sparks go."

"That's a shame. He did excellent work."

"Yeah. But he had personal problems. I'll try to get to your place myself. Let's see." He shuffled through the papers on his desk and found the calendar that Maureen kept. "Best I can do is four days from now. Monday. That work for you?"

"Fine," said Victoria.

Victoria disconnected and, still feeling exasperated with Nancy and her hair dryer, went into the bathroom to see what damage her guest had done in there. She was about to turn on the light to look when the phone rang. She hustled to answer before the machine picked up. It was her granddaughter, Elizabeth.

"Hi, Gram. I'm calling from work. I need to pick up some stuff at the boatyard, and wondered if you'd like to come along for the ride?"

"Yes, of course. That would be lovely."

"I'll be there in fifteen minutes."

Victoria went back upstairs and told Nancy to move her belongings into the West Room, which was on a different electrical circuit. Nancy continued to apologize and assured Victoria she would never, never again use a hair dryer in her house.

Once Victoria had settled Nancy into the room across the hall, she went downstairs again to wait for her granddaughter. She slung her blue coat over her shoulders and stood at the top of the stone steps with her worn leather bag and the lilac-wood walking stick Elizabeth had carved for her. Victoria felt no need for the walking stick, but she didn't want to hurt Elizabeth's feelings by not using it.

It was a mild May day, with the scent of lilacs in the air. The top was down on Elizabeth's convertible. Victoria got into the passenger seat, feeling quite sporty. On the way to Vineyard Haven, she lifted her great nose to breathe in the sweet smell of spring, different at each turn in the road. New-mown grass, lilacs, winter-wet leaves pushed aside by green shoots. They crossed the bridge over Mill Brook and she caught the scent of ferns and skunk cabbage.

"We bought new lines for the harbor launch at the boatyard's marine store," explained Elizabeth, who worked as dockmaster in the Oak Bluffs harbor. "They spliced eye loops in the lines so we can simply drop a line over a piling without having to tie it each time."

"Splicing takes a bit of skill," said Victoria, who understood boats. "Who does the work?"

"Emily Cameron. She runs the computer at the boatyard store and splices most of the lines."

At the boatyard, they parked next to a black-hulled sailboat that was high up above them on a cradle. Inside the store, Elizabeth checked out the new lines while Victoria went around the partition that made a kind of office for Emily Cameron. Emily, a painfully shy young woman, could use a boost in her self-esteem.

"I wanted to tell you how impressed I am that you do the boatyard's splicing, Emily."

Emily blushed at the compliment. "It's nothing much." She turned back to her computer. She was a thickset girl with glasses and dark hair tied back in a ponytail. Long bangs touched the top of her glasses frame.

"You're working late, aren't you?"

"It's that time of year, Mrs. Trumbull." Emily looked up. "We're open until seven every night, getting ready for the season."

She smiled, and when Emily smiled, she could be almost attractive, Victoria thought. "How's your mother? We missed her at church Sunday."

"Much better, thanks. She's back at work. It was just a nasty cold."

Victoria was sympathetic. "Spring colds can be miserable. How's the job going?"

"Great. I love working here. Computers, boats." Emily lifted her hands, palms up, as if to say that's all anyone needed. She turned her chair away from the computer to face Victoria. "And, Mrs. Trumbull, I've got a boyfriend!" She blushed again.

"Wonderful. Who's the lucky man?"

"Jerry Sparks. He works at Watts Electrical Supply."

Victoria decided not to mention that she'd spoken to LeRoy Watts less than an hour before and he'd told her he'd fired Jerry Sparks. "Jerry did some work for me several months ago. He seems like a nice boy."

"He's wonderful, Mrs. Trumbull. We're celebrating our anniversary tonight."

"Anniversary?"

"We've been seeing each other for three weeks."

"Oh," said Victoria.

At that point, Elizabeth came around the partition, her arms laden with lengths of nylon line. "Nice job with the eye splices, Emily." She held up one of the loops in the soft line.

Emily pushed her glasses back into place. "I'll print out the paperwork for the harbormaster."

Paperwork in hand, Victoria and Elizabeth left the boatyard and drove to the harbor, where Elizabeth dropped off the lines, and they headed for home.

"You're kind of quiet, Gram. What's up?"

4

Victoria settled her coat under her before she answered. "Emily tells me she has a boyfriend."

"That's news all right. Who?"

"Jerry Sparks."

"That loser? What does she see in him?"

"He's quite a good electrician."

"When he's not high on something."

"I called LeRoy Watts this afternoon for a small problem," said Victoria.

"Electrical problem?" Elizabeth glanced at her grandmother with concern.

"Minor," Victoria assured her. "LeRoy is coming by on Monday to fix it."

"What happened?"

"Our guest used a hair dryer in the upstairs outlet."

"And tripped the circuit breaker," Elizabeth finished. "We need to have that room rewired."

"LeRoy's taking care of it. He told me he'd fired Jerry Sparks. I didn't know whether Emily knew or not. She seems very fond of him."

Elizabeth made a wry face. "Poor Emily. I don't think she's ever had a steady boyfriend before."

They'd reached the edge of the state forest and Victoria gazed at the silvery snags of dead pine trees, beautiful in an austere way. She mulled over the first lines of a poem she might write. A villanelle, with its interesting rhyme scheme, would lend itself to the starkness of the scene.

"Jerry Sparks is a leech," said Elizabeth, breaking into Victoria's thoughts. "Emily's naïve and not terribly bright, and he's taking advantage of her."

After he'd made a note to stop by Victoria Trumbull's on Monday to check that electrical outlet, LeRoy Watts prepared to leave for the day. It was a pleasant evening, a Thursday. Weekend coming up. Maybe he'd go fishing on Saturday. The stripers were running at South Beach.

The back door of the shop slammed.

Heavy, unsteady footsteps trudged into the showroom from the back entrance. LeRoy smiled. One of his sons pretending to be Godzilla or something. He looked up and his smile faded.

"So. It's you, Sparks. What are you doing here? I told you I don't want to see you again."

Jerry Sparks's voice was slurred, the pupils of his eyes were tiny black dots. He was wearing a grimy knitted headband of an indeterminate color and an equally grimy green hooded sweatshirt. "I want my job back, man."

LeRoy retreated to the counter. "Sorry, Sparks. I warned you. No drugs."

"C'mon, man," Sparks whined. "I need money." He edged farther into the showroom. "Taking my girl out tonight."

The one-way traffic on Circuit Avenue moved slowly past the shop. The scent of lilacs wafted into the showroom through the open back window. LeRoy, who usually noticed such things, watched his visitor instead.

"I want my job back."

LeRoy opened the top drawer of the file cabinet next to the cash register. "Look at you," he said with disgust. "You stink. Pissed in your pants."

"I'm broke. I'll stay off the stuff."

"Get out, before I call the cops."

Sparks held out a hand. "A loan. Couple hundred? Pay you back Wednesday."

"Get out." LeRoy reached for the phone on the wall.

Sparks sobered. "Calling the cops?"

"Right," said LeRoy.

"You do that. Guess what I'm telling them." Sparks grinned suddenly.

"What are you talking about?"

"Go on, call. Bet they'd like to know what I know. Bet your wife would like to see what I've got." Sparks bared his teeth.

LeRoy set the phone on the counter. "I said, what are you talking about?"

"Thought you had a secret?" Sparks jammed both hands into the pockets of his jeans and thrust out his pelvis. "Go ahead. Call the cops. I'll tell them a thing or two."

"You're crazy. The cops going to believe some drugged-out loser I fired? Or me?" LeRoy pointed to his chest. "A guy who runs a business. Who, hey?"

Sparks fished a cell phone out of his sweatshirt pocket. "I'll show them." He opened up the phone and held it above his head. "Documentation." He grinned. "Now, how about a loan?"

"What've you got there?" Leroy held out his hand.

"No you don't." Sparks put the cell phone back into his pocket. "Insurance, that's what." He patted the pocket. "Downloaded the pics onto my computer, too. Never can tell when you might need extra insurance."

"You're bluffing."

"Think so?" Sparks laughed. "You know what you know. And I know what you know. And the cops would like to know what I know that you know. Go ahead. Call." Sparks slouched forward, closing the space between them. "And what do you think your wife will do when I show her, hunh?"

"Get away from me, asshole," said LeRoy.

Sparks's bleary expression changed. "What'd you call me?" He started toward LeRoy, hands raised in fists.

LeRoy reached into the drawer he'd opened.

Sparks brightened. He held out a hand, palm up. "Couple of hundred'll do it."

Instead of bills, LeRoy brought out a blocky metal weapon that looked like a ray gun.

Sparks lowered his hand and backed up. "A Taser? Where'd you get a Taser?"

LeRoy aimed the weapon at Sparks. "I'm counting to three. You better be out of here. One . . ."

Sparks held his arms up. "Don't Taser me!"

"Two . . ."

"Couple hundred . . . ?"

"Three!" and LeRoy pulled the trigger.

Instantly, Sparks slumped to the floor and landed on his back, his face contorted in pain. His body jerked, his stomach arched. His mouth formed a noiseless shriek.

"Don't you threaten me again, punk." LeRoy pulled the trigger again, and again, and again. "Get up and get out of here. Now. You stink up my place. Out." LeRoy came from behind the counter and kicked Sparks in the ribs. Sparks lay still, his face a ghastly mask.

"Faker!" shouted LeRoy, and kicked him again. "Get up, Sparks, and get out of here!"

Sparks didn't move.

LeRoy bent down over him. "Oh, shit!" he said. "Goddamn! Oh, shit!"

CHAPTER 2

What to do? Should he call the police? Tasers were nonlethal, weren't they? He hadn't actually killed Jerry Sparks, had he? He hadn't meant to. Better call the cops. He couldn't. It was illegal to own a Taser. And whatever Sparks claimed was on his cell phone . . . LeRoy had a feeling he knew what it was. If the police checked the phone . . . No way could he involve the police. What did Jerry Sparks mean about his wife? He went to the back door and locked it.

The office phone rang. LeRoy let the answering machine pick up.

"Mr. Watts? It's Maureen. Just checking to see if you're still there. When I got home, I found I'd left my purse in the office. I've got my key. Bye," and she hung up before LeRoy could get to the phone to tell her he'd stop by her place with her purse, no trouble.

He had to get rid of Sparks's body before Maureen got here. Where? The van? He was shivering, a steady shaking from his chattering teeth to his clenched toes. Yet he felt feverish. Sweat trickled down his back and from under his arms, and his sweat already stank of fear. He looked at his watch. Maureen would be here in ten minutes or so.

He'd never killed anything before. Never went hunting. Never even saw a dead person before, except his grandmother at her funeral. LeRoy looked at the grimacing dead face and turned away. His stomach roiled.

The van. Put him in the van and cover him with a tarp. Take care of it later.

But first, the Taser darts. He ejected the cartridge from the weapon and gathered up the strands of thin wire. He'd have to pull the darts out. He yanked the wires that led from the Taser cartridge, and the tiny darts, no more than three-eighths of an inch long, came out of Sparks's clothing with a slight tearing sound. He gathered up the cartridge with the two wires that ended in darts, dropped the whole thing into his toolbox, and slammed the lid shut. He'd get rid of the spent cartridge later.

Sparks's cell phone. He had to do something with the cell phone. LeRoy wrapped his handkerchief around his hand, felt around in Sparks's sweatshirt pocket, past wadded-up tissues and sticky candy wrappers. Just as he found the phone, it emitted a loud burst of rap music and LeRoy dropped it.

"Shut up!" LeRoy shouted at the insistent rap music. "Shut up, shut up!" He picked up the phone and fumbled for the off button.

Someone pounded on the back door.

"Hell!" muttered LeRoy. He wrapped the still-blaring cell phone in his handkerchief and thrust it into the bottom file drawer and slammed the drawer shut.

Bang, bang! Slap, wham!

"Be right with you!" shouted LeRoy. The supply closet. He took a deep breath and heaved Jerry Sparks onto his shoulder, still warm, like one of his sleeping kids after a day at the beach. Sparks was a small man, skinny from the drugs. Easy to carry. But the smell. How could he have stood himself?

Wham, wham! "Daddy! Open up!"

His kids! Back from practice. Early. Shit!

"Just a second, Zeke!" He opened the supply closet with the hand that wasn't supporting the dead legs and dropped Jerry Sparks onto the floor, wiped his hands on his jeans, and shut the closet door. He started toward the back door. No, first he'd have to lock the closet.

"Daddy! I have to go to the bathroom!" Pound, pound.

"Daddy, Zeke hit me!" cried Jared.

The key. Where in hell was the key? Leroy fumbled through Maureen's top desk drawer and found it.

"Stop shouting, kids. The neighbors . . ." He twisted the key in the lock. The key broke off. "Damn!"

"Daaaaaddy!"

"Zeke's gonna wet his pants," said Jared.

"Use the bushes, Zeke!" Sweat was dripping into LeRoy's eyes and he was having trouble seeing.

"Daaaaaaddy!"

He glanced around. Had he overlooked anything? Seemed okay. He went to the back door and opened it. Zeke was dancing from one foot to another. "Sorry, kids. Had to tend to something."

"Why'd you lock the door?" Jared asked. "You never lock the door."

His two boys, twins, tumbled in, hot and sweaty from baseball, a dirty-clean nine-year-old-boy smell.

"Pee-yew! Something stinks!" said Jared.

Zeke unzipped his jeans and raced for the toilet.

"Did the coach buy you pizza?" LeRoy searched for his handkerchief to wipe his forehead, then realized it was wrapped around the cell phone in the file drawer.

Jared nodded. "All of us guys. Pepperoni."

"What did you have to drink?" LeRoy snatched a paper towel off the stack on the counter and mopped his brow.

"Lemonade." Jared made a face. "He never buys Cokes."

"Lemonade's healthier," said LeRoy, crumpling up the paper towel and putting it into his pocket.

Zeke reappeared. "What stinks, Daddy?"

"Something I'm working on," said LeRoy, wondering how he could get the corpse out of the supply closet, now he'd broken the key, and when he'd be able to get it into the van, and where he could leave the body of Jerry Sparks.

As he was wondering how he could dispose of the corpse, Le-Roy heard a gentle rap on the front door and the sound of a key turning, and Maureen, his office manager, entered. She was a comfortable woman in her early sixties and had been with him since he'd started the business eight years ago. "You're still here, Mr. Watts?" She glanced around. "Heavens! What on earth is that smell?"

"Coach bought us pizza, Maureen!" said Zeke, dancing around her.

"That's nice." She advanced into the showroom. "I've never forgotten my purse before. Getting old, I guess. I was carrying that spider plant Mrs. Avery gave me, and I totally forgot."

The office phone rang, and before LeRoy could stop her, Maureen answered it. "Watts Electrical Supply."

LeRoy couldn't hear the voice of the caller.

"I'm sorry, ma'am, we're closed." Maureen listened, then put her hand over the mouthpiece. "Emily Cameron. She wants to know if her, um, *friend*"—she emphasized the word—"Jerry Sparks is still here. He's not answering his cell phone, she says." She removed her hand from the mouthpiece.

"Afraid not," said LeRoy, reaching for a paper towel.

Maureen reported that to the caller, listened, then turned to LeRoy again. "She says he was going to stop by."

"He's not here now," said LeRoy, not looking at her.

"Sorry, Emily," and Maureen hung up. "I don't understand why such a nice girl has anything to do with that dreadful man. Do you know her?"

"She's done some baby-sitting for us. She just got a job at the boatyard."

"A lovely girl." Maureen shook her head. "What goes through some people's minds, I'll never know." She headed toward the file cabinet. "I'll get my purse from the bottom drawer and leave." She sniffed. "What *is* that smell?"

"It's not us," said Zeke, pinching his nose between finger and thumb.

Just as Maureen was reaching for her purse, the cell phone in the file drawer uttered a loud rap phrase.

"Good heavens!" Maureen laid her hand on her chest. "How that startled me!" She found the cell phone, still swathed in LeRoy's handkerchief, and the phone burped out its rap phrase. "Whose phone is this?" She held it up.

He looked away. "Customer must have left it."

"I suppose I should answer?" The phone burped out its rap phrase. "Maybe it's the owner, trying to trace it."

"No!" said LeRoy sharply. "Sorry. Didn't mean to snap at you. Bad case of nerves today. I'll take care of it."

Maureen shrugged. "Not like you to be nervy, Mr. Watts. I hope you're not coming down with something?"

"Me, too," said LeRoy.

She switched off the cell phone and wrapped it again in LeRoy's handkerchief, put it back in the drawer, and slammed the drawer shut. Then she headed toward the supply closet. "I promised I'd get those bills out this week, Mr. Watts. I'll take a box of billing envelopes home with me and work on them tonight."

"No, no! Absolutely not," said LeRoy, moving between Maureen and the closet. "I won't have you working at home. You go on now. Water that new spider plant."

Maureen laughed. "Did anyone ever tell you what a nice man you are?" Before she got to the front door, she turned. "Bye, bye, boys. Have a wonderful evening, Mr. Watts. You and your lovely family."

CHAPTER 3

Zeke squirmed into his seat at the kitchen table. "Macaroni and cheese, yum."

Sarah set down her knitting and got up from the table. "You got another call from your secret admirer."

"She say anything this time?"

"She hasn't since the first couple of times. She whispers 'LeRoy! LeRoy!' like that. Find out who she is, will you? She's driving me crazy."

"The phone company can put a tracer on the calls, but if she's on a cell phone . . . Aren't you eating?"

"I've already had supper."

"Zeke almost wet his pants," said Jared. "Daddy locked the shop door and wouldn't let us in."

"Jared!" warned LeRoy.

"He never locks the door," said Zeke. "He told me to use the bushes, but I didn't."

"You told him to *what*?" said Sarah.

"Zeke!" snapped LeRoy. "Enough!"

Sarah sat down again at the head of the table with her knitting. "I take it you had a tough day."

LeRoy grunted.

"Why don't you take the boys fishing this weekend?"

Zeke bounced in his seat. "Yay! Fishing!"

LeRoy hung his jacket next to the refrigerator and sat in his usual place at the end of the table.

"Did you wash your hands, Roy?" Sarah asked.

"Oh. Yeah." LeRoy got up and stumbled to the sink. He turned on the hot water full blast and scrubbed his hands with the nailbrush and more soap than he needed.

Sarah studied him. "Are you feeling all right?"

LeRoy splashed water on his face and dried it with a dish towel. "Something at work."

"*Don't* use the dish towels to dry your face, Roy. You know how hard I try to keep things nice."

Zeke said, "Daddy's shop stinks."

" 'Cause of you." Jared jabbed his twin with his elbow.

"Stop it, boys," said their mother. "You're upsetting Daddy." She turned to LeRoy, who'd seated himself again. "What's bothering you anyway?"

"Nothing," said LeRoy. "I've got to go back to work after supper, finish up a job." He tugged his napkin out of its plastic ring and spread it on his lap.

"This is exactly what I mean." Sarah thrust her knitting needle into the next stitch. "You spend far too much time at work. It's affecting our family and it's affecting your health."

"Stop bugging me," snapped LeRoy.

"I'm only thinking of you." Sarah changed the subject. "We had a busy day at the library."

"Yeah?" LeRoy scowled, got up from the table, and tossed his napkin onto his untouched plate of food. "I suppose you were telling the librarians how to run the place, as usual." He snatched his jacket from the peg.

"LeRoy, that's uncalled for. . . ."

He strode out of the kitchen, through the living room, out the front door, which he slammed shut, got into his van, started the engine, and backed out of the driveway.

The Watts lived in West Tisbury, in a small house at the end of one of the many dirt roads that branched off Old County Road.

LeRoy tramped down on the accelerator and the van jounced over the speed bumps. He turned onto Old County Road without thinking to look for oncoming cars.

Christ, he was going crazy. Jerry Sparks, dead in the supply closet. An accident. Call the police? Not after all this time. And whatever Sparks had on his cell phone . . .

In the state he was in, he'd better be careful driving. What if a town cop stopped him for speeding?

He slowed down, turned onto State Road, and drove carefully to Vineyard Haven. He passed the boatyard where Jerry Sparks's girlfriend worked, passed the fuel tanks and the boat-rental place, still closed for the season, and continued on into Oak Bluffs. He parked behind his shop and let himself in with his key, made sure the shades were drawn in front, then turned on the lights in back. He found a pair of needle-nose pliers in his tool chest, knelt down beside the closet door, and went to work on the broken key.

There was a series of loud raps on the door. "Anybody here?" A male voice. "Watts?"

LeRoy got to his feet. "Be right there."

He turned on the lights in the front of the shop, opened the door, and gasped. A gigantic uniformed police officer stood there. Tall, broad, face shadowed by the visor of his garrison hat. He's come for me, thought LeRoy. Then with a sudden wash of relief, he recognized the officer. He caught his breath and formed his mouth into a sick grin. "Hey, Smalley. Didn't expect you. C'mon in."

Sergeant Smalley of the State Police stepped inside. His boots reflected the overhead lights. "I was coming from a meeting and saw your lights on in back. Blinds drawn. Just checking to make sure everything's okay."

"Thanks. Had some work to tend to. Guess you're still on duty. Can I get you a Coke or a Pepsi?"

"As a matter of fact, I'm not on duty. I'm on my way home. Got something stronger?"

"Jim Beam do?"

"Sounds good." Sergeant Smalley removed his hat and set it on the counter. LeRoy's tool chest was next to the supply closet. Smalley looked at the chest and then up to the lock. "I see you broke off the key."

"Yeah." Had he seen the Taser cartridge? "I need to get the billing envelopes out of the closet for Maureen."

"Here, let me have those pliers."

"No way!" barked LeRoy. "You sit down. I'll pull Maureen's chair over."

"Won't take but a minute to fix," said Smalley.

"How are things with you?" asked LeRoy, getting off the subject of the key as quickly as possible. He shoved the chair toward the sergeant. "You still seeing that woman doc from the mainland? How's that going?" He went to the bottom drawer in the filing cabinet, hoping Jerry Sparks's cell phone wouldn't ring, then remembered with relief that Maureen had turned it off. He brought out the bourbon and two plastic tumblers.

"Who knows," said Smalley. "I could go for her, but like they say in the personals, 'GU.' Geographically undesirable. The mainland might as well be Australia, as far as dating is concerned."

LeRoy poured a couple of fingers of bourbon into each of the plastic cups and passed one to Smalley.

"Here's to you!" Before Smalley took a swallow, he sniffed. "What are you working on? Smells like stale piss."

LeRoy seated himself on the stool behind the counter. "Kids. You know. Baseball practice . . ." His voice trailed off. Smalley, he knew, didn't have kids. Wasn't married.

West Tisbury's police chief, Mary Kathleen O'Neill, otherwise known as "Casey," and Victoria Trumbull, her deputy, were driving up Circuit Avenue on their way home from the All Island Law Enforcement Officers meeting, the same one Sergeant Smalley had attended.

Victoria raised her cuff to look at her watch. "It's almost eight. I wonder why the light is on in the electrical store. It seems late for LeRoy to be working."

"We might as well check, since we're driving right past," said Casey.

Victoria leaned forward. "The State Police cruiser is out front. Sergeant Smalley may need our help."

"I doubt it." Casey pulled in next to the cruiser.

Victoria opened the door and eased out. Sitting down, she appeared short, but when she stood up, she was just shy of six feet. Her height was in her long, still-fine legs.

"I'll go first, Victoria, just in case. You wait."

But Victoria followed close behind. Casey knocked briskly on the door. "Hello, everything okay?"

Inside the shop, Victoria heard what sounded like a chair falling over.

LeRoy Watts opened the door. His eyes darted from Victoria to Casey and back. "Mrs. Trumbull . . . Monday . . . ? The outlet . . . ?"

"Monday's fine," said Victoria. "We were driving by and saw your lights on."

"I see the State Police vehicle is here," said Casey.

Sergeant Smalley stood up. "Social call, Chief. Stopped by on my way home. Some meeting, hey? Good speaker."

"Excellent. I didn't realize stalkers can have more than one way of going after their prey, like the paparazzi who follow, phone, and photograph celebrities."

Victoria added, "And the fact that most stalkers are perfectly ordinary people otherwise."

LeRoy shifted his weight from one foot to the other and

cleared his throat. "Smalley and I are having a nightcap. Can I offer you something?" He backed into the room and picked up the stool that had fallen over.

"Not me," said Casey. "Victoria?"

Victoria was studying LeRoy. "No, thank you."

"Everything's under control, then?" said Casey.

"Thanks for stopping by." LeRoy brushed his forehead with the back of his hand. "Good to know the Island's law-enforcement officers are on their toes."

"Is there anything we can do before we leave?" Casey asked. "Sure you're okay?"

"No. No, yes. Thanks," said LeRoy.

Casey opened the door. "Guess we'll be going, then."

"Thanks again," said LeRoy. "See you Monday, Mrs. Trumbull."

"See you," said Smalley, and resumed his seat.

Back in the Bronco, Victoria said, "Something didn't seem quite right."

"I agree." Casey reversed out of the parking space and continued up Circuit Avenue. "Maybe because we caught Smalley drinking in uniform."

"It wasn't that, I'm sure. There was an odd odor in the shop, not at all like electrical goods."

"You pick up on a lot of stuff I miss, Victoria," said Casey. "But Oak Bluffs is out of our jurisdiction, as you well know. We've got enough to keep us busy in West Tiz." She looked at her watch. "It's late. I've got to get home."

CHAPTER 4

Earlier that evening, the mathematical knitters' group had met at the West Tisbury Library. Eleven members were in the group altogether, but only eight were present this Thursday. Maron Andrews, the newest member, a honey blonde with wide-set brown eyes, had graduated from MIT at eighteen the previous June and was now doing graduate work in rock mechanics at the Oceanographic Institution in Woods Hole.

She laid her knitting down, a fat figure eight that resembled a brain coral. "I can't concentrate," she said.

"What's the trouble?" asked Casper Martin, one of two male members of the group. "All those good-looking guys pestering you?" Casper himself was an attractive man in his late thirties with the broad shoulders of a swimmer and was wearing funky little round glasses.

"Ha, ha," Maron grunted. "Not funny."

"Sorry. I was trying to be complimentary."

"Well, it wasn't." She picked up her knitting.

Jessica Gordon, a radiologist at the hospital, set her own work aside. "Come on, you two. I've got enough on my mind without your bickering." Jessica was a nicely built redhead with a scattering of freckles across her nose.

Casper pushed his glasses back into place and looked up. "Still having problems with your boyfriend, Jess?"

"Bucky's long gone," she said. "I threw him out a couple of weeks ago."

"What's the problem, then? Sounds like you got rid of a hundred ninety pounds of deadweight," said Casper.

Jessica shrugged. "Ever since he left, I've been getting these weird phone calls."

Alyssa Adams, another of the younger members, dropped a steel needle on the floor. It rolled under the library table and fetched up against a table leg with a metallic clink. Alyssa didn't move.

"Are you okay, Alyssa?" asked Elizabeth Trumbull, yet another member of the group.

"I'm fine." Alyssa bent down and picked up her needle.

"Who's the caller, your ex-boyfriend?" Casper asked.

"It's not Bucky," said Jessica.

"What kind of calls?" asked Maron.

"I don't want to talk about it. Sorry I mentioned it."

Maron set her work in her lap. "This is, like, really weird. I've been getting creepy phone calls, too. That's why I'm having trouble concentrating."

"From a male or a female?" asked Fran Bacon, one of the founders of the group, a mathematics professor retired from Northeastern University.

"It's hard to tell," said Maron. "I honestly can't tell whether it's a man or a woman. A man, I suppose. Heavy breathing, then whoever hangs up."

"What about you, Jessica?" asked Fran.

Jessica sighed. "Could be either a man or a woman. This disgusting sick voice says, 'Jessica,' then breathing, like panting, and I hang up. What's weird is, I have an unlisted phone."

"Me, too!" exclaimed Maron. "I started getting these calls about a month and a half ago, so I changed to an unlisted number, and he's still calling me."

"You might get caller ID," said Casper.

"I've got it," Jessica said.

"I do, too," said Maron. "He's blocked his number."

Jessica added, "I've called the telephone company. I've called the police. They don't seem to be able to do anything about it. Apparently, the guy is calling from a disposable cell phone. I'm going crazy!"

"Disposable phone," Fran repeated thoughtfully. "The calls are probably from someone you don't pay much attention to, for example, a grocery store clerk or someone working on the ferry. Are you aware of anyone like that?"

"Not really," said Jessica.

"Me, either," said Maron.

Fran continued to knit. "I've done quite a bit of research on stalkers," she said. "At Northeastern, I was the student advisor on ways to deal with the problem. One suggestion was to sit down with the stalker and a third party, a mediator or a member of the clergy, and discuss the situation openly."

"But the caller never identifies himself," said Maron. "How can we discuss anything with him? Someone I may or may not know is watching my every move. It's creepy."

"It's likely to be someone you've had some dealings with," Fran continued. "Someone you may not even remember."

"Now, I almost want Bucky back," said Jessica. "This phone creep didn't start calling until after Bucky left. As if he was watching my place or something."

Casper spoke up again. "I hate to say this, girls—"

"Women," Maron corrected.

"—but stalkers often get worse with time. They need more and more stimulation to get satisfaction."

"How come you know so much about stalkers?" asked Jessica.

Casper shrugged. "I'm interested, that's all."

Alyssa stood up and put her knitting in her basket. "I'm sorry, I've got to leave." Her face had become so pale, it was almost green.

"Are you feeling okay?" asked Elizabeth. "Would you like me to drive you home?"

"No, thanks. I'm fine," and Alyssa headed toward the library's front door.

"She doesn't look fine to me," said Casper. He stood up, tugged off his glasses and put them in his pocket, and left his knitting on his chair. "I'll walk her out to the parking lot, make sure she can drive safely."

Back at Watts Electrical Supply, Sergeant Smalley relaxed, drink in hand. He chatted about local politics, state politics, national politics, baseball, fishing. LeRoy, half-seated on the stool, half-listening, set his feet on the floor and jammed his fists into his pockets, his drink untouched.

At last, Smalley got up, pushed the chair back to Maureen's desk, put his hat back on, and adjusted his belt. "Thanks, Roy. Nice pick-me-up. Don't work too late. Sure you don't want me to fix that broken key? I've had some experience along those lines. Won't take me a minute." A nod toward the supply closet.

LeRoy suppressed a shudder. "Thanks. I'm all set."

"Good night, then."

"Night." LeRoy locked the door behind Smalley, and reached for another paper towel.

He turned out the lights again in the front of the shop and went to work on the broken key, trying to extract it with the needle-nose pliers. At last he got the broken-off part out, but the door was still locked.

"Hell. Damnation," muttered LeRoy. He fished through the toolbox and found a paint scraper, slid it through the crack in the door until he came to the latch, and, suddenly, the door opened, releasing the full aroma of Jerry Sparks, several hours riper than it had been at five o'clock this afternoon.

Where the hell could he take the body? Where, where? LeRoy

thought of State Beach, but after a mild day like today, people might be out for an evening stroll, even though the night had turned chilly. Maybe take Sparks to a beach up-Island. There were still remote places there.

Then he remembered the book shed at the West Tisbury Library, where his wife was a library trustee. Volunteers stored used books there for the summer book sale. He'd installed electricity in the shed last fall, done it for the cost of materials because of Sarah. Perfect spot. No one would question his being there. The shed was about the size of a small garage, with not much in it but cardboard boxes of books. It would look as though Sparks had sheltered there and died of an overdose.

Jerry Sparks dead. LeRoy couldn't get his mind around the concept.

He hoisted the body onto his shoulder and carried it out to the van, opened the back door with one hand, and gently laid the body on the mat.

"Hey, Mr. Watts!"

LeRoy slammed the van door and spun around. One of the older kids from the baseball team had come around to the back of the shop.

"Yeah?" said LeRoy. "What are you doing up so late?"

"It's not so late. One of the twins left his coat at the field. My mom picked me up after the game and we were driving by and saw your light. She told me to bring the coat to you."

"Thanks," said LeRoy. "Thanks a lot. Looks like Zeke's coat all right. Thanks."

"My mom had to go to a meeting and said maybe you'd give me a ride home."

LeRoy took a deep breath. "Sure. Sure, I'll take you home. You're Henry, right?"

"No, sir. Hugo. Hugo A. Blinckmann."

"Sure. Sure, Hugo. Hop in."

"I'll get in back," said Hugo. "I like riding in back." He reached for the handle of the back door.

"No! Stay away!" shouted LeRoy.

Hugo turned in astonishment.

"Sorry, Hugo. Didn't mean to be so sharp. No seat belt back there. Get in front. The front seat." The kid wouldn't be able to see into the back, would he? LeRoy wiped his eyes. He started the engine and Hugo climbed in. The boy wrinkled his nose and leaned around the seat toward the back of the van.

"Hey," said LeRoy, pointing out of the windshield. "That cat has something in its mouth."

"Where?" asked Hugo, turning back to the front and sitting forward. "I don't see it."

"It moved fast. Keep an eye out. We might see a deer."

From then on, Hugo was eyes front. LeRoy followed Circuit Avenue to the end, kept going until he came to Barnes Road, where Hugo lived, and dropped the kid off. "Thanks for bringing Zeke's coat. Take care."

"Good night, Mr. Watts. Wish I'd seen that cat."

CHAPTER 5

LeRoy continued down Barnes Road to the end and turned right onto the Edgartown–West Tisbury Road. He passed the airport, where the runway lights made a path for incoming planes. The lights looked menacing tonight for some reason. A small plane came in for a landing, right over the road. Right over him. He ducked his head as the engine noise grew to a roar, then faded quickly as the plane touched down at the end of the runway. LeRoy pulled over to the side of the road. He couldn't see to drive. His hands were shaking and sweat trickled down his forehead into his eyes. He put his hand over his chest. His heart was beating irregularly. He turned off the motor. Was he having a heart attack right here? Would the EMTs find him with the body of Jerry Sparks in the back?

After a few minutes, LeRoy felt calmer. He turned the key in the ignition and started up.

A couple of miles from the airport, he passed Victoria Trumbull's big old house. Her lights were on downstairs and he could see someone moving around inside. LeRoy shuddered when he thought of the way she'd inspected the shop and him. She'd sensed something. He mustn't forget to fix that outlet of hers on Monday. He prayed that she wouldn't question him any more about Sparks.

He checked his speedometer as he passed the police station. The Bronco was parked out front. He braked at the hand-lettered sign by the Mill Pond—SLOW! TURTLE CROSSING!—stopped at the stop sign on Brandy Brow, then continued up the hill and turned into the library's parking lot. The lot was full of cars. Damn. Movie night. Tonight it was open until nine. A woman came out with an armload of books and waved at him. A small girl skipped alongside her.

There was no way on heaven or earth he could move Jerry Sparks to the shed until the library closed. He'd have to drive around and kill a half hour or so.

It was almost nine o'clock when Elizabeth returned home and parked her convertible under the maple tree. She bounded up the stone steps and into the kitchen. After her divorce, Elizabeth had moved in with her grandmother—for just a couple of weeks, she'd said months ago. She settled into Victoria's life, and now Victoria, who'd always cherished her solitude, couldn't imagine life without her.

Victoria was sitting at the cookroom table, opening mail she hadn't gotten to earlier.

"Hi, Gram, I'm home."

Victoria handed an unopened envelope to Elizabeth. "You have a letter from your mother."

Elizabeth made a wry face.

"She means well," said Victoria. "Don't judge her so harshly."

"Was she always like this? I mean, trying to run everybody's life?"

"She was very caring, even as a little girl," said Victoria. She pushed aside a full-color catalog of scanty underwear. "Such a waste of paper."

" 'Very caring' translates into *busybody*. I'm in my thirties, for Pete's sake. Doesn't she realize that?"

"Our children never stop being our children."

"You don't interfere with her life. You never have."

Victoria changed the perilous subject of mothers and daughters.

"How was the knitters' group?" She understood Elizabeth's feelings. Amelia could be difficult.

"Great. You wouldn't think you could knit something that looked exactly like coral, would you?"

"I'd never thought about it before. Are you referring to the quilt you're making?"

Elizabeth nodded. "We have to finish it by mid-June, so it can go on tour with other quilts. We're going to meet every night from now on."

"How many quilts are entered so far?"

"Close to a hundred, I think. People all over the country are working on reef quilts. Ours is three-dimensional. We're knitting stuff like coral and sea anemonies." Elizabeth ran water into the teakettle and put it on the stove. "Tea, Gram?"

"That would be nice."

While she waited for the water to boil, Elizabeth sat at the table with her grandmother. "How was the law enforcement meeting?"

"Interesting," said Victoria. "A speaker from off-Island talked about stalking and stalkers."

"Really!" Elizabeth sat up straight.

"Apparently, it's become a problem on the Island." Victoria indicated the stack of catalogs she'd separated out of her mail. "Would you please drop these into the recycling bin?"

"Sure." Elizabeth took them away and returned shortly. "Just tonight, two of the women in the knitting group told us they're getting calls from a breather. He sort of pants, then hangs up."

"Who are the women?"

"Jessica Gordan and Maron Andrews."

"I know Jessica," said Victoria. "She has beautiful red hair. I don't know Maron."

"Maron's really bright, as well as pretty. She's just turned nineteen and she's doing grad work at the Oceanographic. Jessica broke up with her live-in boyfriend a couple of weeks ago, and a few days later she started getting these calls."

"Have they done anything about the calls?"

"Jessica didn't do anything the first time, figuring it was a wrong number, but after the second call, she contacted the phone company and they put on a tracer."

"Were they able to identify the caller?"

"No. He's calling from a disposable cell phone."

"A disposable phone?" asked Victoria. "I've never heard of such a thing."

"You can buy them at the Stop and Shop or off-Island at places like Walmart. Vineyard Electronics probably sells them. They cost about twenty dollars."

Victoria sat back in her chair. "The tea water's boiling. Then let's hear what your mother has to say."

Getting the body into the book-storage shed was going to be a nightmare. The movie tonight was *Citizen Kane*, a classic old black-and-white film. LeRoy drove around for a half hour, along South Road, then onto one of the dirt roads that connected with Middle Road, checking the time every few minutes. At 9:15, he figured everybody must have cleared out, so he turned off the dirt road onto Middle Road, followed it to the Panhandle, which became Music Street, followed that until he came out onto South Road, and then he was a short hop from the library.

There were still half a dozen cars in the parking lot. Several people milled about. He couldn't pull away again without being too obvious, so he parked off to one side and turned off the engine.

There was a tap on his window. LeRoy started. A teenager. Whit something. What was the kid's last name? Manter. Whit Manter.

"How're ya doing, Mr. Watts? Are you gonna need help this summer? I'm looking for a job."

"Talk to Maureen, Whit. She handles hiring."

"Thanks, Mr. Watts."

"I'm not promising anything," LeRoy called to Whit's departing back. But then he recalled, with an odd feeling, he would need an extra hand.

As he rolled up the window, a woman was about to tap on the glass. Diana. Another Manter. Whit's third cousin.

"I'm glad I saw you, LeRoy. I wanted to let you know I voted for your wife. She's just wonderful as head of the library trustees."

LeRoy nodded. "I'll tell her, Diana. Thanks."

"Also, it's my dishwasher."

"Mice eat the wiring again?"

"I think so."

"They like the white wiring. Call the shop, Diana, and talk to Maureen. She makes out the schedule."

He'd rolled the window up partway when he saw someone else, a woman, walking toward the van. The woman looked familiar, but he couldn't place her right away. She was stocky and wore a mannish buffalo-plaid shirt over jeans. Her hair was pulled back into a ponytail and she had long straggly bangs. Then he recognized her. Emily Cameron, their baby-sitter.

"Hi, Emily," said LeRoy. "Can I help you?"

"Hello, Mr. Watts. Have you seen Jerry Sparks?"

LeRoy shuddered. "Jerry Sparks?"

"He was supposed to meet me here."

LeRoy reached into his pocket for his handkerchief. Hell, his handkerchief was in the bottom drawer of the file cabinet, wrapped around Jerry Sparks's cell phone. "You called the shop earlier this afternoon, didn't you?"

She nodded and the low lights in the parking area were reflected in her glasses, so he couldn't see her eyes. "Maureen said he hadn't come by, but when he left me around four-thirty, he said he was going directly to the shop."

31

"Maureen told me she hadn't seen him," said LeRoy.

"I hoped maybe you had," said Emily. "We had a date to go to the movie tonight. He was supposed to meet me here, and he never showed up. It's our anniversary. We've been together three weeks."

"Congratulations," said LeRoy. He hoped she'd go away before she scented the distinctive smell of Jerry Sparks in the back of the van.

She sighed and turned away. "Yeah. Thanks."

"Want me to give him a message if I see him?"

She looked over her shoulder at him. "Don't bother, Mr. Watts. It's not the first time he's stood me up."

LeRoy kept the window open after Emily Cameron left, despite the cool night. Once the parking lot cleared, he waited a few minutes longer until the lights went out in the library, then went around to the back of his van. He'd better carry Jerry Sparks from here, rather than driving to the shed. If he drove, someone might remember seeing him there. He was just about to open the back door, when he heard footsteps crunching on the gravel surface of the parking lot.

"Night, Mr. Watts."

He swiveled around. Lucinda Chandler, the librarian.

"Good night, Lucinda." He put his hand on his chest. "You had a busy evening."

"It's not usually this busy, but it was a great movie, and the knitting group is working on their coral-reef quilt."

"A what?"

"You should see it. It's really amazing. It's to raise awareness of global warming."

"Knitting?"

"Mathematical knitting." Lucinda examined the keys she had on a ribbon, then put the ribbon around her neck. "Projective planes and Klein bottles. That sort of thing. Non-orientable surfaces. Möbius strips."

"Global warming?" LeRoy, his mind on the corpse in the back of the van, was having trouble concentrating.

"Global warming affects coral reefs all over the world."

"So I've heard," murmured LeRoy.

"Come on in and I'll show you the quilt. It's not finished, but you can see what it's going to look like." Lucinda pulled her key on its cord out of the neck of her fleece jacket.

"I'd like to, but . . ." He wiped his forehead with the back of his hand and looked at his watch.

"Are you using the wireless?"

"Wireless?" Was she referring to the Taser?

"People park here all kinds of crazy hours to log onto the wireless. Used to be lovers. Now it's computer geeks."

Lucinda seemed to require some response, so LeRoy laughed politely and thought fast. "Nope. Just wanted to check out the electric meter after you closed the building. See how much current you're using at low load."

"Oh," said Lucinda. "Thanks. You're just wonderful. With electric rates what they are . . ."

"Right," said LeRoy.

"Let me know what you find out, and when you've got time, I'll show you the quilt." She dropped the key on its cord back into the neck of her pink jacket, zipped it up, slipped her recumbent tricycle out of the bike rack, and pedaled off.

So that's what those characters are knitting, thought LeRoy. A coral reef.

CHAPTER 6

Before he opened the back door of the van, LeRoy looked around once again, then tugged Jerry Sparks out feetfirst. The body had stiffened into a grotesque shape. He'd only read about rigor mortis. He slung the rigid body over his shoulder and made his way to the book shed behind the library. He laid Jerry Sparks facedown in a cleared space in the center of the shed and shut the door.

He drove home the long way, with the windows wide open.

Sarah was waiting up for him, knitting. "What took you so long?"

"Had to finish up something at work. I told you."

She wrinkled what LeRoy used to think of as her pretty nose. "I hope you're planning to take a shower."

Later that same evening, Alyssa's mother called out to her from the kitchen. "How was the knitters' group, honey?"

"Okay, Mom."

"I've made lasagna. Would you like some?"

"I'm not hungry, thanks." Alyssa took her sweatshirt from the rack in the front hall and pulled her headband over her cropped hair. "I'm going out again."

"Where are you going now?"

"Just out."

"You need to eat something, honey." Her mother stopped in the doorway, holding the pan of lasagna.

"Maybe later, Mom." Alyssa opened the door. Her mother was still talking, so she waited.

"You've lost weight, Alyssa. You've got to eat."

"I can't deal with food now, Mom. See you later."

"When will you be home?"

"I don't know. Don't wait up," and Alyssa shut the door gently.

Victoria answered the knock on her kitchen door. "Well, good evening, Alyssa."

"I'm sorry to be coming here so late, Mrs. Trumbull."

"It's not late. Have you had supper yet? I've got some nice soup." Tendrils of savory-smelling steam wafted up from a pot simmering on the stove.

"Thanks, Mrs. Trumbull, but I don't want anything. I hope I'm not bothering you?"

"Of course not." Alyssa was the granddaughter of one of Victoria's childhood friends. She resembled her grandmother so much that Victoria had a feeling of time running backward. The young woman was probably in her twenties, but seemed like a teenager. Her hair was cut short like a boy's and she had a boy's slender build. "You look as though you could use a little warmth. There's a fire in the parlor."

Alyssa was wearing her hooded navy sweatshirt with TRI-TOWN AMBULANCE printed on it in large white letters. She'd pulled the sleeves down over her hands.

Victoria led the way through the dining room and into the parlor, where McCavity lay stretched out, his soft belly fur toward the fire. Victoria settled herself into her mouse-colored wing chair. Alyssa stood uncertainly by the coffee table, hugging herself.

"Have a seat." Victoria indicated the horsehair sofa, and Alyssa perched on the edge.

"I hope we don't have a frost tonight," said Victoria, wondering why Alyssa had come to her.

"Yes, ma'am." Alyssa looked down at her hands, which were clasped together between her knees.

"You never can predict what Island weather will do," said Victoria.

Alyssa nodded.

"I think you need a glass of sherry." Victoria got up from her seat and headed for the kitchen.

She returned a few minutes later carrying a brass tray with a bottle of sherry, two glasses, and crackers and cheese. Alyssa had moved from the couch to the floor, where she sat with her legs crossed, stroking McCavity.

"Be careful not to pat his stomach," warned Victoria. "He turns into a wildcat."

Alyssa held up her hand. Thin red lines extended from knuckles to thumb. "He's already explained that to me."

"There's witch hazel in the bathroom," Victoria said. "Don't you want to put some on that scratch?"

Alyssa got to her feet. "I'd probably better."

She returned, holding a soggy cotton pad on her hand. Victoria breathed in the clean, pungent smell of witch hazel, a remembered cure-all for childhood scratches and mosquito bites. Alyssa dropped to the floor again near McCavity. He rolled over on his back, belly exposed.

She smiled and moved her hand away.

Victoria put a chunk of cheese on a cracker and Alyssa took it absently.

"You remind me so much of your grandmother," Victoria said softly. "When she had something on her mind, it took her a long time to get around to talking about it."

Alyssa nodded.

Victoria handed her a glass of sherry. "Do you remember her?"

"Not very well," she said, accepting the wine. "I was only five or six when she died."

"You look like her. She was very beautiful."

Alyssa blushed and looked down at McCavity.

Victoria waited.

Alyssa said nothing for some time. She ate the cracker Victoria had given her, sipped her sherry, and helped herself to another cracker. The fire blazed up. McCavity shifted away from the heat.

"Two women in the group are getting phone calls from a breather," Alyssa said at last.

"So I heard. Jessica Gordon and Maron Andrews."

"I didn't want to say anything at the meeting tonight." Alyssa stopped.

"Go on," said Victoria.

"I'm getting phone calls, too, Mrs. Trumbull. The guy says disgusting stuff before I can hang up."

"Oh," said Victoria, and waited.

Alyssa wiped her eyes with the back of her hand. "I need your advice, Mrs. Trumbull. I think I know who the breather is, and I'm scared."

LeRoy couldn't sleep. He tossed from side to side and from his back to his stomach. Before dawn, Sarah switched on the light. "I might as well get up. You've kept me awake all night." She put her hand on his hot forehead. "You're sick. I knew something was wrong."

He sat up, swiveled his feet over the side of the bed, and put his head in his hands. "Leave me alone, will you?"

"You'd better see Doc Jeffers. If you're coming down with something, I don't want the boys to catch it."

LeRoy got up, dressed, and left the house before the twins were up, without waiting for breakfast.

He drove through Vineyard Haven, quiet this early in the morning. Only a few shops on Main Street were lighted. His was the only car on Beach Road. As he drove, the sky turned from night black to gray. The horizon emerged and he could see boats magnified by their reflections in the still harbor. Circuit Avenue was deserted; his shop was dark.

LeRoy couldn't think of yesterday's event as anything but an incident. The Jerry Sparks incident. He'd have to remember to get rid of the Taser cartridge he'd stashed in his toolbox. He felt groggy and hungover, although he hadn't even taken a sip of the Jim Beam he'd poured last night, had poured it back into the bottle, in fact.

He let himself into his shop, then made sure both the front and back doors were locked before he turned on the lights and opened the bottom file drawer. He unwrapped the cell phone and tucked his handkerchief into his pocket. It took him awhile to figure out where Jerry Sparks might have stored photos.

He checked everything on the cell phone, glancing at his watch every couple of minutes. Only an hour before Maureen would arrive and open up.

Messages from Emily Cameron, the girlfriend who'd spoken to him in the library parking lot. Their baby-sitter. Addresses, jokes, dates, notes. Pictures of Emily. No other photos. He finished before the hour was up. Sparks had lied to him. No photos. No videos.

Had he lied, too, about downloading the photos onto his computer? About having any pictures at all?

Someone knocked at the back door.

"Be right there," LeRoy called out, and quickly stashed the phone back in the bottom drawer. He'd have to tend to the Taser cartridge later. He looked at his watch. Eight o'clock, the time he usually opened. He got up, kicked the file drawer shut, and made it to the back door.

It was the tall guy who worked at the Steamship Authority, directing cars onto the ferries.

"Hi," said LeRoy. "Just opening up. Can I help you?"

"I'm looking for Jerry Sparks," the guy said.

LeRoy glanced behind him, as though Jerry Sparks might materialize. "He doesn't work here anymore. Sorry." He was about to shut the door.

The guy held up a large hand to keep the door from closing. "Name's Beany. Sparks told me he's working here part-time."

"He doesn't work here anymore," said LeRoy, backing away from the door. "Sorry."

"Give him a message, will you?" said Beany. "That's a damned piece of junk he sold me and I want my money back."

"Sure, but I don't expect to see him anytime soon," said LeRoy. "Sorry about that, buddy."

"No problem," said Beany. "When you see him, tell him I said, 'Or else.'" With that, Beany turned away and stepped off the three back steps in one long stride.

"Sure. Okay," said LeRoy to Beany's departing back.

A key turned in the front door lock and the door opened. LeRoy swiveled around, expecting to see Jerry Sparks.

Maureen put her key back into her purse. "I didn't realize you were here, Mr. Watts. The door was locked."

"Sorry, I forgot."

Maureen studied him. "You seem to have an awful lot on your mind, Mr. Watts."

LeRoy nodded. "I've got a couple of errands to do, Maureen." He had to find Sparks's computer, and soon. "I'll be away from the shop most of the morning. I broke off the key in the supply closet, so the door's unlocked. Need to get a new key. Call me if something comes up. I've got my cell phone."

It was another fine, bright morning with a brilliant blue sky and the scent of spring in the air. LeRoy was too preoccupied to notice. He checked his watch. After 8:30.

After 8:30. Victoria had been working in her garden for more than an hour. Last summer, she had sowed seeds of touch-me-not near a lush growth of poison ivy that thrived in a damp spot on the other side of her vegetable garden. She'd gathered the seeds from plants that grew alongside the brook on the other side of Doane's pasture. When she was a child, even before she could read, she'd loved to touch the seedpods that popped like birthday favors, shooting seeds into the air and water and earth like tiny missiles. Last summer, she'd felt almost guilty, touching as many of the fat pods as she could reach to watch the exploding seedpods and the way the emptied pod split and snapped back into tight curls. It still seemed magical. Touch-me-not grew in the same places poison ivy did and was an antidote. You merely rubbed touch-me-not on your skin where it had been exposed to poison ivy, and the itchy rash wouldn't develop. Or that's what they said.

She got slowly to her feet. Eight-thirty wasn't too early to call her attorney friend, Myrna Luce. Her legs had cramped from kneeling too long. But she'd found the green leaves of touch-me-not poking out of the dirt where she'd planted them. A good discovery for this fine morning.

She limped back to the house, her muscles gradually easing, and called Myrna. "I need to talk to you," she said. "Unofficially."

Myrna laughed. "I won't charge you, if that's what you're asking. Come about four, and I'll break out the sherry. Do you need a ride?"

"No, thank you. I've got transportation."

CHAPTER 7

Jerry Sparks lived, or had lived, in a basement room in a house off Wing Road, a place owned by old Mrs. Rudge. He'd done work for her in the past. LeRoy parked in the driveway, went up to her kitchen door, and knocked.

Mrs. Rudge shuffled to the door in her bedroom slippers, a wiry woman in her seventies, cigarette hanging from her lips, eyes half-closed against the smoke.

She held the door partway open. "Yeah?"

"Mrs. Rudge, I'm LeRoy Watts, your electrician. Is Jerry Sparks in?"

"Haven't seen him for several days. He owes me rent."

"I need to get something he borrowed from me. Mind if I take a look in his place?"

Mrs. Rudge removed the cigarette from her mouth with thumb and third finger and flicked the ashes onto the floor. "Be my guest."

"Thanks. Is his place locked?"

"I doubt it," and Mrs. Rudge shut the door.

LeRoy went around to the outdoor basement entrance and tried the door. Not locked, of course. Nothing much in the place. An unmade futon with a greasy pillow and a wadded-up blanket, empty carryout cartons containing dried-out Chinese food, a couple of pizza boxes with week-old cheesey dough stuck on the lid. A crappy easy chair he didn't want to touch. A bare lightbulb hung from an extension cord wrapped around an overhead pipe. No computer.

While he stood there wondering where Jerry Sparks would have kept the computer, Mrs. Rudge barged in, bringing with her the smell of stale cigarette smoke. "Found what you was looking for?" She lit a new cigarette from the end of one that had burned down to the filter tip, breathed in the fresh smoke, and blew it out.

LeRoy shook his head. "Don't see it anywhere."

"He had a couple of good things, like a stereo and a radio, but he sold them."

"A computer?"

"One of his drinking buddies took that away."

LeRoy felt his stomach lurch and put his hand over his chest. "Do you know who it was?"

Mrs. Rudge took another drag. "Don't know his name. Tall, skinny guy. Works for the Steamship Authority. I got no idea where he is. If you see him, tell him he doesn't pay his rent, I'm moving his stuff out. I gotta live, too, you know. I'll give him another week; that's it." She flicked the ash off the end of her cigarette. "How much longer you gonna be?"

"I'm done here, I guess."

"You hear of anybody wants a nice room, tell them to call, okay?"

"I'll do that."

LeRoy trudged back to his van. Before he opened the door, Mrs. Rudge called out, "You tell him to move that junker car of his outta here. I'm not running a parking lot, you know."

LeRoy opened the van door and stepped up into it. He'd cleaned the inside, swept it out. A green cardboard tree hung from the mirror, and the van smelled like pine.

So Beany had Sparks's computer. He didn't know Beany's last name. He'd go to the Steamship Authority on Monday when the office opened and find out from them.

On the way back to the shop, LeRoy stopped at Shirley's Hardware. Mary—he never could remember her last name, although he'd known her for the entire eight years he'd had his shop—cut a new key for him and he returned to work. He gave the key to Maureen, who tucked it under a plastic pencil tray in her top desk drawer.

"Mr. Watts, you really should see the doctor," she said. "Yesterday I was sure you were coming down with something. You go on home. I'll take care of things. The weekend's coming up. Get some rest."

"Guess you're right," said LeRoy, thinking if he didn't find that computer soon, he was in deep trouble.

After lunch, Victoria dressed in her green plaid suit, put on the clip earrings that matched her outfit, and found her leather purse under a pile of papers on the dining room table. She considered whether or not she should take her lilac-wood walking stick, and decided that if she got a ride in a pickup truck, she'd like a bit of support.

At half past three, she marched around to the front of her house and crossed the road. Within a few minutes, a vehicle approached from Edgartown and she held out her thumb. It wasn't a car after all, but a shiny new blue dump truck that slowed and stopped, as she knew it would.

The driver lowered the window on the passenger side. "Afternoon, Mrs. Trumbull." The driver was Bill O'Malley, a man she occasionally saw at the selectmen's meetings. He leaned across the seat. "Nice to see you on a fine day like this. Where're you heading?"

"Myrna Luce's law office in Vineyard Haven," said Victoria. Through the open window she heard O'Malley's radio playing something with a banjo and harmonica and a high male voice wailing a country-music ballad.

"At your service." O'Malley slipped out of the driver's side, truck engine still running, and went around to the passenger side. He was a tall, well-built young man in his mid-forties, with dark, unruly hair streaked with silver. Victoria admired men with nice flat stomachs. He brought out a black plastic milk crate and set it down for a step. "I keep it here just for you. By the way, how's your granddaughter?"

Victoria smiled. "Elizabeth is fine. She likes her job. You know Myrna, don't you?"

"Sure. Everyone does. She handled my second divorce."

Victoria tucked her stick under her arm, grasped the metal handhold on the side of the truck, stepped up onto the milk crate, and, with a boost from O'Malley, swung up into the high passenger seat. She straightened her skirt over her knees. "Thank you."

"Anytime," said O'Malley as he stowed the milk crate behind her seat. "I'll take you right there."

He slammed the door shut, got back into the driver's seat, and shifted into gear. "Where's she working?"

"Who?" asked Victoria, then immediately realized she was being dense. "Elizabeth's working as dockmaster at the Oak Bluffs harbor."

"I'll run my boat around there sometime, see how she's doing."

"I'm sure she'd like that."

As they approached Vineyard Haven, O'Malley turned off State Road and followed a series of lanes until they reached what was once a small house, now tripled in size with a new two-story addition.

"Myrna's law office is on the first floor," explained Victoria. "She has a dance studio on the second."

"That woman has almost as much energy as you do, Mrs. T.,"

O'Malley said as he helped her dismount. "I've got a couple of errands to run, and can stop by in about an hour, if you'd like a ride home."

"That would be fine," said Victoria.

As she went up to the front step, a short, stout black woman opened the door. Her hair was twisted into long dreadlocks entwined with beads. She greeted Victoria with a warm bosomy hug.

Victoria, usually not much of a hugger, embraced her, then turned to O'Malley, who'd waited to see her safely met. He lifted a couple of fingers from the steering wheel in acknowledgment and drove off.

"It's been too long, Victoria." Myrna indicated with her beringed hands for Victoria to go first, and they entered her new law office.

African sculptures and carvings were displayed on low columns between windows that looked out on woodland. The wall to the right was lined with law books. Oriental rugs covered the polished wood floor.

Myrna seated Victoria on a satin-striped couch next to a ficus tree and sat across from her.

After they'd exchanged pleasantries, Myrna said, "Tell me what brought you here—besides Bill O'Malley's cobalt blue dump truck." She laughed and sat forward, her fingers laced so that her rings seemed to form a solid gold band. Her ears, too, were outlined in gold rings.

Myrna laughed again when she noticed the way Victoria was examining her. She shook her head and beads clicked.

"I know you're involved with women's issues," Victoria began. "Do you still run the shelter for battered women?"

Myrna nodded and waved at a door in the book-lined wall. "That leads to my house. It's not easy for batterers to get to their victims, since they'd have to go past me." She bared her teeth in a smile. "You indicated on the phone that a woman you know is being stalked. Illegal, of course. I can get a restraining order for her."

"It's more serious than that," said Victoria. "Three women. Possibly more."

Myrna pursed her lips. "I see."

Victoria told her about the breather.

"I recall your granddaughter was being stalked by her ex-husband."

"That was frightening. He's a sensible, well-educated man. I don't understand what gets into some people."

Myrna nodded. "More women are willing to come forward these days. Men, too. Stalkers are not just males."

"I wanted to come in person rather than phoning," said Victoria. "I suppose my interest stems from Elizabeth's problems. Do you have any clients who are being stalked?"

"You know I can't divulge names."

"I don't want names," Victoria assured her. "I need to know if our stalker reaches beyond the knitters' group."

"Have the women notified the police?"

"They've talked with Casey, who's not sure anything can be done beyond notifying the phone company, and they've done that. Last night, I attended a lecture on stalking and learned it can escalate into something quite dangerous."

Myrna nodded. "Two of my clients are hiding out from ex-husbands who've gone beyond telephoning." She looked thoughtful, then stood. "I'll go through my files and see what I can find." She arose from her seat and went over to a file cabinet near the bookcase, unlocked a drawer, and ran her fingers through a sheaf of folders. While Victoria waited, she pulled out four or five.

She returned to her seat with the folders and opened them one at a time. "These are stalking cases. Only one woman is getting phone calls from an unidentified man, a breather. The others know who the stalker is, ex-husbands or former boyfriends."

"Would you be willing to meet with the women from the knitters' group?"

"Anytime, Victoria. Let's make it some evening, to be sure I'm not in court."

They spent the rest of the time catching up on family news until the blue dump truck rumbled to a stop in front of Myrna's office.

"Thank you," said Victoria, and strode out to her waiting ride.

CHAPTER 8

LeRoy didn't recall how he spent the rest of Friday. By the time he got home, the boys were fed and in bed. Sarah was knitting. Always knitting.

"Soup's on the stove," she said. "*She* called again."

"I notified the phone company. Not much they can do." LeRoy helped himself and sat down at the table opposite Sarah.

"Who is she, Roy?"

"How am I supposed to know? What're you making?"

"Thought you'd never ask. Sweaters for the boys. She must know you."

LeRoy shrugged.

"Some former girlfriend?"

"For God's sake," said LeRoy. "Get off my back."

"I'm the one who gets the calls." Sarah looked up. "Unless she calls when you're here and you answer?"

"Yeah." LeRoy ate his soup to the sound of clicking needles. The woman had called when he'd answered, a soft voice he didn't recognize. Told him she'd dreamed about him. What she'd like to do with him. Teach him a few things. He'd hung up. He slathered butter on a chunk of homemade bread, mopped up the last of his soup, and stood up. Who the hell was she?

"I baked the bread this morning," said Sarah.

"Great." LeRoy yawned, stretched, and tossed his napkin onto the table.

"How about putting your napkin in your napkin ring? I have enough laundry—"

"Okay, okay," said LeRoy, and stuffed the napkin into the green plastic ring that identified the napkin as his.

Sarah set down her work. "I've already showered."

"I can take a hint." LeRoy headed for the bathroom.

"How about clearing your dishes first?"

"Oh, for God's sake." LeRoy returned to the kitchen, put his bowl and spoon in the dishwasher, slammed it shut with a thunk, and turned to her. "Anything else you want?"

"Did you go to the doctor today?"

"No."

"You don't need to be so snippy." Sarah put her work away and stood. "What's the matter with you anyway?"

"I'm going fishing tomorrow. Early." He followed her into their bedroom.

"It's supposed to be nice. I'll get the boys up."

"I'm not taking the boys."

"You promised."

"Well, I'm not taking them." LeRoy opened a bureau drawer and took out the clothes he planned to wear the next day, a plaid shirt and jeans, and laid them on the blanket chest at the foot of the bed.

"They'll be disappointed, Roy."

"Can't help that," said LeRoy. He added a T-shirt, wool socks, and clean underwear to the pile.

"They can't go with me," said Sarah. "I'm helping Lucinda move books downstairs in the library."

"Take the kids with you."

"Two nine-year-old boys stuck in the library?" Sarah's voice rose. "When they'd rather be fishing with their dad?"

LeRoy made a fist and smacked it into the palm of his left hand. Sarah flinched.

"All right!" she snapped. "I'll take them."

LeRoy got up before dawn and dressed in the clothes he'd laid out the night before, then drove to Edgartown and down the street that led to the ferry. His van was first in line for the minute-and-a-half crossing to Chappaquiddick, an island that had been connected to the Vineyard by a slim barrier bar until the ocean cut through.

"Morning, Roy." The ferry captain slipped wooden chocks under the front wheels of LeRoy's van.

"Morning, Bart."

"Raised the rates again," said Bart, collecting the fare. "The current's wicked since the ocean cut through the bar. Burns more fuel, and fuel's outta sight."

The ferry crabbed against the fierce new current, and in less than two minutes Bart nosed the ferry into the dock on the Chappaquiddick side, took down the chain at the bow, and removed the chocks from LeRoy's wheels.

"The blues are running pretty good at Wasque," said Bart, pronouncing it WAY-squee, the way Islanders do. "I like a baked bluefish."

"I'll save a couple for you," said LeRoy. "Too oily for my taste."

LeRoy drove off the ferry onto the paved road and continued to the end of a dirt road, where he parked. He hiked the short distance through the pines to the wooden steps that led down the cliff face to the beach. There he stopped to watch the sun rise out of the wild sea, lighting the pond at the foot of the cliff and beach beyond.

Suddenly, he heard the voice of Jerry Sparks and turned around. Nothing. No one. Only a catbird, mocking him.

Shaking with the thought of Jerry Sparks's ghost calling to him, he carried his fishing gear down the steep steps, taking in deep breaths of clean salt air. He hiked along the wooden walkway that skirted the pond, then trudged the half mile down the beach to the outermost corner of the Island. Every few steps, he looked around to see what was behind him.

The southeastern corner of Martha's Vineyard forms a sharp right angle, where the ruler-straight south-facing beach meets the equally ruler-straight east-facing beach. There tidal currents clash in confusion, stirring up bait and attracting blues and stripers.

A half dozen fishermen lined up in the surf. He knew a few by sight and he joined them, keeping his own distance to avoid tangled lines. He greeted Janet Messineo, the Island's number-one fisherman, who nodded.

"Great fishing today," she said, casting.

At noon, he drank water and ate a peanut butter and jelly sandwich. He could see the blues going after baitfish in the surf. Though everyone else seemed to have luck, he caught nothing.

He worked the surf all day, even after the tide changed and all the rest left with their quota of blues.

He came home after Sarah and the boys had gone to bed, weary, sunburned, and feeling rotten. He fixed himself a bacon and egg sandwich, drank a Bud, and crawled into bed. Sarah moved away from him.

When Sarah awoke on Sunday, LeRoy was gone. Fishing again, she supposed. She was in a foul mood. He hadn't taken the twins fishing this morning, either. She might as well be a single parent. Worse, because Roy had been in such an ill temper lately, she'd found herself snapping at the boys, who'd done nothing wrong. She was making breakfast when there was a knock on the door. It was Emily Cameron, who occasionally baby-sat for them. She was holding a plastic shopping bag.

Sarah dried her hands on a paper towel. "Morning, Emily. What can I do for you?"

"I hope this isn't a bad time, Mrs. Watts."

In the kitchen, the twins were fighting over a box of cereal. A chair fell over.

"Boys!" Sarah called over her shoulder. "Whatever you're doing, stop it!"

"I can come back later," said Emily.

"Don't pay any attention to the kids. Come on in." Sarah moved away from the doorway.

"Is Mr. Watts here?"

Sarah grunted and turned back to the kitchen, where the twins were scuffling on the floor. "Get up, both of you. Behave yourselves." And to Emily, "My husband's gone fishing. At least I think that's where he is."

"I wanted to return a couple of DVDs to him."

More squabbling from the twins.

"Boys, eat your breakfast and go out and play."

"We haven't done our homework yet."

"You were supposed to finish your homework on Friday. This is Sunday."

Both boys stood up, both looked down at their feet.

"Get upstairs and do it, then. I don't want to hear another peep out of either of you."

The boys shambled off, and Sarah turned to Emily. "Sorry about that. Anything to avoid homework. Sit down, Emily. What are the DVDs?"

"I don't know what they are. My boyfriend, Jerry, left them at my place a couple of weeks ago." Emily took two thin plastic cases out of the Stop & Shop bag. They were labeled in black marker pen: "WATTS 1" and "WATTS 2."

Sarah took the cases and examined them. "That's not my husband's writing. Did your boyfriend tell you they belonged to LeRoy?"

Emily looked confused. "No. I was straightening up my place and came across them again. I just assumed . . ."

"My husband hasn't mentioned any missing DVDs," said Sarah. "Did your boyfriend tell you to give them to LeRoy?"

Emily pushed her glasses back into place. Her magnified eyes looked red, as though she'd been crying. "We broke up, I guess."

"I'm so sorry. That's too bad." At the moment, Sarah was thinking breaking up wasn't so bad at all. She poured a mug of coffee and handed it to Emily. "Here. You need this. There's the cream and sugar, and a spoon."

Emily brushed bangs out of her eyes. "He promised to go to the movies with me Thursday, and he never showed up. I haven't seen him since." A tear trickled down her cheek. Sarah handed her a box of tissues and Emily took one.

"There are lots of other nice boys on the Island," said Sarah. "Since your boyfriend—Jerry?"

Emily nodded.

"Since Jerry didn't tell you to return the DVDs to LeRoy, they might be his, training films LeRoy copied for him. Let's see what's on them, okay?" She looked at Emily's tear-streaked face. "I'm sure he'll be back, Emily."

Emily shook her head miserably.

"The TV is in the living room. Bring your coffee with you and we'll see what we've got."

Sarah removed "WATTS 1" from its plastic case. A slip of paper fell out and she picked it up. Penciled on it in barely legible writing was "Copied from LeRoy Watts laptop by Jerry Sparks," and the date, two months ago.

"Jerry Sparks," said Sarah thoughtfully, turning the paper over to see if anything was written on the other side. "I didn't realize your boyfriend was *that* Jerry."

Emily nodded.

"Well, I guess we're about to be lectured on how to deal with electricity without electrocuting ourselves," Sarah said with a smile. She slipped the disc into the DVD player and turned it on.

A blurry pinkish image came into focus on the screen. There was the sound of running water in the background and a warbling voice singing slightly off-key. Sarah sat forward and stared at the fifty-inch high-resolution plasma screen, which showed every drop of water, every hair, every mole, every eyelash, every freckle on the skin of a young woman taking a shower. The screen proceeded with intimate details of her washing herself.

"Oh my God!" Sarah sprang out of her chair and flipped off the television, ejected the DVD, tossed it onto the coffee table next to the sofa, and dropped into her chair.

There were a long few minutes of silence.

"I don't know what to think," Sarah said at last.

Emily's face was a dismal red. "Me neither."

"Just what did Jerry say when he gave these to you?"

"Only that . . ." Emily had trouble speaking. Her voice came out in a sort of squeak. "He told me," she began, then stopped. "He told me to hang onto them for safekeeping. That's all he said."

Sarah got up and picked up the DVD she'd cast aside. "That notepaper said Jerry copied it from Leroy's laptop. Could Jerry have made those videos?"

"No way." Emily shook her head. "He knows less than I do about cameras."

"My husband fired him last week. Did you know that?"

Emily looked down at her hands.

Not sure Emily had understood, Sarah repeated, "Did you know my husband fired Jerry?"

"He has a problem," Emily said. "Drugs."

"I see."

More silence.

"He's a really great guy when he's not . . ." Emily didn't finish.

"Thank you for bringing these to me, Emily." Sarah moved away from the coffee table. "I don't see any need for you to tell anyone about them, do you?"

Emily shook her head and got up stiffly. "I'm sorry, Mrs. Watts. I guess I shouldn't have brought them to you."

"Yes, you should. You did the right thing." Sarah held out her hand. "Here, I'll take your cup."

Emily stumbled to the door, Sarah shut it behind her and went back to the television set. She inserted "WATTS 1" again and watched it all the way through, fast-forwarding after each woman appeared. An hour of various women, seven or eight of them, all young, all taking showers, all completely unaware of someone spying on them. No one she knew.

She thought "WATTS 2" would be more of the same. But then she recognized one of the women. Then another. She simply couldn't watch their private ablutions. She continued to fast-forward.

Something told her she had to view this to the end. She recognized several more of the women. The twins' kindergarten teacher. The girl who taught riding at the stable. The Brazilian checkout woman at Cronig's. All young women, ranging in age from teens to mid-twenties. She could hardly believe what she was seeing, videos that Roy had taken? *Had* Roy taken them? Her husband Roy? The upstanding civic leader, the town's electrical inspector, scout leader, baseball coach? How long had he been filming naked women? She'd had no inkling of this hidden twist of his—that is, *if* Roy had taken those pictures. Would she, could she, even talk to him about this? What was she going to say? Or do?

She had another thought. Was this a game that was going both ways? One or more of the women calling Roy with suggestive talk?

If this was Roy's little game, clearly Jerry Sparks had known about it. An awful thought crossed her mind. Was Jerry Sparks blackmailing Roy? That would explain Roy's mood lately.

The Island's grapevine unearthed deeply hidden secrets, seemingly without human intervention. The fact of Roy filming naked women in their showers would be all over the Island like—she couldn't imagine anything with which to compare the speed of the Island grapevine.

CHAPTER 9

LeRoy had arisen early on Sunday, before Sarah awoke. He showered and shaved, then spent another full day fishing. He caught nothing. And nothing helped the sick feeling in his gut. All day, Jerry Sparks had perched on his shoulders.

When he got home, his wife and kids were eating supper. His wife turned away from him.

LeRoy put his gear away and hung up his waders in the mudroom. He washed his hands and face in the kitchen sink and looked for a towel.

"Don't use my clean dish towels," snapped Sarah.

He dried his face and hands on a paper towel and threw it in the trash. "You move the books okay?"

"She called twice yesterday." Sarah still didn't look at him. Probably mad at him. Who the hell was the caller?

Supper was leftover macaroni. Zeke and Jared squabbled and whined over nothing. Sarah stared at her plate.

LeRoy got a dish out of the cabinet and served himself from the casserole in the oven and sat at his usual place. Sarah continued to eat in silence.

"Something bothering you?" asked LeRoy.

"It's nothing."

"Suit yourself," said LeRoy.

"Emily Cameron came by."

"Who's she?" Then he remembered. The baby-sitter. Jerry Sparks's girlfriend. "Never mind. I know who she is. Lumpy girl with glasses and bangs." LeRoy speared a forkful of macaroni and shoveled it into his mouth. "What did she want?" he asked, his mouth full.

"The 'lumpy girl,' as you call her, is trying to locate Jerry Sparks. It seems he's disappeared."

"Lucky her."

"Jerry can be perfectly nice."

"I've heard enough about Jerry Sparks." LeRoy tossed his napkin onto his scarcely touched supper and got up from the table. The macaroni and cheese he'd shoveled into his mouth had stopped halfway to his stomach in a glutinous mass.

"She brought something to show me," said Sarah to his departing back.

"Lucky you," he said over his shoulder.

"Now where are you going?" Sarah asked.

"Out." LeRoy slammed the front door behind him.

He drove to the unlighted parking area near the bike path in the state forest and made himself a nest in the back of his van with his sleeping bag and some plastic tarps. He twisted and turned all night, and the sleeping bag wrapped itself around and between his legs. As the night moved on, the cold metal of the van floor got harder and colder and the ghost of Jerry Sparks breathed his foul breath into his face and there was no place he could think of where he could escape.

When the dawn chorus began early Monday morning, first a robin, then doves, chickadees, cardinals, and blue jays, LeRoy, who hadn't slept at all, shuffled off his sleeping bag and climbed into the driver's seat. He had to get to the Steamship Authority office when it opened. He was exhausted. His mouth felt as though it was full of half-composted moss and the smell of Jerry Sparks clung to him.

———

Around the same time LeRoy was getting ready to head to the Steamship Authority office, Victoria Trumbull was hiking the quarter mile to the police station. She used the tip of her lilac-wood stick to turn over leaves to see what interesting plants were sprouting underneath.

This was the day LeRoy Watts had promised to come to fix the outlet her guest had blown up with her hair dryer. Fortunately, Nancy had decided to leave a day early.

Across the road to her left, grass had greened in Doane's pasture, seemingly overnight. They'd be cutting the first hay in another few weeks. A catbird called from the wild cherry tree next to the road and another catbird answered. She breathed in deeply. The scent of lilacs was everywhere. Her own lilacs reached almost to her second floor and were laden with blossoms. Neil Flynn, who owned Katama Apiaries, had set up seven beehives in her pasture, and the lilacs hummed with his bees.

She paused to catch her breath before turning in at the parking area in front of the station. Ducks rose as she approached, and waddled off toward the Mill Pond.

Victoria straightened up, lifted her head, and climbed the steps into the station house. Casey was at her desk, scowling at something on her computer.

She turned, her scowl softening. "Morning, Victoria. You're up early."

"I've been out in my garden since the sun rose. My touch-me-not is going to bloom this season."

"The year of touch-me-not and stalkers," said Casey.

Victoria seated herself in the wooden armchair and unbuttoned her blue coat. "Is something wrong?"

"Stalking." Casey picked up her stone paperweight and hefted it from one hand to the other. "Exactly what the speaker on Thursday was talking about. Jessica Gordon and Maron Andrews called me again to complain. I can't do anything; the telephone company can't do anything. They put a tracer on the calls."

"And, I suppose, the stalker is using a prepaid disposable cell phone. Almost impossible to trace."

"Where on earth did you learn that?"

"I get around." Victoria laced her hands on the top of her lilac-wood stick. "We need to talk. Three women in the knitters' group are getting unwanted calls."

"Three? Who's the third?" asked Casey.

"Alyssa Adams."

"The EMT?"

"Yes."

"The guy's not threatening them, is he?"

"Mostly heavy breathing. Occasional obscenities."

Casey swiveled in her chair. "It's distressing for the women, I know, but unless they're getting threats, we can't do anything. Even with overt threats, there's not a lot we can do." Casey stood up. "Let's make our rounds, Victoria. Too nice a day to be inside worrying about stuff we can't do anything about."

"Can't calls be traced somehow?"

"Every cell phone has a way of being identified for billing purposes," said Casey. "But with disposable phones, you buy cards with minutes on them that the phone itself deducts. Can't be traced."

"Aren't the calls relayed by a cell tower?"

"Yeah, sure," said Casey. "I guess so."

"That means we can locate the caller," said Victoria.

"'We,' Victoria? Hardly. You're talking about an entire army of technicians," said Casey. "Before you get any more bright ideas, let's get out of here."

LeRoy opened a can of Mountain Dew from his cooler, rinsed his mouth with it, and spat it out onto the ground. Still feeling grungy, he drove to the ferry terminal and went into the men's room, where he cleaned himself up.

The woman at the ticket counter who always looked cheerful and always had a great smile, greeted him. "Morning, Mr. Watts. Going to be a beautiful day. Can I help you?"

LeRoy attempted a smile in return. "I'm trying to remember Beany's last name."

"That's funny. I just know him as Beany. Wait a sec." She turned away from the ticket window and called out to another ticket seller. "Mike, what's Beany's name?"

"Albion. He's a Fereira. Lives in Edgartown."

"Oh, sure," said LeRoy, not being sure at all. "I've done some work for them. Thanks."

"No problem, Mr. Watts. Have a great day!"

"Thanks," mumbled LeRoy. "Same to you."

Back in his van, he started to page through the Island directory he kept in the glove compartment, when he remembered he'd promised to repair Victoria Trumbull's upstairs outlet. He scribbled a note to himself to call her. First, though, he looked up Fereira in the phone book. He found listings in the directory for a dozen Fereiras. Four in Edgartown. No Albion.

He considered going back to the ticket office, and decided against making too big a deal out of trying to locate Beany. He took out his cell phone and punched in the number for the first Fereira in Edgartown.

"Beany? You want Irma, his mother," said the woman, and gave him the number. "He in trouble again?"

"No, ma'am," said LeRoy. "At least not that I know of. Thanks for the help."

He checked the number in the directory, found a listing on Pine Street, and dialed.

"Beany's my son. Haven't seen him for a while."

"Does he have a new computer?"

"No idea. Why?"

"He stopped by my shop on Friday, complaining about something one of my employees sold him. I was wondering if it happened to be a computer."

"Want him to call you if he shows up?"

"I'm close by," said LeRoy, thinking he could cover the eight miles to Edgartown in fifteen minutes. "Mind if I stop in and take a look?"

"Well," said Irma. "I guess that's all right. You know where I live?"

"Yes, ma'am. I believe I did some electrical work for you a couple of years ago."

"Oh, sure, I remember you, I think."

LeRoy closed his phone and headed toward Edgartown.

He made the trip in fifteen minutes and parked in front of the Fereira house. An Island car was out front, a green Citation held together with duct tape. The rear window was a sheet of plastic stuck in with more duct tape.

He knocked, and a short, plump woman wearing a flowing muumuu printed with magenta flowers came to the door. Her salt-and-pepper hair was pulled away from her face and held with plastic butterfly clips.

"Mrs. Fereira? LeRoy Watts."

"Come in. Beany just got home." She turned and called, "Beany! Some man to see you."

"Who is it, Ma?" The lanky guy who'd come to the shop appeared from the back of the house. He wore a faded Red Sox cap and was drinking a Diet Coke.

"This man called about a computer," said Mrs. Fereira.

"Yeah, Jerry Sparks's boss. How're ya doin'?"

"Not bad," said LeRoy, who felt awful. "You said Jerry sold you some lemon. Was that his computer?"

"Come on in, Mr. Watts," said Mrs. Fereira. "Don't let all the warm air out."

LeRoy entered the stifling house and shut the door behind him.

"Yeah, I bought his stinkin' computer. Piece of junk." Beany took a last swig of his diet Coke and crushed the can. "I put an ad up on the Cronig's bulletin board and some guy came by and bought it after I talked to you. Sold it for more than I paid."

"Who'd you sell it to?"

"I never got his name. He paid cash. What's up?"

LeRoy thought for a moment. "I knew you were upset with Sparks. Wanted to help if I could."

Beany lifted his cap and scratched his head. "The guy who bought it lives in West Tisbury. Drives an old white Volvo station wagon, if that helps any."

"It's not important. Thanks anyway."

CHAPTER 10

Victoria stood at the foot of the station house steps, waiting for Casey to finish a phone call, when Howland Atherton pulled into the parking lot.

"Good morning, Howland," she called out to him. "We were just leaving to do our rounds."

"Morning, Victoria. Before you go off, I need to talk to you and the chief." Howland was wearing his usual khakis with a dark knit shirt. A lanyard was looped around his neck, with a small metal object dangling from it.

Casey appeared and greeted Howland. "You look worried."

"I am."

"Come in, then. Our rounds can wait."

Back inside, Victoria returned to her armchair, and Howland moved Junior Norton's seat next to her and straddled it, his arms folded on the back. Casey returned to her desk and placed her hands flat on top of her large desk calendar. "Well?" she asked, turning to Howland.

Howland said, "A couple of days ago, I bought a used computer from Beany, one of the guys who works for the Steamship Authority. He'd acquired the computer from a buddy who needed some cash in a hurry, he told me."

Casey picked up her beach-stone paperweight and rubbed the smooth surface. "Go on," she said.

"Beany used the computer for a few days and decided it was a piece of junk."

"Who's the buddy he bought it from?" asked Casey, looking up.

"Jerry Sparks."

"Oh," said Victoria. She sat forward, hands on top of her lilac-wood stick.

Casey turned to her. "Jerry Sparks again."

"You know him?" asked Howland.

"His boss—his former boss, LeRoy Watts—is coming to my house sometime today to repair an outlet." Victoria stroked the smoothly sanded surface of her stick and settled back into her chair.

"Former boss?" Howland unwound himself from the chair and went to the window overlooking the Mill Pond, hands thrust into his pockets.

"LeRoy told me on Thursday he'd fired Jerry Sparks."

"What about the computer?" asked Casey.

Howland turned from the window. "I went through the hard drive to see what was on it. Delete files I didn't need, that sort of thing. One file was encrypted. I didn't want to delete it until I knew its contents. When I finally did decode it . . . Well, that's what I need to show you."

Outside, the ducks quacked a few times, then settled down again. Through the window, Victoria could see wind riffling the surface of the Mill Pond.

"A police matter?" asked Casey.

"I'll let you decide," Howland replied, returning to his chair. "The file consists of a dozen or more short videos, apparently taken by a camera or cameras hidden in bathrooms and showing women taking showers."

"Cameras installed without the resident's knowledge?" Victoria asked. "Was the installer Jerry Sparks?"

"No way of knowing," said Howland. "The videos were on his computer. I downloaded them onto this thumb drive." He lifted the lanyard with the inch-and-a-half-long metal object. "They're disturbing, to say the least."

"Jerry Sparks has free access to the places he works," said Victoria. "I certainly have never watched over him. I suspect most people don't."

"Sparks has done work here in the police station," said Casey. "He seemed competent enough." She pushed her swivel chair away from her desk and stood up. "Can you download the videos onto my computer?"

"Sure," said Howland.

"There's something I should tell you," Victoria said to Casey. "Alyssa Adams came to see me on Thursday evening." She turned to Howland and explained. "She's a member of the mathematical knitters' group, and she, too, has been getting calls from the breather." Victoria turned back to Casey. "Alyssa believes she knows who's making the calls."

"Not Jerry Sparks?" said Casey.

Victoria nodded.

"Double whammy, if he's the one," murmured Casey. "Phone calls *and* videos."

"Did she recognize his voice?" asked Howland.

"He didn't speak. But a couple of months ago, she had a movie date with Jerry that ended unsatisfactorily, and she's been getting calls since then."

"Did he ever identify himself?" asked Howland.

"He did in the first couple of calls. Jerry apologized and invited her on another date. She accepted the apology and declined the date. He called two or three times after that, getting more and more insistent."

Casey shifted the beach stone from one hand to the other and back again.

"And after those first calls?" asked Howland.

"There was a period of several weeks when she didn't hear

from him, and then the calls started again, but this time they've consisted of heavy breathing or muttered obscenities."

"How often does she get the calls?" asked Casey.

"At irregular intervals, two or three times a week."

"The videos were filmed over several months," said Howland. "Dates are noted on the right side, near the bottom. He may have used only one camera and moved it around. Many of the videos seem to have been taken in the same bathroom. Possibly a rental unit, or a gym or fitness center."

"Where is Jerry Sparks now?" asked Victoria.

"I wouldn't know," said Howland. "Never met the guy."

Casey swiveled her chair. "How long will it take you to bring the videos up on my computer?"

Howland got up from his chair again. "No time at all."

LeRoy left Beany's with no clue as to the whereabouts of Jerry Sparks's computer except that the guy who'd bought it drove a white Volvo station wagon. LeRoy got back into his van. He had to find that computer before the police did. Sparks had lied about downloading the videos onto his cell phone, but LeRoy couldn't take a chance that Sparks had also lied about downloading those pictures onto his computer.

When LeRoy called Victoria Trumbull, the answering machine kicked in with a message from her granddaughter. He told the machine he was on the way and would take a look at the upstairs outlet.

When he got to Victoria's, no one was home. He knocked several times on her kitchen door, then went upstairs to the guest room, where he checked the blackened outlet and the smoky patch on the wall above it. He'd have to come back later when he had more time. It was a wonder Mrs. Trumbull hadn't burned her house down long ago.

He finished rewiring what he could with the tools he'd

brought with him, making her house somewhat safer. Since he'd stashed the Taser cartridge in his toolbox, he decided to leave it at Victoria's, where no one was likely to discover it. Even if she did look inside, she wouldn't recognize a spent Taser cartridge. That way, he could dispose of the cartridge later. He kept out a couple of tools he might need in the meantime, a screwdriver and a pair of pliers. A wrench. A flashlight.

He then went downstairs and left Victoria a note on the kitchen table, telling her he'd made temporary repairs to the outlet but not to use it. After that, he went outside and stood at the top of her stone steps, thinking.

Banks of lilacs—not mere shrubs, but tall trees—surrounded Victoria's weathered house, and the branches were heavy with blossoms. He breathed in deeply and thought about his life before the death of Jerry Sparks.

He was so tired. His eyes felt scratchy and his clothes were rumpled. If only he could go back in time and redo that confrontation. He hadn't meant to kill Jerry Sparks. Tasers weren't supposed to kill. That's why he'd bought one. Guns killed people, not Tasers. He'd never wanted a gun around that his kids might play with.

Why did he have to be the one in hundreds or thousands to kill with a Taser?

The Taser. Would an autopsy determine how Sparks had died? He didn't think the tiny darts had penetrated the skin. They didn't need to. Perhaps the medical examiner would conclude that Jerry died of a heart attack, which was probably what had happened. Too many drugs, not eating right, that's what they'd think. He had to get rid of the damned cartridge as soon as he could. No one would find it at Mrs. Trumbull's, and if, by some chance, she looked into his toolbox, she'd think it was some piece of electrical equipment. Which it was, in a way. The Taser itself, he'd left in the top file drawer. God, how his stomach hurt.

Before he did anything, he had to find that computer.

He'd parked his van in Victoria's drive. The gold lettering on the side was dusty, and he wiped it with his handkerchief before he got in.

As he passed the West Tisbury police station, he saw a white Volvo station wagon parked out front. Could this be the guy who'd bought the computer? A lot of Volvos in the village, but not many white ones. Did he dare meet the owner face-to-face, in the police station, of all places?

Best defense is a good offense, he thought, and made a U-turn around the triangle at Brandy Brow and pulled into the parking area, stopping next to the white Volvo.

He went to the back of his van for his toolbox, then remembered he'd left it at Victoria's. Lucky he'd thought to keep out a couple of tools. He put the screwdriver and pliers in his shirt pocket, brushed past the ducks squatting on the oyster shells, and went up the steps and into the station house.

Chief O'Neill was at her desk, talking with Victoria Trumbull. A distinguished-looking guy stood up when LeRoy came in. The chief stood, too, and held out her hand.

"Mr. Watts," she said. "You know my deputy, Victoria Trumbull, don't you?"

"Of course. I was just at your house, Mrs. Trumbull."

"Were you able to fix the problem?"

"I'll have to come back when I have more time. It's going to take some work."

"I was afraid of that."

"By the way, I left my toolbox there. Hope you don't mind."

"Of course not." Victoria nodded and said to Casey, "LeRoy and Jerry Sparks worked for me in the past."

Jerry Sparks, thought LeRoy. Jerry Sparks, Jerry Sparks!

"I understand he's not with you any longer," said Casey. "I'm sorry about that. He seemed to do good work." She turned to

Howland. "By the way, Mr. Watts, do you know Howland Atherton?"

"How're you doin'?" LeRoy held out his hand.

Howland shook hands. "The owner of Watts Electrical?"

"Yes, sir," said LeRoy.

"How can we help you?" asked Casey.

"I was driving past, Chief, thought I'd stop in to see if the work Sparks did is okay."

"You know where the breaker box is," said Casey.

She sat down again, as did Howland. LeRoy went to the far wall and opened the metal circuit-breaker box. He checked the breakers and listened to the conversation.

"Where did you get the computer?" he heard Casey ask.

"Saw an ad posted on the bulletin board outside Cronig's," said Howland. "The guy I bought it from got it from Sparks. He couldn't make it work, so he sold it."

LeRoy dropped the screwdriver and it rolled on the linoleum floor in a half circle, making a clicking sound.

Casey called over her shoulder, "How does it look?"

"Everything looks fine." LeRoy bent over and picked up the screwdriver and put it into his pocket. "Mr. Atherton, did I hear you say you'd bought Jerry Sparks's computer?"

"That's right."

"I've been trying to track it down. I didn't realize he'd sold it." LeRoy closed the breaker box. "I gave him the old office computer when I bought a new one for Maureen. Then after I let Sparks go, I wondered if he had work-related stuff on it."

"Be glad to let you check it out. It's in my car. I was taking it to The Computer Lab for a tune-up."

"Kind of presumptuous of me, but any chance I can borrow it for a few hours? I'll bring it right back."

"No problem," said Howland.

"And, Mrs. Trumbull, I'll stop by later this week and work on that outlet. Don't use the electricity in that room until I take care of it."

"Thank you," said Victoria.

Howland and LeRoy went out to the parking area, past the ducks, which moved aside to make way for them, and LeRoy transferred Howland's newly acquired computer to the back of his van.

"Appreciate this, Mr. Atherton," said LeRoy.

Casey stood in the doorway. "Again, thanks, LeRoy."

"Part of the service." LeRoy wiped his hands on his handkerchief.

"I'm sorry you had to let Sparks go," Casey added.

"He'd been a good worker before he got into drugs."

"It's a serious problem." Casey shook her head.

LeRoy said, "Thanks for letting me borrow your computer, Mr. Atherton. Want me to return it here to the police station when I'm done?"

"Sure. That would be fine."

"Be seeing you, then," and Leroy took off.

CHAPTER 11

Around 9:30 that same morning, Monday, the phone rang at the Watts's house. Sarah figured it was that woman caller again, so she let it ring. Or maybe it was Roy. Well, he can wait. Wonder where he spent last night? On the fifth ring, before the answering machine kicked in, she set down her knitting and picked up the phone, ready to tell either her or him a thing or two.

"Well?" she answered.

"Mrs. Watts? This is Joanne, the secretary at the West Tisbury school."

Sarah immediately readjusted her thinking. "The twins? Has something happened to the twins?"

"The boys are fine, but you need to come in right away. We tried to reach Mr. Watts, but he was out of the office and his office manager didn't seem to know how to reach him. Shall we say twenty minutes or so?"

"Yes," said Sarah. "Of course. What's the matter?"

"I'm sorry, Mrs. Watts. I can't discuss it over the phone," and Joanne disconnected.

Sarah dialed LeRoy's office. The answering machine kicked in. "You've reached Watts Electrical. . . ." She slammed down the phone. Maureen must be away from the shop.

She went into the bedroom and changed quickly from her sweats to jeans and a long-sleeved blouse with an old-lady floral print. She dabbed on lip gloss, which she seldom used, ran a comb through her thick hair, curled tightly in the humidity. She tied it back with a black ribbon so she would look more serious, then decided to change out of her jeans and into black slacks. She tried calling LeRoy's cell phone, got the robotic voice that told her to leave a message, asked LeRoy to call the school, and darted out the side door. She started up the Volkswagen and flew over the speed bumps toward Old County Road and the school.

What on earth had the boys done that would cause the school to demand to see her and LeRoy? And right away.

She parked, walked quickly to the office, and followed the secretary to the principal's office. Mrs. Parkinson, the principal, stood up as Sarah entered.

"My boys?" Sarah blurted out. "Where are my boys?"

Casey and Howland went back into the station house after LeRoy left with Howland's new computer.

"You wouldn't find an off-Island electrician making sure stuff was done right like that," said Casey.

Victoria looked thoughtful.

"Is something bothering you, Victoria?" Casey asked.

"LeRoy's usually so tidy. This morning, he was disheveled and hadn't even shaved."

"I bet he's been busy since he let Sparks go." Casey moved papers off her desk. "Let's check out the videos."

Howland took the lanyard with the dangling metal piece from around his neck. "I downloaded the videos onto this and, without thinking, deleted them from Sparks's computer." He rubbed his nose. "Stupid of me. I know better."

"Oh?" said Victoria. "You have the copy, don't you?"

"If we ever apprehend the guy who made the videos, I've destroyed evidence that might be important. My copies will never hold up in court." He turned away from the desk and paced the few steps to the window, and looked out at the pond. "I was too eager to delete the damned things."

Casey moved away from her desk to give Howland room.

Howland sat in her chair and inserted the thumb drive into her computer, tapped keys, and the videos, complete with sound, popped up onto the screen.

The first was of a young woman taking a shower. She faced the camera, which was somewhere above her. Clearly unaware of being watched, she soaped herself and held her head up to the spray, eyes closed, hands cupping her breasts. She was singing.

The screen went blank for a second. Then there was a second scene of a different young woman. And then another scene and yet another.

"Enough!" said Casey. "I've seen enough. He's got to be stopped." She picked up the phone. "Sparks lives in Oak Bluffs. Since it's out of my jurisdiction, I'll have to call the OB police."

"Why does LeRoy need to check Jerry Sparks's personal computer?" asked Victoria. "You wouldn't think Jerry would have business files on it."

"He didn't," said Howland. "All personal stuff, including those videos. At least one good thing came of my deleting the files—Watts won't have to view them."

When LeRoy got back to his office with the computer, Maureen was on the phone. She glanced up as he pushed the back door open with his hip, holding the operating unit against his stomach. The computer still had the flower stickers that Maureen had attached in an attempt to make the machine look less formidable.

She finished her call and disconnected. "Isn't that my old computer? I thought you gave it to Jerry Sparks."

LeRoy grunted and set the operating unit on the floor.

Maureen studied him. "You look just awful, Mr. Watts. You haven't even shaved. Go home and make yourself some hot lemonade with honey and get to bed."

"I've got to check something out."

"You worked much too hard last week, Mr. Watts. It's going to catch up with you one of these days." She straightened papers on her desk. "By the way, the school called while you were out. They want you to call back."

"Thanks. I'll take care of that later."

"It sounded important, Mr. Watts."

"Right," said LeRoy.

He unplugged wires from his computer and attached them to the unit he'd borrowed from Howland, and booted it up.

"Can I help you with something, Mr. Watts?"

"No, that's okay," said LeRoy. "Why don't you take off for lunch now. I'll be around the office for the next couple of hours to take any calls."

"It's only eleven o'clock."

"Take a couple of hours, then," said LeRoy. "Go shopping or something."

"If you're sure?"

"Take your time," said LeRoy.

"Don't forget to call the school, Mr. Watts," and with that, Maureen left.

He went through the files and menus on the computer that had belonged to Jerry Sparks, checked everything that Jerry could possibly have copied from his, LeRoy's, computer, and found nothing. He went into the washroom and shaved, brushed his teeth, washed his face, and combed his hair. He was a different man.

Maureen returned a little after 12:30.

"No calls," said LeRoy.

"Did you take care of Mrs. Trumbull's outlet?"

"I looked at it. I'll need to spend a couple of hours. It's a wonder she didn't have a fire. Old wiring."

Maureen examined him. "You look better, Mr. Watts. I'll make you a nice cup of tea." She turned before she got as far as the hot-water maker. "Did you call the school?"

"I will. Tea sounds good." He checked the files once more. Nothing. Nothing at all. Sparks's personal stuff, period. Sparks had lied to him. He'd bluffed. LeRoy felt a surge of relief. He'd panicked over nothing.

Maureen brought him a mug of strong tea with sugar, which he didn't usually take, but he drank it anyway and his spirits lifted. He'd wasted time worrying about those damned videos, and he needn't have.

"Almost forgot. Isn't tomorrow your birthday?"

"Thank you for asking, Mr. Watts. Actually, it's the day after tomorrow. My daughter and her husband and my two grand-babies are coming tomorrow. I was going to ask you if I might take two days off."

"What a cad I am!" LeRoy smacked his hand on his forehead. "I should have remembered. Of course you can take off both days. Thursday, too."

"Thank you, Mr. Watts, but I really should get those bills out no later than Thursday."

"The bills can wait another day. Have a great birthday. Relax. We'll see you on Friday, then."

"Two full days of grandbabies is enough. I'll be back on Thursday."

"Well, if you're sure. How old are the grandkids now?"

"One's two and the other's six months."

"Time flies," said LeRoy. He unplugged all the wires so he could return the unit to Howland Atherton, who must be wondering why he was so concerned about the computer.

Maureen laid some papers on his desk and smiled at him. "You look much better, Mr. Watts. Nothing like a cup of strong, hot tea."

"You're a gem, Maureen," said LeRoy. "I appreciate all you do for me." He waited until she'd gone back to her desk and was on the phone before he opened the top file drawer to take out the Taser.

The Taser didn't seem to be in the top drawer. Had he put it in a lower drawer? He opened the second, then the third drawer. Not there. Not in the bottom drawer, where Jerry Sparks's cell phone lay like a dead mouse. He felt the blood drain out of his face.

Maureen finished her call, set the phone down, and it rang immediately. "Watts Electrical Supply," Maureen answered. "Just a moment, please." She pushed the hold button and set the phone down. "It's the school again, Mr. Watts." She glanced over at him. "Oh my Lord, Mr. Watts! What's happened? You look awful!" She put her hands up to her mouth.

LeRoy, wild-eyed and deathly pale, leaped up from his chair and dashed out the back door. The door slammed behind him.

Maureen followed him to the door. "Mr. Watts, the school has to see you right away! Mr. Watts . . ."

LeRoy scrambled into his van and tore out of the parking area.

What had he done with the damned Taser? Where had he put it? He had to find it, and now. Right now.

CHAPTER 12

"Your boys are with a teaching aide in the faculty room, Mrs. Watts," said Mrs. Parkinson. The principal was an imposing figure in a tailored gray suit and white silk shirt. Her silver hair was perfectly coifed and she wore pale pink lipstick and matching pink nail polish.

"I've called the police. Chief O'Neill should be here momentarily with Mrs. Trumbull. I wanted to speak to you and your husband privately."

"The police!" Sarah gasped. "What happened?"

"Please, sit down," said Mrs. Parkinson.

Sarah continued to stand. "Tell me what's going on!"

Mrs. Parkinson, still standing, pointed to the chair in front of her desk. "I think you'd better sit down."

Sarah slumped into the chair, not aware that she had done so. Mrs. Parkinson, too, sat.

"We wanted your husband to be here, but as you know, we were unable to reach him."

Sarah sat on the edge of her chair. "What's—"

Mrs. Parkinson held up her hand and Sarah sat back. "The boys came to school this morning with what they claimed was a toy gun. According to them, your husband's office manager gave it to them."

Sarah edged forward and put her forearms on Mrs. Parkinson's desk, hands clasped. "Maureen knows we don't allow the boys to play with toy guns. She knows that!"

Mrs. Parkinson held up her hand again. "Let me finish, please." She waited for a few moments.

Sarah, feeling as though she herself were in fourth grade, moved her arms off the desk.

"At recess this morning, the twins were taking turns showing off this so-called toy gun, pointing it at other children and pretending it was a death ray." Mrs. Parkinson folded her own hands on her desktop. "The teacher's aide took the weapon away from them and brought it to me."

Sarah gawked at the principal.

"The so-called gun is actually a Taser, a sophisticated police weapon."

Sarah sat still.

"Do you know what a Taser is, Mrs. Watts?"

Sarah shook her head. "I've never heard of it."

Mrs. Parkinson reached into her desk drawer and brought out a blocky weapon that looked like a cartoonist's drawing of a ray gun. She set it down on her desk with a heavy metallic clunk.

"Do you have any idea where the boys might have obtained such a weapon?"

"N-no." Sarah stared at the Taser.

"Or where your husband's office manager might have obtained such a weapon?"

Sarah didn't respond.

Mrs. Parkinson pressed a button on her phone, and when a voice said "Yes?" she asked that the Watts boys be brought to her office.

Zeke and Jared slunk in on either side of a teacher's aide, a young man barely out of his teens with short, neatly combed brown hair.

"We weren't shooting anyone!" Jared exclaimed as soon as he saw his mother.

"You won't tell Daddy?" said Zeke.

"Sit down, boys," said Mrs. Parkinson. She dismissed the aide with a nod and a "Thank you, Charles." When the boys were seated, she said, "Why don't you tell your mother and me how you got the weapon."

The twins looked at each other.

"Where did you get that thing?" Sarah's voice verged on hysteria. "Did Maureen give it to you?"

"Please, Mrs. Watts. Let the boys answer." The principal turned to one of them. "You're Zeke?"

"No, ma'am, I'm Jared."

"Tell me from the beginning, Jared, when you went to your father's shop and he wasn't there but Maureen was."

Jared nodded but looked down at his sneakers.

"Well?" asked Mrs. Parkinson.

"Maureen gave it to us to play with."

"Look at me, Jared," said Mrs. Parkinson. "Are you sure Maureen gave that gun to you? Think again. You must tell the truth."

"My boys don't lie," said Sarah.

"Mrs. Watts!" warned Mrs. Parkinson. "Well, Jared?" When Jared still looked at the floor, she turned to Zeke. "Would you like to tell me exactly how you happened to have this gun, Zeke?"

"Yes, ma'am," said Zeke, so softly that even Sarah wasn't sure she heard him.

"Speak up, please," said Mrs. Parkinson. "Was the weapon in your father's desk?"

"No, ma'am."

"Where, then?"

"In the filing cabinet," said Zeke.

Jared spoke up. "In the top drawer."

"How did you find it?"

"We was—"

"Were," said their mother.

Zeke glanced at his mother, then down at his feet. "We were

looking for paper to draw on. Maureen keeps scrap paper in the file drawer."

"And that's when you saw the weapon?"

"Yes, ma'am," said Jared. "We didn't take it then."

"We took it when Maureen went to the post office," said Zeke.

"Where did you hide it then?" asked Mrs. Parkinson.

"In Zeke's book bag," said Jared.

"This was on Friday?"

"Yes, ma'am," the boys said together.

"And you brought the weapon to school this morning?"

The boys looked at each other and nodded.

"You know it's serious to bring a weapon to school?"

"We thought it was a toy gun."

"We don't allow toy guns in school."

"Yes, ma'am."

Mrs. Parkinson's phone buzzed. She picked it up and Sarah heard the school secretary say, "Mrs. Trumbull and Chief O'Neill are here, Mrs. Parkinson."

"Send them in."

When Sarah arrived home, feeling badly beaten up after her confrontation with the principal and the police, the phone was ringing. Her two boys dragged along behind her, heads down, hands in their pockets, scuffing their sneakers in the gravel path. She hurried to answer the phone, pointing at the mat just inside the door. "You two stand right there. Don't move from that spot."

The caller was her sister Jackie. "Sarah, I've been trying to reach you all morning. I've got to talk to you." Jackie lived on the Edgartown–West Tisbury Road, not far from Victoria Trumbull.

"I can't talk to you now, Jackie."

Jackie's voice rose. "This is really, really important. I'm coming over to see you."

"Don't even think about it." Sarah plopped herself down at the kitchen table, the phone held to her ear. "The boys got into trouble at school. I've just come back from a lovely session with that dragon lady principal. This is not the time to pester me with one of your damned crises."

"Sweetie, this is one hell of a lot more important than your nine-year-olds getting into mischief, I promise. I'll be right over," Jackie said, and hung up.

"Shit!" Sarah got up and slammed the phone at the wall cradle. It fell to the floor and a robotic voice told her that she hadn't disconnected.

She glowered at the boys, standing exactly where she'd told them to stand, shifting from foot to foot.

"Go to your room!" She pointed to the stairs. "Homework! Not a sound from you until your father comes home. Understand?"

"Yes, ma'am," said Jared.

"Can I go to the bathroom?" asked Zeke.

"You'd better hurry."

There was a soft shuffling up the stairs. After a minute, the toilet flushed and their door shut.

On the floor, the robotic voice on the phone said, "Your call cannot be completed as dialed. Please hang up. . . ." Sarah started to kick that voice, thought better of it, picked up the receiver, and hung it up. What could Jackie have on her mind that was so important? Jackie, the alarmist. Her twice-married, twice-divorced younger sister. The glamour girl. How would *she* deal with two nine-year-olds who'd somehow acquired a serious police weapon and brandished it around the school yard?

Sarah cleaned up the breakfast dishes she'd left when the school called. She poured a cup of coffee, put it in the microwave, and was about to push the button that read BEVERAGE, when the door burst open and Jackie flew in, her golden hair attractively awry, her large blue eyes looking helplessly appealing. Sarah had seen it all before.

"Well?" Sarah pushed the microwave button.

"Look at this!" and Jackie flung down a small camera.

Sarah turned and glanced at the camera. She opened her eyes wide and stared at it. With a sick feeling, she knew what was coming. She turned back to Jackie. "What's that supposed to be?"

"A video camera, sweetie." Jackie folded her arms under her perfect breasts, covered modestly by a blue sweater that exactly matched her eyes.

Sarah sat. "So it's a video camera. So what?"

Jackie slipped into another chair at the kitchen table, sitting across from her sister. "Mark found it."

"Who's Mark?"

"My new boyfriend. Don't you remember meeting him?"

"Apparently not."

Jackie sighed. "Well, he was in the john and saw this camera hidden in the heating duct. Aiming at the shower."

Sarah looked away. Too much was happening. The boys and that gun. And just yesterday, Emily Cameron had given her those two DVDs, "WATTS 1" and "WATTS 2." Jackie hadn't appeared on either one, but then, the videos were dated two months ago. How many women had Roy filmed?

"Motion-activated," Jackie continued. "It's a remote sensor. Sends pictures to a receiver somewhere."

The microwave beeped and Sarah got up to retrieve her coffee. She needed those few seconds to regain her composure. She returned to her seat. "Taking pictures of you showering? Why would anyone want to do that?"

"What do you mean?" Jackie sat up straight.

"Oh, come off it. Who put it there, Mark?"

"No, of course Mark didn't put the camera there. He found it. He removed it."

"Then who do you think *did* put it there?"

"I'm getting to that. I need a drink."

Sarah pointed to the coffeepot. "Help yourself."

"A drink, I said."

"Are you kidding? It's not even noon."

Jackie strode over to the cabinet next to the sink, opened it, and brought out an almost full bottle of Scotch. She reached down two glasses from the cabinet above the counter and set one in front of Sarah and one at her place.

"Ice?" she asked.

"Don't bother. You're right. I guess I *can* use a drink after all. The boys . . ." She held her glass up and Jackie poured.

"What about the boys?"

"Never mind. It's a long story. How do you think someone snuck a camera into your bathroom?"

"You want to guess?" Jackie took a large swallow and brushed her golden hair out of her eyes.

Sarah said nothing.

"Your ever-lovin' husband, LeRoy Watts. That's who put the spy camera in my bathroom."

That was exactly what Sarah didn't want to hear. She stood up and pushed her glass away. "What are you talking about?"

"Roy's been spying on me."

"You arrogant bitch!"

"He's been trying to make out with me for a looong time, sweetie." Jackie examined her nails, painted a metallic lavender. "Since he didn't get anywhere, he's getting his jollies long-distance."

Sarah pointed to the door. "Get out."

Jackie remained seated. "Don't you want to know how I found out?"

"No. Get out. Leave!"

Jackie didn't move. "Roy and his whacked-out assistant did some electrical work for me a month ago. That camera's been there a month, Sarah. Your creepy husband has been salivating over me every night for a damn month. Taking my shower."

"You . . ." Sarah knew Jackie was right. "How dare you accuse Roy!"

At that, Jackie laughed. "Striking a sensitive note, are we?" She lifted her glass and drank. "I don't suppose Roy watches *you* in the shower, does he?"

Sarah collapsed back into her seat. What was she going to do? Confront Roy the minute he came home? What?

"He was installing an extra outlet in the hall outside my upstairs bathroom. Actually, they were."

"Roy and Jerry? Why two people?"

"How should I know? Ask them. I wasn't even home."

Sarah pulled her glass toward her. Her face had regained some color.

"Frankly, Sarah, I never trusted that bastard husband of yours."

Sarah ran her finger around the rim of her glass. "You're so prejudiced against Roy, you haven't even considered Jerry. *He's* the creep."

"Ha!" said Jackie.

CHAPTER 13

Now that the knitters had decided to meet every weekday afternoon to finish their quilt by the mid-June deadline, this was the first time they'd met on a Monday.

Maron and Jessica sat side by side on the black-and-white-striped couch, Fran Bacon in the matching easy chair, and Elizabeth Trumbull at the table across from Casper Martin and Jim Weiss. Casper had shifted the pile of atlases and reference books to the floor to give them room to spread out their work.

Reverend Judy MacDonald, the Unitarian minister, sat in a rocking chair, where she had a view of the library's entrance. Two young women breezed in. One was what Victoria Trumbull would call "pleasingly plump." She was just over five feet tall, with short, curly dark hair, bright apple red cheeks, and violet eyes. The other woman was tall and slender, with straight light brown hair and matching brown eyes. She seemed pale by comparison to the first woman.

"Well, hello, Cherry, Roberta," said Reverend Judy.

"Sorry we missed the last couple of meetings," said violet-eyed Cherry. "Roberta and I were invited to present a paper on tube worms at the Oceanographic."

"On *what*?" asked Elizabeth.

"Tube worms," said Roberta.

"Oh," said Elizabeth.

"Pogonophora," said Jim Weiss, a researcher at the Marine Biological Lab. "Long, skinny deep-sea worms."

"You don't find tube worms on coral reefs, or we could knit some for the quilt," said Cherry.

Roberta sat down near Reverend Judy and pulled her knitting out of a basket.

"Where's Alyssa?" asked Cherry. She set her knitting bag on the table and pulled up a chair next to Elizabeth. "I'd like to see how she's doing with her kelp."

"She had to respond to an emergency call," said Elizabeth. "Somebody hit a tree on State Road. She called and said she'll try to get here before we break up."

Jessica tossed her knitting off to one side. "I dropped a stitch five rows back. I can't concentrate."

"Now what?" asked Casper.

"I got another call last night."

Fran Bacon, the retired professor, spoke up. "You know, girls, we really must concentrate on our work. We don't have much time."

"What can we do? We've tried everything," said Jessica. "The phone company and the police can't trace the calls. He's calling on a prepaid disposable phone."

"It has to be someone who knows us," said Maron.

Cherry's needles stopped abruptly. "What phone calls are you talking about?"

"A breather is calling Maron and me a couple of times a week," said Jessica.

"No kidding!" said Cherry. "Me, too."

"That makes three of us," said Maron.

Roberta set her knitting in her lap. "This is strange. I got a call the night before last."

"Just that one call?"

Roberta nodded.

"A man?"

"I assume so."

"Four of us, then. Someone knows all four of us."

Jim glanced at Casper.

"You know," said Casper, concentrating on his fringed anemone, "Anemones are carnivorous."

The group was silent.

Casper adjusted his glasses. "An anemone can capture small fish."

"Really!" said Reverend Judy, breaking the silence. The other knitters, heads down, worked intently.

Casper lifted the realistic pink woolen tentacles he'd been working on. "These tentacles have stinging cells that fire a tiny dart connected to a thin filament into its prey. Sort of like a stun gun."

After several moments of silence, Jessica said, "Don't tell me to change my phone number again. I did that already, and the creep actually said, before I could hang up, 'changing your number won't help, girlie.' "

"Definitely a man?" asked Fran.

"No question about it."

Casper set down his anemone. "Let's be up-front, shall we? You're thinking Jim or me, aren't you? One of us."

There was a murmur from the group, denying any possible suspicion.

"Well, rule me out. I'm not into that kid stuff."

Fran Bacon checked her watch. "If we're serious about finishing our quilt by the deadline, people, we simply must concentrate. Mid-June is only a few weeks away."

"What do you girls have in common besides this group?" asked Casper.

"Women," said Jim.

"Church? Health club? Bars?"

For the next hour, the group was quiet. Needles clicked. Through the double doors separating the reading room from the main library, came the sound of library patrons conversing softly. Outdoors, a car started up. Children's voices drifted over from the playground across the road.

A few minutes before six, Casper looked at his watch. "My wife is picking me up early today. Want a ride, Jim?" He folded up his anemone, wrapped tissue paper around it, and packed it and his needles into his briefcase. "She should be here any minute."

"Great, Casper. Thanks." Jim tucked his coral into a green cloth bag marked THINK GREEN.

"Good night, all. See you tomorrow," said Casper.

"Night," said Jim, and waved.

"Please, don't think anyone is pointing a finger at you, Casper. Or you, either, Jim," said Fran.

Casper nodded.

"Good night," said Jim.

"Bye."

"Night."

"See you."

The door closed behind the two men, and the women continued to work.

After awhile, Jessica set down her knitting. "Well, what do you think?"

"What do you mean?" asked Maron.

"*Is* it Casper? Or Jim?"

"Good grief, no," said Cherry.

"Well, why not?" asked Jessica.

"We're all members of this group," said Maron. "That's the connection. The caller knows who all of us are."

"Much too obvious," said Reverend Judy. "Besides, Jim and Casper are both too, well, normal."

"Mathematical knitters? Like, *normal*?" said Maron.

Reverend Judy laughed. "Point well taken."

"Girls! Please!" said Fran.

Jessica laid her arm along the back of the couch. "Then how do we rule them out?"

"Thanks for the ride," Jim said to Casper once they were outside the library. "Damned uncomfortable in there." He sat on the top step and Casper leaned on the railing. "What's with Fran?"

"What do you mean?"

"She claims she was student advisor on how to deal with stalkers, yet she keeps avoiding the subject."

"She's preoccupied with the quilt deadline. Feels responsible, since it was her idea in the first place."

It was six, a bright May evening. Bees hummed in the lilacs by the door, planted by the Friends of the Library. A breeze wafted the fragrance around them.

Jim said nothing.

Casper unhooked his glasses from his ears and breathed on the lenses. "Four women in our group are getting obscene phone calls." He polished the lenses with his handkerchief and hooked his glasses back on. "I know all four." He bent down and pulled up a stem of grass that was growing beside the steps and stuck the end in his mouth.

"We both know all four," said Jim.

"How old is your daughter?"

"Sixteen," said Jim, smiling. "Lily. Apple of my eye." Jim fished his wallet out of his back pocket and flipped it open to a photo gallery of his daughter. "We were married ten years before she was born."

Casper studied the pictures. "She has your wife's looks, fortunately. Shame to lose her mother like that."

"It's tough," said Jim, looking away from the photos.

"She have brains to match the looks?"

"Honor roll. Straight *A*'s." Jim put his wallet away.

"What would you do if she got calls from some guy—"

"I'd kill the bastard. I swear to God, I'd kill him." Jim smacked a fist into the palm of his hand.

Casper nodded. "Same here. My daughter's only two, but I can't imagine how I'd feel." He crossed his ankles. "The caller knows who the women are. The four youngest. He isn't bothering Fran Bacon, who's in her sixties, or Reverend Judy, who's in her fifties."

"Or Victoria Trumbull's granddaughter." Jim clasped his hands between his knees and gazed at the bees working the lilacs. "He doesn't want to tangle with Mrs. T."

"Clearly, he's observed all four in the library."

Jim looked up at Casper. "Have we seen anyone suspicious around the library? Cleaners?"

Casper shook his head. "Two Brazilian women."

"Maintenance people?"

"Walter, who's in his late sixties," said Casper. "Not that that rules him out."

"Except for Steve Bronski, the library staff is all women. What about Steve?"

"He's been in Florida the past two weeks."

"Painters? Carpenters? Electricians? Plumbers? Roofers? Booksellers? FedEx or UPS drivers?" Jim unclasped his hands. "Landscapers? Pavers? Who?" He jerked his head at the library building behind them. "The atmosphere in there is so thick, you could cut it with an ax."

"Who the hell is making those calls?" said Casper.

Jim said, "I don't intend to quit the group simply because of this growing hostility."

Casper sat down on the step next to Jim and tossed the grass stem he'd been chewing off to one side. "You mentioned electricians. You know, LeRoy Watts's wife, Sarah, heads the library trustees. Watts Electrical does a lot of work here at the library, right?"

"Right," said Jim. "LeRoy Watts is here several times a week, working all over the building. He must know who's here regularly, have a feeling for what's going on. What do you say we enlist his help?"

"See if he can shed some light on this?" said Casper.

"Very funny," said Jim.

"Let's talk to him," said Casper. "He's a great guy. I'm sure he'd love to help us get our hands on the bastard who's making the calls."

A red Chevy turned into the library parking lot. "This your wife?" asked Jim.

"Right on time. How about having supper with us? We can drop off my wife, go on to Watts Electrical, and have supper after we talk to him. He's usually open late."

"I want to get home to my daughter," said Jim.

"Another time, then. We'll invite Lily." Casper started down the steps. "I wouldn't mention this to the girls."

"Women," Jim corrected.

CHAPTER 14

Shortly after Casper's wife picked up her husband and Jim, Alyssa arrived at the library. "Sorry I'm late. A moped accident on State Road."

"Already?" asked Jessica. "The season hasn't even begun yet."

Alyssa slumped into her usual seat and took out her knitting. "It was a guy with his eight-year-old daughter on the back." She shook her head. "He skidded on a patch of sand and went into a tree."

"Are they all right?" asked Reverend Judy.

"The father's in pretty bad shape. They medevaced him to Boston. The little girl was hysterical." Alyssa pulled out a length of yarn and jabbed her needle into a stitch. "She'll probably be okay, at least physically. Skinned hands and legs. They'd never been on a moped before. They didn't have a clue about how dangerous mopeds are." She knit fiercely. "I had to come here tonight, even though I'm late. Get my mind off the accident." She looked around. "Where are Jim and Casper?"

Jessica, sitting next to Maron, replied. "Casper's wife picked him up early and they gave Jim a ride."

"We're being unfair to them," said Reverend Judy. "There's no reason to believe either one is the caller."

"Casper made a joke about anonymous phone calls," said Maron. "It's not a joke."

"It's certainly not a joke. But that's his usual way of trying to lighten a serious situation."

"Girls!" said Fran. "We're on deadline. We can't let anything sidetrack us now."

"Four of us are getting calls," said Jessica. "Maron and me, now Roberta and Cherry. Casper thinks he's so clever with his snide remarks."

Alyssa was silent. She looked down at the set of typed instructions in her lap and moved stitches along the needles, apparently counting.

Fran said, "Your kelp looks wonderful, Alyssa. Very realistic. You seem to be coming along nicely."

"Thanks."

"Let's keep up the good work, everyone. We've got eight or nine different corals, several anemones, sea stars, sea urchins, squid, and half a dozen sponges. And kelp, of course."

"These phone calls . . ." Roberta began.

"We can't let those phone calls distract us," said Fran somewhat testily. "Our deadline is only three weeks away. We have work to do."

"Whoever is calling knows all of us," said Jessica. "He's not calling Elizabeth."

"He'd better not," Elizabeth said. "My grandmother would take care of him."

"Obviously he knows that," Jessica said. "He's not calling Fran or Reverend Judy, either, our senior members. What about you, Alyssa? You've been awfully quiet."

Alyssa tossed her knitting aside. "I went to see Mrs. Trumbull after last Thursday's meeting." She looked down at the brown-and-green woolen kelp on the seat next to her.

"Mrs. Trumbull?" asked Jessica.

Alyssa took a deep breath. "I'm getting calls, too."

Several pairs of eyes turned to her.

"That's why you were upset on Thursday," said Jessica.

Alyssa nodded.

"You should have said something. We told you someone's calling Maron and me."

Alyssa didn't answer.

"And we just found out that Roberta and Cherry are getting calls, too."

"Why Mrs. Trumbull?" asked Maron.

"She has a lawyer friend who specializes in women's issues." After a few moments, Alyssa added in a small voice, "I know who's making the phone calls."

Needles stopped clicking.

"Who?"

"Why didn't you say so earlier?"

"Casper or Jim?"

"Who?"

"It's not Casper or Jim."

"Who is it, then?" asked Maron.

"The guy who works for Watts Electrical Supply, Jerry Sparks. I got a heavy-breathing call today, just before I got paged for the moped accident."

"I know Jerry," said Maron, nodding. "He's whacked-out on drugs half the time."

"He's done electrical work for me," said Jessica.

"Me, too," said Cherry, looking around at the others.

Roberta nodded.

"Are you sure it's Jerry Sparks?" asked Reverend Judy.

Alyssa looked down at her work. "I'm pretty sure."

"The creep."

"Slimeball!"

"Sicko."

"What do you say we track him down and give him a taste of his own medicine?" said Maron.

"A lesson or two," added Roberta.

Fran held up a hand for silence. "Please, girls. We don't have time for this."

"What made you decide Jerry Sparks is the caller, Alyssa?" asked Reverend Judy.

Alyssa told them about her movie date with Jerry Sparks and his follow-up calls.

"He's been going with Emily Cameron for the past couple of weeks," said Maron. "Why would he hassle us?"

"Girls, the quilt," said Fran. "The quilt!"

Jessica stood up. "Let's find him, right now."

Reverend Judy pushed her glasses back into place and continued to knit. "Don't do anything rash."

"Rash!" said Jessica, heading toward the back door. "I'm simply going to take my scissors with me and . . ."

Reverend Judy stood up, holding her knitting.

"Five of us against one puny little geek," said Cherry.

"We're coming with you," said Maron, setting her knitting aside.

The five headed out the library's back door, followed by Reverend Judy and Fran.

"Girls! Come back, right now!" Fran called to them.

"It's too late," said Jessica. "Does anybody know where he lives?"

"We can take my car," said Cherry.

"Tar and feather him!" said Maron.

"Girls! Girls! Stop!" Fran called to them, but they piled into Cherry's red Jeep.

"Let's go!" someone shouted, and the Jeep took off in a swirl of dust, long hair flying around eager faces.

Fran hurried back into the library, her hands pressing on either side of her head as though she were trying to hold it together.

Reverend Judy followed more slowly. She laid her knitting on the rocking chair and headed to the front of the library, where there was a phone, calling back to Fran, "I'm phoning Victoria Trumbull."

Fran didn't respond. She was still holding her head with both hands.

Elizabeth, who'd been dutifully working on her sea sponge, set it down and went to her. "We'll be all right, Fran. The quilt is almost finished. It'll be fine." She put her hand on Fran's back to calm her. Fran shuddered.

At the front desk, Reverend Judy was on the phone. "We've got a problem, Victoria. Five of the knitters have formed a posse to go after Jerry Sparks."

"How did this happen?" asked Victoria.

"Alyssa convinced the others that he's the breather."

"I was afraid of that," said Victoria. "Can you stop them?"

"It's too late. They left with Cherry DeBettencourt."

"She has a red Jeep, doesn't she?"

"Yes."

"Casey is with me now. We're about to leave for Oak Bluffs. We can intercept them."

"There's no evidence that Jerry Sparks is the caller, Victoria. They went off like a lynch mob."

"I don't blame them for being upset," said Victoria. "We've got to prevent them from doing something foolish, though. I'll see what we can do." Before she hung up, she added, "I hope you've noticed the sky. We're going to have a lovely sunset."

The entire sky, from horizon to horizon, was turning a bright rosy red. The sunset brought shopkeepers out of their stores along Circuit Avenue to gaze at the magnificent display.

LeRoy Watts was too preoccupied to notice.

He'd left the shop to search for the Taser, and he'd searched everywhere. Where was it? Had he been so shaken after the Jerry Sparks incident that he'd hidden it in his van? He'd cleaned the van with disinfectant after he'd transported Jerry Sparks to the library book shed. He simply couldn't remember. He was sure he'd put it in the top file drawer, but his mind was acting funny lately. He had to think. Think! Where would he have put it?

The rose color slowly drained out of the sky and the shopkeepers went back to their stores. LeRoy's head hurt from trying to work out where he'd put that damned Taser.

The bell at the front door of his shop jangled. LeRoy looked up. Two men entered. One was a tall, slim man in his fifties with dark hair, white on the temples, and a white beard. The other was younger and shorter, with round glasses and broad shoulders.

LeRoy's first thought was that they were from the FBI, and he stood up, knocking his coffee mug onto the floor, where it smashed. Then he saw they were dressed in jeans and sweatshirts, not like FBI agents at all. And then he recognized the shorter man. Casper Martin, the math teacher at the high school. He bent down and picked up the larger pieces of his cup and dropped them into his wastebasket.

"Evening, Roy," Casper said. "Sorry. We startled you."

"No problem, Mr. Martin," said LeRoy, his voice quavering. Where was that Taser? "I was distracted is all. How can I help you?" He kicked the remaining pieces of his coffee mug into a pile under the desk.

"Mr. Watts, I'm Jim Weiss." Jim held out his hand.

LeRoy wiped his hand on his jeans before he shook.

"Jim's a biologist at the Woods Hole lab," said Casper. "You got a few minutes to talk?"

LeRoy looked from one to the other, puzzled.

"We belong to a mathematical knitting group that meets at the West Tisbury Library," Jim began.

LeRoy gasped and felt the blood drain from his face.

Jim paused. "Is something wrong?"

LeRoy thought fast. "I heard about—" Then he stopped. What could he possibly have heard about? "Have a seat. Can I offer you some Jim Beam?"

Casper gave him a look, as though he thought LeRoy had gone crazy. Maybe he was going crazy. That Taser . . .

"No, thanks," said Casper. "Not for me. You go ahead." He pulled up a chair next to LeRoy's desk.

Jim took the other seat. "Casper and I thought maybe you could help us solve something that's been puzzling us."

LeRoy nodded. "Whatever I can do, sure."

Jim sat forward. "Some of the women in our group are getting phone calls from a breather and we're trying to track him down."

"Is that right?" LeRoy avoided their eyes.

"We know you do a lot of work for the library. Have you noticed anyone suspicious, taking too much interest in the women in our group?" asked Casper.

Jim added, "Most of them have unlisted numbers. The telephone company and the police are no help at all. As an electrician, you might be able to tell us how he could have gotten their numbers. A way to track him down."

LeRoy took a deep breath and looked down at his hands, which he'd clasped on top of the big calendar on his desk. When was all this shit going to stop?

"You seemed a good person to start with," Casper broke in. "The caller must be familiar with the library."

LeRoy looked up at that.

"Since your wife is head of the library trustees and, as we've said, you've done electrical work there—"

"Contributed it, in fact," Jim interrupted. "We appreciate all you've done for the library."

"—you might have some ideas," Casper finished.

"Ideas . . ." LeRoy picked up a pen from his desk and examined it. "Does this, um, person call other women?"

Jim looked at Casper, who shrugged.

Jim leaned forward. "Listen, LeRoy, the five women are suspicious of us, Casper and me. We've got to find this guy. Deal with the bastard. The cops are powerless. We need your help."

"That's not my . . . I don't think . . . Let me . . ." LeRoy's voice trailed off.

Jim studied him. "We have some ideas on ways to deal with him without involving the police."

LeRoy's face, which had regained some color, went white again.

Casper stood up. "Let's go, Jim. We obviously caught Roy at a bad time."

Jim, too, stood. "We'll talk to you tomorrow, give you time to think it over."

Casper extended his hand.

LeRoy pushed his chair back and stood, wiped his hand again on his jeans, and they shook.

"This breather is a piece of slime," said Jim. "We're ready to string him up by the you know whats."

LeRoy looked away.

"Think it over, Roy," said Casper.

The bell on the door jangled as the two men shut it behind them.

CHAPTER 15

"We've got to hurry before it gets dark," Cherry said. "I don't want to get stopped by the cops. My front left headlight is out."

After conferring with one another, the five women made their way to Jerry Sparks's last-known address. They pulled up to the house and got out of the Jeep. Mrs. Rudge appeared at the open front door, cigarette dangling from her lower lip, arms folded, the sunset bathing her in a kindly rose-colored glow.

Before Cherry had a chance to say anything, Mrs. Rudge called out, "You women lookin' for Jerry Sparks? He's not here." The cigarette stuck to her lower lip when she spoke.

"Do you know where he is?" asked Cherry, who was in the lead. The other four knitters cowered behind her.

"Nope," said Mrs. Rudge.

"Any idea where we can find him?"

"What's this, some popularity contest? Everybody wants Jerry Sparks?" Mrs. Rudge removed the cigarette, flicked the ash off to one side, removed a speck of tobacco from her tongue, and stuck the cigarette back in her mouth.

"We want to tell him something," said Cherry.

"Try the Rip Tide," said Mrs. Rudge, and turned her back on them, went inside, and slammed the door behind her.

The five women looked at one another.

"The Rip Tide?" Maron asked Cherry.

"That sleaze bar on Circuit Avenue," Cherry replied. "Figures. Let's go, girls!"

After the two men left, LeRoy thought about the bottle of Jim Beam in the bottom file drawer. Tempting. He could use a good slug of bourbon. But he didn't dare cloud his thinking. Those two suspected him. Of what? Surely not of making phone calls to those women?

The Taser. He had to find that Taser. Whatever they suspected about the phone calls had to wait. And Jerry Sparks's body was still lying undiscovered in the book shed. Lucky the weather had been cool.

Where had he put that Taser? He'd gone through the file cabinet, his desk, Maureen's desk, the supply closet, the van, his toolbox. . . . Where else, where else?

After Mrs. Rudge went back inside her house, the five knitters piled into the Jeep again, flip-flops slapping against bare heels.

"Ouch!" one of them cried. "You just stuck your elbow right in my boob!"

"Don't get in my way, then."

"Stop it, girls!" shouted Cherry.

"This wreck wasn't made for this many people."

"Get out and walk if you don't like it!"

Cherry shifted into gear and headed to the Rip Tide, one of the more decrepit hangouts on Circuit Avenue, not far from Watts Electrical Supply. The sunset glow was fading.

The bell at Watts Electrical Supply jangled again, and LeRoy looked up. His first impression was of two uniformed cops, and he nearly passed out.

Then he realized it was Chief O'Neill and Victoria Trumbull, who was wearing a police hat with gold stitching.

He stood up. "Well," he said, trying to sound cheerful. "Twice in one week. How can I help you?"

Casey's expression was solemn, all professional cop. "We were at your boys' school this morning, sir. The school had been trying to reach you."

"The school?" asked LeRoy, thinking about the phone calls he'd ignored. "Jesus! I forgot. My kids . . . ?"

"Your wife took your boys home."

LeRoy plopped down into his desk chair.

Victoria looked around and sat in the still-warm chair Jim had vacated.

Casey said, "We won't take up much of your time."

"I've been out of the office." LeRoy leaned forward, elbows on his tidy desk. "Cell phone . . . must have been a dead spot." He looked at Casey's cop face. "My boys?"

"They're not hurt, sir, but they're in trouble."

"My boys? Trouble?" He sat up straight.

"They went to school this morning with what they thought was a toy gun, and were showing it off at recess."

"Toy gun? We don't allow . . . The school doesn't allow . . . Oh my God!"

"Sir," said Casey in her cop voice, "the weapon they were playing with was a Taser."

LeRoy half-rose from his chair. "Where in hell did they get it?"

Casey said, "Your boys claimed at first that your office manager had given it to them to play with."

"Oh no!" LeRoy moaned.

"An aide confiscated the weapon in the school yard and took it to the principal. He had no idea what it was. The principal recognized it as a Taser." Casey paused. "She called me and tried to reach you. She finally got your wife, who came to the school."

"Oh my God!" LeRoy slumped back in his chair.

"After questioning, the boys admitted they'd taken it from your file cabinet."

LeRoy put his elbows on his desk, his head in his hands. "The boys?" he mumbled.

"The school has a clear policy and will determine how to discipline them. No guns, no toy guns, nothing that looks like a gun permitted in school."

LeRoy took a handkerchief out of his pocket and wiped his forehead. He swiveled his chair. Casey remained standing. Victoria looked around the shop.

Outside on Circuit Avenue, the bar crowd was arriving, couples and single guys strolled down the sidewalk, women in twos and threes laughed and called to one another, stopped to look in the windows of closed shops.

"In Massachusetts, as I'm sure you are aware," Casey went on, "it's illegal for an individual to own a Taser."

LeRoy's forehead shone in the overhead light.

"A heavy fine and possible jail time," Casey continued. "There's even some question about the legality of Taser use in law enforcement in Massachusetts."

LeRoy decided to take the offensive. He sat up straight. "I purchased a Taser instead of a gun because I didn't want to kill anyone." He put his handkerchief back into his pocket. "Tasers are nonlethal. Not supposed to have any aftereffects." His voice rose. "They're safe!"

"Not entirely, sir." Casey reached into an inside pocket and brought out folded papers. "I have here a receipt for the Taser, a notice of the violation, and a summons for your appearance in court. Please sign them." She handed the papers to him one at a time.

"But . . ." said LeRoy.

"Sign here, sir." Casey indicated the line. "Date it."

LeRoy's hand shook so hard, his writing looked as though he'd just learned to hold a pen.

Casey tore off the back pages of the notice, summons, and

receipt and gave them to him. "Your copies, sir. We'll see you in court."

Casper and Jim had gotten back into Casper's wife's car and driven to where Circuit Avenue became two-way. Casper turned left toward Nantucket Sound. Whitecaps stirred up by the brisk northwest breeze glistened in the fading light. He made a U-turn, pulled over to the side of the road, and parked, facing the Steamship Authority's dock, shut off the engine, and turned to Jim. "Well. What do you think?"

Jim nodded. "Same thing you do, I imagine."

Casper held his hands high up on the steering wheel. "The guy's scared of something."

Jim nodded.

In the distance, they could make out the ferry, a string of white lights coming from Woods Hole to the Island. They watched in silence.

After a while, Casper said, "When you told him the caller is someone familiar with the library and he was around the library a lot, things clicked into place. Did you see the look on his face?"

"Guilty," said Jim. "Guilty of something at least."

"Why in hell would LeRoy Watts make those calls?" asked Casper. "What a stupid adolescent thing to do."

"Stalking is a sickness," said Jim. "A stalker will jeopardize everything when he's obsessed by someone."

"And the way he wouldn't meet our eyes. Didn't offer to help. Looked as though he wanted to run."

"I'd like to know how he gets their unlisted numbers," said Jim. He cranked down the window on his side. The wind coming off the sound riffled papers in the backseat.

"While we were talking, I thought about that," said Casper. "It makes sense. Electrical boxes are usually next to phone boxes.

No one thinks twice about an electrician opening a box to check the meter or whatever."

"I suppose the phone guy pencils the number next to the connection so he doesn't have to look it up."

"They're not supposed to," said Casper. "But they do."

Gulls, white flecks in the distance, trailed after the ferry. Wings white against the darkening sky, the gulls dived after fish stirred up in the wake or snapped up morsels passengers tossed into the air.

"So," said Casper, turning back to Jim. "What can we do about it?"

"Good question," said Jim. "We've got to stop him."

"Any suggestions?"

"Yeah, but none of them is legal."

The two sat still. Casper tapped his fingers on the steering wheel; Jim rested his elbow on the window frame.

"How do you get to a guy like that?" Jim said. "He's got a nice wife, nice kids, nice house, prosperous business, good reputation, active in community affairs."

"No one will believe us," said Casper. "All we have is a gut feeling." He started the car, checked behind him, and pulled away from the curb. While they'd talked, cars had lined up for the ferry.

Casper was quiet until they were clear of ferry traffic. Then he said, "We've got to stop him, and soon."

Chapter 16

By the time Cherry found a parking space several doors from the Rip Tide, the sun had set. The five women entered the bar and conversation stopped. All eyes examined them, from heads to flip-flopped feet.

"Hi, can I help you?" asked the bartender, a woman about the same age and with the same well-rounded shape as Cherry. The mostly male clientele watched.

"We're looking for Jerry Sparks," said Cherry.

"Can I buy all of yous a beer?" asked a husky guy with an American flag bandanna wrapped around his head and tattoos from shoulder to wrist.

Cherry started to say, "Yes, thanks . . ." but Alyssa interrupted. "No, thanks. We need to find Jerry Sparks."

"Haven't seen him for a couple days, hon," said the bartender. "Let Dude buy you a beer. He doesn't drink, but he likes to see other people drink."

"Well . . ." said Cherry.

"We're in a hurry," said Alyssa. "Do you know where he might be?"

"You try the place he stays?" asked Dude.

Alyssa nodded.

"Not at the shop?"

"We haven't tried there."

Dude studied them with bright blue eyes. His crossed arms

showed off serpent tattoos that writhed when he moved. Cherry sighed.

"The boss might still be there," said Dude. "LeRoy Watts. Works late. You can walk there. Only a couple blocks."

"Sorry we're not more help, hon." The bartender dipped a cloth into the sinkful of soapy water under the counter, wrung it out, and wiped the already-clean bar. "If you don't find him, drop by later. We're open until two."

The five knitters conferred and decided to try the electrical-supply store, since it was close.

Victoria glanced down Circuit Avenue as they were leaving Watts Electrical Supply. She shaded her forehead against the last of the fading light with a hand. "It looks as though a red Jeep is parked beyond the Rip Tide bar," she said.

"There are at least a hundred red Jeeps on this Island, Victoria."

"Cherry DeBettencourt has a red Jeep."

"Okay, Victoria. Since Circuit Avenue's one-way, it'll take us a few minutes to drive around to there. Hop in."

Except for the bars, most of the businesses along Circuit Avenue had closed for the night. After Chief O'Neill and Mrs. Trumbull left, LeRoy locked the door and turned out the lights in the front of the shop. He went back to his desk to read the copies of the papers Casey had left with him that he'd signed earlier without reading.

The five knitters walked quickly up the street. A light was still on in the back of Watts Electrical Supply. Cherry tried the door. Locked. Maron cupped her hands against the glass and peered in. "Someone's in there." She banged her fist on the side of the door. "Hello! Mr. Watts? Can we come in? We're looking for Jerry Sparks!"

"Is it Jerry Sparks?" asked Jessica.

LeRoy could barely make out the shape of a woman with her hands cupped against the glass, peering in. Damn, he had to get out of here before anyone else showed up. He stood up and headed for the back door, forgetting the papers on his desk in his haste to get away.

"It's only Mr. Watts." Maron banged again. "He must not have heard us. He's headed for the back door."

"Let's go around," said Cherry. "Come on, Alyssa!"

"He probably doesn't want to deal with anyone this late," said Alyssa.

"It's not late. Come on, we'll just ask him where we can find Jerry Sparks."

When the two reached the alley that ran behind the back entrance, LeRoy was standing at the top of the steps, locking the door.

LeRoy turned around. Two women stood at the foot of the steps, blocking him and shouting at him. All he could hear were the words "Jerry Sparks! Jerry Sparks! Jerry Sparks!"

"Mr. Watts!" called Cherry.

"What do you want?"

"We're looking for—" Cherry began.

"We need to talk with you," said Alyssa.

"I'm in a hurry," said LeRoy.

"We want to ask you about Jerry Sparks."

At the latest mention of Jerry Sparks, LeRoy jerked back and dropped his keys, which bounced off the top step and clattered to the ground. "Oh shit!" He threw both hands up to his forehead.

"Jerry Sparks," Cherry repeated. "You know, Jerry Sparks?"

"Mr. Watts, we're just trying to find Jerry Sparks is all."

"Jerry Sparks," said LeRoy.

"Yes. We have something we want to tell him."

"I—I—I—" stuttered LeRoy. "I can't tell you where he is." He scrambled down the steps and picked up his keys. "I've got to go."

"Wait!" shouted Alyssa, but LeRoy was already in his van, with the door shut.

"We've got to get back to my Jeep," said Cherry. "I saw a police car go past behind your shop and I can't afford another ticket."

LeRoy had shoved his way past the two women, muttering something to shut them up. But all he could think of was getting away, getting as far away as he could. Anywhere. He'd stumbled to his van, climbed in, slammed the door shut, and had torn out of the parking area.

It took almost ten minutes for Casey to drive the Bronco around the back streets that returned them to the foot of Circuit Avenue. Although it was still early, the barhopping crowd was out, sauntering down the middle of the narrow street, singing lustily.

By the time Casey arrived at where the Jeep had been parked, she had trouble finding even a place where she could leave the police vehicle. After another five minutes, she found a handicapped slot and pulled in. She and Victoria walked back to where Victoria had seen the red Jeep. It was gone.

"I suppose we can ask at the Rip Tide if they've seen any of the five women," said Victoria. She and Casey pushed the door open and went into the bar. Conversation stopped.

The bartender said, "Hi, Chief. Hi, Mrs. Trumbull. Can I help you?"

"We're looking for five young women who were in a red Jeep," said Victoria. "Have you seen them?"

A tall, very broad, very muscular man strode forward, tattooed arms crossed. "Evening, ladies," he said. "Five girls were asking for Jerry Sparks, say ten, fifteen minutes ago. I told 'em to try the electrical shop up the street." He nodded in the direction of Watts Electrical Supply.

"We've just come from there," said Victoria.

"Must've just missed 'em."

"Thanks," said Casey. "You wait here, Victoria. I'll go back to the shop."

"Buy you a beer?" asked the big man.

"Thank you," said Victoria, and perched on a bar stool. "Just a half glass, please. I'm on duty."

Casey returned moments later. "Closed up tight. No one around."

Out of ideas and with darkness falling, the five knitters returned to the library, where they'd left their own vehicles.

"Where do we go from here, girls?" asked Roberta.

"He must be somewhere," said Maron.

"We'll find him," said Jessica. "Tomorrow, for sure. And when we do . . ."

Where was Jerry Sparks?

CHAPTER 17

LeRoy came to his senses when he found himself tearing along the narrow strip of beach separating Sengekontacket Pond from Nantucket Sound. He glanced at the speedometer. Sixty-five in a thirty-five mile zone. A wonder he hadn't been pulled over. He lifted his foot from the accelerator, then remembered the papers he'd been served. They were in plain view on his desk.

He'd go home, talk to the boys. They knew not to go into his filing cabinet. Why in hell did they take the Taser to school? He'd have to think of a punishment. They were good kids, but this was beyond anything. He'd ask the chief to give them some hours of community service, or ask the sheriff to have them tour the jail. Jail. The kids needed to know how serious a little thing could be.

He made a U-turn and headed for home.

The minute LeRoy stepped through the kitchen door, Sarah charged at him. "Where's Jerry Sparks?"

"Jerry Sparks, Jerry Sparks!" he snapped. "Where are the god-damned twins?" He hadn't meant to be so sharp.

"Don't you dare speak about my boys like that."

That did it. "*Your* boys, eh? Stealing something from my office and taking it to school—*your* boys?" LeRoy's hands were in tight fists by his sides.

"What those children took from your filing cabinet was a deadly weapon. A deadly weapon," she repeated.

LeRoy snapped, "Tasers are nonlethal weapons," then realized what he'd said and turned away.

"Not according to our chief of police," said Sarah. "The children—*children*," she repeated—"brandished that thing around the playground, knowing the school doesn't tolerate even toy guns. You look at me!"

LeRoy shuddered, his back still to Sarah.

"And you stuck it in the drawer with their crayons and drawing paper. Of course they thought it was a toy gun."

At that, LeRoy faced her. "The boys know the school's rules. Where are they?"

"Upstairs. Doing their homework. Where were you all day when the school was trying to reach you?"

"Working."

"Working? Or taking pictures of naked women?" Sarah's voice rose. "What kind of father are you . . . you pervert!"

LeRoy's face went dead white.

"Oh, yes. Emily Cameron stopped by on Sunday. While you were fishing." Before he could respond, she added, "And that woman called. This time, she said she wants to teach you something. Who *is* she? And where's Jerry Sparks?"

"What lies has Emily Cameron been telling you?"

"She didn't need to tell me a thing. She showed me the movies you've been taking. Pornographic movies."

"What are you talking about?" LeRoy was shouting now.

"Naked women taking showers, that's what. Pictures you took with a hidden camera. With sound, even."

"Where did she get those?" LeRoy felt ice-cold.

"Never mind where she got them. Jerry Sparks gave them to her for safekeeping, and now Jerry Sparks is missing."

"Sparks must have taken those pictures," said LeRoy, starting to sweat again.

"Right after I came back from school, when no one could find

you and you'd let the boys take that . . . that . . . weapon"—
Sarah's voice rose—"who should stop by but my sister Jackie
with a video camera her boyfriend found in her shower. Explain
that, if you can!"

"Daaaddy?" came from upstairs. "Jared's kicking me. I can't
do my homework!"

"Am not!" said Jared. "Liar!"

LeRoy spun away from his wife and started up the stairs. "I
have a thing or two to settle with you two," he shouted up to
them.

"You have a thing or two to settle with me first," Sarah shouted
back, "or I'm calling the police."

LeRoy stopped mid-flight. "You're what?"

"I said, come right back down here or I'll call the police." She
lifted the phone out of its cradle.

"The devil you are!" shouted LeRoy, dropping down the stairs
in two long steps.

He hadn't meant to smack Sarah so hard. He'd never hit her before, ever. Never understood guys who hit their wives or girl-
friends. He felt sick when he thought of how she'd stumbled back
against the kitchen sink, looked at him, held her hands to her
face, and dropped to the floor.

He'd left her slumped against the cabinet and headed back to
the shop. On the way, he decided he had to calm down before
reading those papers he'd signed. Owning a Taser illegally, a court
date, a fine, possible jail term. Jail! He couldn't think. He was a
perfectly normal guy, a college graduate, degree in electrical engineering, a respected businessman, a father, a husband. . . .

He decided to drive along State Beach, park and walk along
the shore, let the lapping waves calm him before he faced those
papers and what they meant.

The road along State Beach was dark. He could see a line of

lights on the distant mainland, four miles away. In between was blackness. Blackness, he thought. Blackness.

He'd better make peace with Sarah. Take her flowers and a box of Chilmark Chocolates. Get down on his knees and apologize. Beg her forgiveness, swear it would never happen again, and it wouldn't. He'd broken that unthinkable barrier and hit her.

Then he thought of the way she'd looked at him when he smacked her. Hatred. Not just because he'd hit her but because Emily Cameron had showed her the videos. Because her sister despised him. He thought of Sarah slumped against the sink, and suddenly a chill hit him in the gut. Had he killed her? Without meaning to, had he killed *again*?

He pulled across the left lane and parked, facing the wrong way, got out, and walked up the sand path that cut through the low dune. In daylight, the wild beach roses that topped the dune would show bright green leaves along thorny winter-black stems. He shoved his hands into his pockets and walked along the shore with the gentle swish of the waves on his left. He couldn't see the stones under his feet, but the waves were crested with a line of phosphorescent bubbles that showed him the way.

Why in hell had Jerry Sparks given his girlfriend copies of those videos? And why in hell had Emily Cameron shown those videos to Sarah? What did she think she'd prove by showing them to his wife? And who was that new boyfriend of Jackie's?

What a mess! The Taser. Jerry Sparks. Jackie. The videos. He'd been so secretly proud of them. How had Jerry Sparks managed to copy them? What a loser the guy was. And that girlfriend, too dim-witted to understand what she was doing, showing those videos to his wife.

He'd walked to one of the jetties that projected out from the shore. Sand had built up on one side, washed away a hollow on the other side. What a dumb idea. You couldn't fight nature with some puny line of rocks.

He couldn't have killed Sarah with that one blow. He shivered. Sarah didn't understand, any more than Emily Cameron had. She'd never try to understand. In her way, she'd interpreted his videos as dirty. They were art. Look at the ancient Greek statues, naked women and men. His videos were no different, simply a twenty-first-century version, three-dimensional, in living color and sound. Jackie, he could dismiss. She'd been hitting on him since before he and Sarah were married.

Boat shells had concentrated on the building-up side of the jetty. He recognized the sound they made when he stepped on them, halfway between the crunch of a scallop shell and the clack of a stone. He stooped down and picked up a handful. Slipper shells. Limpets, some people called them. *Crepidula fornicata* was their scientific name. He'd always wondered about the *fornicata* part. He put the shells into his pocket and headed back to his van.

As he reached the crest of the slight dune, he saw flashing blue lights and someone standing next to his van. A police car was parked behind him. Sarah—they'd found her dead body and tracked him down. He hustled along the path and reached the van as the cop was tucking a ticket under his windshield wiper.

"Officer," he gasped, "what's the trouble?"

"I had to give you a ticket, sir. You're parked facing the wrong direction."

LeRoy giggled. Then he laughed. The laugh turned into a hysterical warble that he couldn't control.

"Sir?" said the police officer. "You okay, sir?"

LeRoy nodded, but the disembodied laugh kept going.

"Do you need medical attention, sir?" The officer stared at him, clearly upset. "It's Mr. Watts, isn't it? Shall I call an ambulance, sir?"

That snapped LeRoy out of it. "No, no." He shook his head. The hysteria faded away to hiccups and the hiccups stopped. "No, thanks. I'll be fine."

"Didn't mean to upset you that way, sir. We've been instructed to enforce that parking regulation. It seems silly, I know. This time of year and all. I'd already written out the ticket before you got back from your walk, or I wouldn't have ticketed you."

LeRoy nodded. "It's okay."

The officer said, in an attempt to lighten the situation, "Guess you've never been in serious trouble with the law, right, Mr. Watts?"

LeRoy controlled the hysteria that was bubbling up again and nodded instead. He removed the ticket from under the wiper blade and stuck it in his jacket pocket.

"Have a good evening, Mr. Watts, sir," said the police officer, a young kid who looked about eighteen. "Sorry about the ticket. You sure you'll be okay?"

"I'm fine." LeRoy got into the van. "Good night, Officer," he said to the kid. He made a U-turn and headed back to Oak Bluffs.

His headlights picked up a gull swooping onto the road for a clam it had dropped and smashed on the hard surface. He slowed to avoid hitting it. The gull would soar out of the way, he knew. You never saw dead gulls in the road.

Why couldn't his life be that simple?

CHAPTER 18

"Girls," said Fran at the next meeting of the knitters. It was Tuesday, and the library was closed for the afternoon. "You have a responsibility here. You're part of a team. We have a project to finish." She tapped one of her needles on the library table. "I'm not comfortable with the way you took off yesterday."

"What are you talking about?" asked Casper.

"We never found him," said Cherry. "His landlady hasn't seen him for several days. His drinking buddies at the Rip Tide say he hasn't shown up there, either. Mr. Watts, his boss, was too busy to talk to us."

"LeRoy Watts?" asked Fran.

"Who are you talking about?" asked Casper.

"Alyssa claims he's the caller," said Cherry.

Maron said, "You know, we owe you an apology."

"What's going on?" Casper looked from one to another of the women, puzzled.

"We really didn't think it was you," said Jessica.

"Well, thanks a lot," said Casper. "Who, then?"

"Jerry Sparks," said Maron. "We tried to find him."

"When did you talk to Watts?" asked Jim.

"Around seven," said Cherry. "It wasn't dark yet."

"Jim and I stopped by his shop right after we left here yesterday," said Casper. "Right around sunset. We asked him for his help in identifying the phone caller."

"LeRoy was one of my math students at Northeastern," said Fran. "He'd be a great help. A bright, lovely man."

"The breather obviously is familiar with the library and has singled out members of our group," said Jim.

Casper said, "Because his wife, Sarah, heads the library trustees, he's done a lot of volunteer work here. We thought he might have seen someone suspicious."

"I'm sure he'd be delighted to help," said Fran.

"We know Jerry Sparks is the caller," said Maron.

"I'm not convinced about that," said Casper. "Jim and I came away feeling uneasy about LeRoy Watts."

"That's ridiculous," said Fran. "Preposterous! I've known him since . . . well, since."

"Since he was in college?" asked Maron.

"Yes," said Fran. "Yes."

"It can't be Mr. Watts," said Maron. "He's worked for my family since I was a little kid."

Alyssa spoke up. "I'm sure it's Jerry Sparks."

Casper and Jim looked at each other. Jim shrugged. "Guess we have to find Jerry Sparks."

An hour or so later, Lucinda Chandler, the librarian, was taking an armload of books to the book-sale storage shed when she found the body. She shifted the books to one arm so she could unlatch the door, then pulled it toward herself, careful not to drop her load. The door opened stiffly. After the bright May afternoon, the shed was dark, and it took her eyes a few moments to adjust. There was a foul smell, as though a large animal had died. She'd need to air it out before they sorted the books for the sale.

When her eyes finally adjusted, she didn't immediately grasp what she saw. Some idiot had piled a mound of clothing on the floor. Probably thinking it was a Thrift Shop drop-off. She'd have to get Walter, husband of one of the library volunteers, to make a larger sign.

She started to nudge the pile to one side with her foot, but it was heavier than she'd imagined. And then she realized there was someone in the clothing and the person smelled awful. A man. A book donor who'd brought books to the shed and had a stroke or a heart attack? A drunk seeking a night's shelter?

Lucinda, being a sensible New Englander, set her armload of books on the table and knelt down beside the man, who was lying facedown, to see if he was breathing. She pulled back the sweatshirt hood that covered his face, and then lost her composure. She lurched back, tripped over the sill, caught herself as she started to fall backward, put her hands up to her face, and screamed.

When Lucinda screamed, all of the knitters, who were meeting every afternoon now, stopped what they were doing.

"What in hell was that?" asked Casper.

Alyssa, the EMT, raced out the back door, leaving her green-and-brown Möbius-strip kelp on her seat.

Elizabeth Trumbull set down the sea sponge she was working on and stood up. "Lucinda?"

Others laid aside their work and headed toward the library's rear entrance.

Lucinda was standing by the shed, hands over her mouth. She was tall. Her blond hair, usually pinned up in a French twist, had loosened and fallen to her waist. A hairpin seemed to protrude from her scalp.

"Are you all right?" asked Alyssa.

"Of course she's not all right," said Casper.

"A body . . . in the shed . . ." gasped Lucinda.

"Help me get her inside," Casper shouted to Jim.

"I'll check in the shed," said Alyssa.

"Brandy," said Reverend Judy, the Unitarian minister. "Where does the library keep its brandy?"

Lucinda staggered inside, with Jim and Casper on either side. They led her to the striped couch in the reading room and she slumped onto it. "Call the police," she gasped. "Elizabeth, call your grandmother!"

Elizabeth said, "What shall I tell her?"

"There's a dead man in the shed."

"I'll get her!" Elizabeth left in a hurry.

A few moments later, Alyssa returned, sat down, and lowered her head between her knees.

"What is it, Alyssa?" asked Reverend Judy. She looked around. "Where's the brandy?"

Alyssa mumbled, "I'll be okay in a second or two."

Reverend Judy patted Alyssa on the back, then tucked her coral into her knitting bag and looped the bag over one arm. "I'll guard the shed."

Ten minutes later, Elizabeth returned with her grandmother. Victoria Trumbull strode into the library and greeted the knitters, who stood when she entered. The afternoon light illuminated the gold stitching on Victoria's hat, which read WEST TISBURY POLICE, DEPUTY.

Lucinda was sipping water someone had thought to give her.

"Has anyone called Casey?" Victoria asked.

"Chief O'Neill is on her way," said Jim Weiss.

"You may as well return to your seats while we wait for her," said Victoria, who remained standing. "We don't want to talk about the finding until the police get here."

The knitters sat again, their bags and baskets lumpy with works in progress, and talked in low voices.

Victoria sat at the the library table and waited, her hands clasped in front of her. Before long, blue lights flashed through the window and across the shelves of books, and a few moments later Casey appeared.

"I'm glad you're here already, Victoria." Casey lifted her hair out of the back of her uniform sweater. "I left in a hurry," she explained as she rebuckled her heavy utility belt with its assortment of law-enforcement tools.

Victoria knew most of the knitters and introduced them, eight altogether, including Elizabeth, her granddaughter. Two men and five women, plus the minister, who was guarding the shed.

"Forgive us if we continue to knit," said Fran, the retired professor. "We're working on deadline."

The clicking of needles continued.

"The medical examiner and State Police are on the way," Casey told them. "Wait here, everyone, while I check the shed, see what's what."

Victoria coughed politely.

"Yes, of course," said Casey. "You, too, Victoria."

As they headed for the back door, the sound of steel, aluminum, wood, and plastic needles working wool into sea creatures faded behind them.

On such a fine afternoon, evil seemed far removed. Bees hummed in the wisteria that festooned a trellis near the shed. Mourning doves cooed behind the library. High up in the sky, a hawk cried its plaintive call.

Reverend Judy was seated on a bench by the shed. "Six . . . seven . . ." She looked up briefly and smiled. "Counting stitches. . . . Eight . . . nine. . . . There." She set her work beside her on the wooden bench.

"What are you making?" asked Casey.

"A projective plane. Part of the quilt." Reverend Judy held up a strangely contorted mass. "Terrible about the body." She inclined her head toward the shed and picked up her knitting again. "The group is knitting a coral reef. It's not really a quilt; it's more of an art object. I wonder if it's someone we know." She waved at the closed door, and went back to her knitting.

"What did you say you're making?" asked Casey.

"A projective plane," repeated Reverend Judy. "A twisted sphere. A surface without a boundary. Would you like the pattern?"

"No," said Casey. "Thanks anyway."

Victoria paused at the shed door until her eyes were used to the darkness. She pulled a paper napkin from her pocket and held it over her nose. The body was as Lucinda had described, the hood thrown back, exposing his head. He lay on his stomach, face turned to one side. Dark, greasy hair held back by a knitted headband, large ears, a small nose. It was difficult to grasp any other details.

"Whew!" said Casey. "He's been here awhile. Do you have any idea who he is, Victoria?"

Victoria studied the man. "None whatsoever. What a ghastly expression. What kind of death would cause that?"

"Can't imagine," said Casey.

Victoria leaned on her lilac-wood stick.

Casey held a tissue to her nose. "There's not much we can do right now. We can talk to the people in the library when it's open tomorrow, but I don't imagine anyone saw him enter the shed. Who are the people you introduced me to?"

"Casper Martin teaches mathematics at the high school, Jim Weiss is a marine biologist, one woman is a radiologist at the hospital, and two others teach at the West Tisbury School. Reverend Judy is the Unitarian minister."

"The stuff they're knitting isn't sweaters and socks."

"They're entering their work in a competition to draw attention to global warming."

"Takes all kinds." Casey shrugged. "When Doc Jeffers gets here, first thing we have to do is identify the body. I hope he's got an ID on him."

They returned to the reading room, where the knitters sat, silent except for the incessant sound of needles.

While they waited for the medical examiner, Victoria seated herself at the library table across from Alyssa, and Casey sat on the couch next to Lucinda, who had recovered some of her color. The others continued to work.

Victoria studied Alyssa. "You saw something you recognized, didn't you?"

Alyssa closed her eyes.

"As an EMT, you're accustomed to violent death."

Alyssa nodded. "I went into the shed. . . ."

"Can I get you a glass of water?"

"I'm fine, Mrs. Trumbull."

Victoria could see she wasn't fine. "He was wearing a knitted headband. Was it something you gave him?" Victoria held out her gnarled hands to Alyssa, who took them in hers. "The dead man is Jerry Sparks, isn't he?"

Alyssa nodded.

CHAPTER 19

Victoria was aware of the low murmur of voices in the background. Casey spoke softly to Lucinda, and Lucinda smiled at something she said. The knitters whispered to one another. Victoria looked up at the clock on the wall. Almost six. Doc Jeffers should be here any minute.

Casey got up from the couch, patted the librarian's shoulder, adjusted her belt, and joined Victoria and Alyssa at the table. "I called Sergeant Smalley," she told Victoria. "He'll be here shortly."

"Why the State Police?" asked Maron.

"It's a case of an unattended death," said Casey. "The State Police get called in."

A motorcycle pulled into the library's parking lot. The engine revved and died, and Doc Jeffers strode into the reading room, the chains on his leather boots rattling.

"Where's the chief?" He looked around. Casey raised her hand and stood. He nodded at her. "Where's the corpse?"

"In the book shed," said Casey.

Doc Jeffers removed latex gloves from his black bag, snapped them on, and flexed his fingers. "Lead on!"

"Let's go, Victoria," said Casey.

Outside the shed, Reverend Judy knit peacefully. She greeted them and continued to count stitches.

Doc Jeffers, Casey, and Victoria went into the small building. When he bent down and saw the grimacing face of the body in the shed, Doc Jeffers muttered something Victoria couldn't make out. "Strange," he said, standing up straight. "Either of you know who this guy is?"

Casey held the tissue to her nose. "No idea."

"I believe it's Jerry Sparks, the electrician who worked for LeRoy Watts," said Victoria.

"Oh?" said Doc Jeffers.

"One of the knitters recognized his headband."

"If you don't need us, we'll be outside," said Casey.

"Lucky you," said the doc.

On the bench outside, Reverend Judy moved her knitting to make room. "Have a seat, Victoria. No telling how long the doctor will be."

"Thank you."

Casey radioed Junior Norton to report to the library, then paced the grass in front of the shed.

Eventually, Doc Jeffers came to the door holding up a worn, greasy card. "Right on, Victoria. Jerry Sparks. Worked for Watts Electrical Supply in Oak Bluffs."

"He did some work for me a few months ago," said Victoria. "If it hadn't been for the knit headband, I wouldn't have known who it was."

"Small wonder," said Doc Jeffers.

"Any idea when he died?" asked Casey.

"Can't tell yet. I'd guess four days ago, maybe five."

Casey asked, "Can you tell how he died?"

Doc Jeffers grinned. "I assume you're joking. Could be a drug overdose. The forensics team from off-Island should be here in a couple of hours."

"The shed isn't used much this time of year," mused Victoria. "Such a lonely place to die."

In the reading room, the knitters worked steadily. "It feels odd, you know, working on our quilt with that going on," said

Maron, nodding in the direction of the shed. "It's hard to concentrate."

"Have they identified the body?" asked Cherry.

Alyssa concentrated on her work. "It's Jerry Sparks."

Jessica stopped knitting abruptly. "What?"

"It's Jerry Sparks. Wearing a headband I gave him."

The name Jerry Sparks echoed around the room.

"It's creepy," said Maron. "I mean, just yesterday we were looking for him. . . ." The sentence trailed off.

"Do they know when he died?" asked Jessica. "Or why?"

"That will take awhile to determine," said Jim.

"You're kind of quiet, Alyssa," said Casper. "Can I get you anything? Water?"

"No, thanks."

"I'm sorry he died, I guess," said Jessica. "But that solves our problem about the breather."

"No, it doesn't." Alyssa shook her head, still looking down. The group stopped working. After a pause, Alyssa said, "Last night around ten, I got a call from our breather."

There was silence.

Jim said, "LeRoy Watts. He's the one."

"No!" said Fran. "Not LeRoy."

"Mr. Watts?" said Maron. "Never."

"When Casper and I spoke to him last evening, he was evasive. We both had the uncomfortable feeling that he was hiding something."

Maron shook her head. "It can't possibly be Mr. Watts. Everybody respects him."

Victoria shrugged into her coat. "Let's pick up the mail, Elizabeth, then go home and have drinks by the fire. It's been a long day."

They left the car in the library's parking lot and walked across

135

the road to Alley's. Victoria opened the glass-fronted post office box she had used for three-quarters of a century and tugged out the stack of letters and catalogs. She handed Elizabeth a blue envelope with a neatly typed address. "Another letter from your mother. Two in one week. I hope everything's all right."

"I'll wait until we get home to open it," said Elizabeth. "I kind of dread letters from Mom."

Once home, Victoria lit the parlor fire and Elizabeth brought in two glasses of cranberry juice with rum. When she had settled herself on the sofa, they toasted each other.

"Poor Emily Cameron," said Elizabeth. "She was so angry with Jerry Sparks because he'd left her, or so she thought. She's going to feel awful when she learns what happened to him. I wonder who'll tell her?" She took the blue envelope out of one pocket, her knife out of another, and neatly slit the top.

Victoria was sorting through catalogs, setting aside the few she wanted to look through, when she heard Elizabeth groan. She looked up.

"Bad news, Gram."

"I'm not sure I can handle any more bad news," said Victoria. But then she saw Elizabeth's obvious distress. "What does your mother have to say?"

Elizabeth passed the letter to her, and Victoria glanced at the first page. "I see she plans to visit. That will be nice. I haven't seen her for a while."

Amelia, Victoria's elder daughter, lived in San Francisco, usually a safe distance away.

"But she's arriving the day after tomorrow. Thursday."

"I wonder what's on her mind," said Victoria.

"She's being 'caring.'" Elizabeth took the letter her grandmother handed her and stuffed it back into its envelope. "She's afraid I'm a bother to you."

"What!" Victoria sat up straight in the wing chair and set her glass on the coffee table. "What is she talking about? What have you said to her?"

"After her last letter, I called and told her I'm a grown woman. That I have a job I like and a life I like, and maybe I said that I like taking care of you."

"You didn't!"

"It was the wrong thing to say, I'm afraid."

"I could have told you that," said Victoria. "I have a prediction for you. She'll arrive with colored brochures describing the delights of assisted-living facilities near her and will lecture me on the many advantages for me." Victoria got up from her chair, took up the tongs, and jabbed a smoldering log to the back of the fire. She set the poker back in its stand and returned to her seat.

"I'm sorry, Gram."

"It's not your fault. She *is* my daughter, after all."

"This couldn't be a worse time, with Jerry Sparks's body being found this afternoon and all. And Fran's freaking out about the deadline for the quilt competition."

"Perhaps you can call her and suggest she make her visit at a later time."

"Good idea." Elizabeth left to dial her mother's cell number. A few minutes later, she returned and plopped back onto the couch.

"What did she say?" asked Victoria.

"It's too late. She's in Denver, visiting her college roommate."

"Is she bringing that friend of hers with her?"

"Frank? The guy who reeks of stale cigarette smoke?"
Victoria nodded.

"She broke up with Frank a month or so ago. That may be part of her problem. She's got to fuss over someone, and we're good targets."

"Well, we still have a day of respite." Victoria held up her empty glass. "Why don't you fix us another drink."

CHAPTER 20

It was Wednesday. For six days, Emily Cameron had waited for Jerry Sparks, wondering what she'd said or done to drive him away. She alternated between worry and anger. Finally, she decided to forget she'd ever known him, that he'd shared her life for three weeks. And now he'd dropped out of her life, just like that. She hadn't heard a word from him. Six whole days! She brushed her bangs out of her eyes and pushed her glasses back into place. Wasn't man enough to tell her to her face that he was breaking things off. Well, she'd show him how much she cared. Nothing, that's what. She simply didn't give a damn. Another woman or those lousy drugs. Which one? She was glad she'd given his DVDs to Mrs. Watts.

She'd gotten to the boatyard early and was at her desk in the back of the marine store, eating a jelly doughnut and entering orders for cordage and hardware into the computer. She was hardly aware of music in the background coming from WMVY, the Island's radio station. Emily got up and poured herself another cup of coffee from the communal pot the boatyard kept going all day. She hadn't slept much since Jerry—well, since Jerry left. She checked her watch. Almost nine o'clock, time for the news. She stood again and turned up the volume on the radio to hear what was going on in the rest of the world. The same old things: the failing economy, the wars, fires in California. Nothing good happening anywhere. When the local news finally came on, she hoped to hear the score for the off-Island game.

Maybe the girls basketball team had won again. Some good news to start the day.

But the first thing she heard was Toby, the local announcer. ". . . A body discovered in the book-storage shed of the West Tisbury Library has been identified as that of Jerry Sparks, an electrician who worked . . ."

"Oh no!" Emily sat again, stunned. There was a ringing in her ears so loud, it drowned out everything else. Toby read details, but she didn't hear them. Her computer seemed far, far away, surrounded by a shimmering red halo. Her hands hung down, almost touching the floor. The numb, tingling things didn't seem to be part of her. She couldn't breathe. Jerry. Her Jerry?

He'd stood her up, hadn't he? Again? That's what she'd accused him of, when all the time he was lying dead. He hadn't called, hadn't stopped by, hadn't left a message on her machine. She'd sworn she'd never speak to him again. Now she never would. She should have known he wouldn't do that to her. Not her Jerry. She moaned.

"Em? You okay?" Gayle came around the partition that separated Emily from the store. "I just heard the news. About Jerry . . ."

"Jerry," Emily gasped. "Jerry!"

"I'll get you a soda. Be right back." Gayle scurried around the partition. Emily was aware of silence. Someone had turned off both of the store's radios. The usual chatter was still. She could hear only the ringing in her ears. Blood pounded through her head. Whether she opened or closed her eyes, she was enveloped in a blinding redness.

Gayle returned and Emily heard the pop of a soda can opening. The rim of the can touched her lips and she drank. Far, far away she heard whispers. The can left her mouth and someone put it into her limp hand and wrapped her fingers around it.

"God, I'm so sorry, Em." She recognized Gayle's voice.

Emily opened her eyes. "I was so angry with him. . . ."

"I know, I know." Gayle was kneeling next to her, stroking her hair.

Another person had followed Gayle to her desk. She heard a man's voice saying something. She had no idea what the disconnected words meant.

"Someone take her home," she heard at last. Mr. Pease, her boss. That's who it was. "Call her brother. He's probably in Oak Bluffs, working on a job. You, Bill. Log off of her computer, will you?"

Emily had no idea how she got home. To her apartment above the T-shirt store in Oak Bluffs. Someone opened up ths sofa bed and eased her down onto it, took off her shoes, and put a blanket over her.

She closed her eyes. Jerry. How could she go on living without Jerry? The only person in the whole world who'd ever cared about her, and here she'd thought . . .

Around one o'clock the same day Emily Cameron learned about Jerry Sparks's death, Victoria had finished her lunch and was hiking to the police station.

The station house fax machine whirred and spit out pages. Casey picked up the first few and glanced at her ancient deputy. "The State Police are sending over the preliminary report from the coroner." She shuffled through to the first page and read, " 'The victim was in poor physical condition, malnourished and dehydrated. Numerous needle marks were noted on his left inner arm, two recent.' " Casey scanned the rest of the page. "Goes on to say a significant but not fatal amount of drugs was found in his system."

The phone rang. Before she answered, Casey retrieved the remaining pages from the fax and handed them to Victoria. "See what you think of this." Then she lifted the phone. "Chief O'Neill speaking."

Victoria picked up the report and studied it.

After a few words, Casey covered the mouthpiece. "I'm on hold, Victoria. Have you found anything interesting?"

"There's a mention of Tasers. The first time I ever heard of Tasers was the day before yesterday. Now the word seems to be everywhere."

"Watts probably bought it from the Internet. Irresponsible leaving it where his kids could find it." She took her hand away from the phone. "Yeah, I'm still here."

Victoria continued to read while Casey finished the phone conversation.

She finally hung up. "Trying to sell me equipment I don't need. Why does the report mention Tasers?"

Victoria wetted her finger and turned pages. "They talk about causes of arrhythmia and give several reasons why a young, underweight, dehydrated man under the influence of drugs might die of a heart attack. One of several causes is that he could have been Tasered. It's certainly a coincidence that Jerry Sparks worked for Watts Electric, LeRoy Watts owned a Taser, and a possible cause of Jerry's death is by Taser."

"Coincidences happen," said Casey, "but I don't believe in them when they occur just as you need one."

"Is there any way to tell if a Taser has been fired?"

"I don't know much about Tasers," Casey said. "I believe they use a disposable cartridge that fires tiny darts on the ends of two wires that carry an electric charge." She made a note on her desk pad. "I'll find out."

"Is it possible that LeRoy Watts used his Taser on Jerry Sparks?"

Casey tapped her pen on her desk pad. "Up until today, I'd have said no way. LeRoy Watts has always seemed such an upright member of society. Graduate of Northeastern, active in the Little League, the library, a bunch of service organizations. Now, I just don't know. We might go back and talk to him again."

"Good idea." Victoria handed the report back to Casey. "The coroner did a drug screen. Apparently, whatever level of drug is in the bloodstream at the time of death remains the same after death."

"Right." Casey flipped through the report. "His drug level wasn't high enough to be more than what they call 'a contributing factor' to his death. 'Death is attributed to cardiac arrest,' it says here. Well, duh," she said. "When the heart stops, you die."

Later that afternoon, after a week of bright skies and mild weather, the sky clouded up and the smell of rain was in the wind. Elizabeth, home from work, gathered up her yarn, needles, and the half-finished coral she was knitting, then hunted up Victoria, who was standing in front of the bathroom mirror, adjusting her baseball cap to a becoming angle.

"Better bring your raincoat, Gram."

Victoria slung the worn trench coat that had belonged to her husband, Jonathan, over her arm, and they took off in Elizabeth's convertible.

Fran, the retired professor, was already in the reading room when they arrived, arranging finished sea creatures on the coral-reef quilt spread on the library table. Casper and Jim were helping her mass the sponges, corals, anemones, and starfish in some aesthetic order.

"My mother's coming to visit, Fran," said Elizabeth. "I may miss the next couple of meetings."

"Your mother?"

"She's a Trumbull, too. We both kept the name."

"Interesting," said Fran. "I'd like to meet her."

Victoria sat where she could view the quilt.

"It's certainly realistic," she said. "I can't imagine sleeping under it, though."

"Good heavens, no," said Fran. "It's art, not utilitarian."

"Will you include a school of fish?" Victoria asked.

"I don't think anyone thought of fish," said Jim.

"A moray eel peeking out of a coral head," said Maron. "Just the thing."

Once the others arrived, shedding raincoats and umbrellas, there was a flurry of talk about the body in the book shed, then a catching up on what needed to be done. The knitters liked the idea of a school of fish, perhaps hovering over the reef on wires concealed in branched coral, and then the group settled into their seats. Work came out of briefcases, bags, and baskets, needles clicked.

"Mrs. Trumbull would like to say a word," said Fran. The group hushed for Victoria to say whatever it was she'd come to tell them.

CHAPTER 21

"Jim, you and Casper talked to LeRoy on Monday evening," Victoria began. "What time was that?"

Jim Weiss and Casper Martin were sitting at opposite ends of the long black-and-white couch.

"Around six-thirty, quarter to seven," said Jim.

Casper nodded. "My wife picked us up around six. Jim and I have been feeling uncomfortable in the group lately. The women clearly suspected one of us was the caller."

"Not all of us," said Alyssa.

"Please let him finish," said Victoria.

"We decided to ask LeRoy for help," Jim went on.

"Why LeRoy?" asked Victoria.

"A logical choice," said Jim. "His wife's head of the library trustees, he's around the library a lot fixing electrical problems, installing new lines. He probably notices people and might have seen someone take an unusual interest in the women in the knitting group."

Victoria nodded.

"We left before Alyssa arrived and so we didn't hear her claim that Jerry Sparks was the caller," said Jim. "At that point, we had no idea who the caller could be. Never occurred to us that it might be LeRoy."

Casper said, "We got to Oak Bluffs just as the sun set and the sky was turning red."

"Why did you become suspicious of LeRoy?"

"He's usually pretty straightforward," said Jim. "But he wouldn't look at us. That's not like him at all."

"Another thing—he kept evading our questions," said Casper. "We thought he could tell us how a stalker might get hold of an unlisted number. Instead, he freaked out."

Jim added, "Since he's in the library a lot, he might have seen someone taking an interest in the women. Then, suddenly, light dawned. He was the caller. LeRoy."

"Casey and I visited LeRoy shortly after you did, close to seven, and gave him some unpleasant news."

Jessica looked up from her knitting.

"The news involved his sons." Victoria hesitated, wondering if she should say anything about the Taser. She looked around at the knitters. "It's public knowledge by now, I'm sure. His sons found what they thought was a toy ray gun in a file drawer in the shop and took it to school. The school was in quite an uproar."

"School policy bans toy guns," said Fran.

"They were playing with the weapon at recess. A teaching aide took the gun away from them and showed it to the principal, who recognized it as a Taser."

"How did Mr. Watts get hold of a Taser?" asked Maron.

"You can get anything on the Internet," said Jim.

"In Massachusetts, possession of a Taser is subject to a heavy fine and a jail term," said Victoria. "We informed Mr. Watts of that."

"Ouch!" said Maron. "Bad news is right."

Casper picked up his knitting and studied it for a moment. "Watts was certainly having a bad day. First we stopped by unexpectedly, took him by surprise. By the time we left, he must have known we were uneasy about the way he was acting."

"LeRoy is the electrical inspector," Jim pointed out. "He works on electrical boxes, which are usually next to telephone boxes. To find an unlisted number, all he needs to do is open the phone box."

"I can't believe it, Jim!" said Maron. "I mean, I've known Mr. Watts all my life. He goes to my church. Sometimes I baby-sat for the twins. He does all this volunteer work."

"I agree with Maron," said Fran. "I've known Leroy for a long time. He's the last person on earth I'd suspect."

Jim shrugged and looked down at his knitting. "If he's such a great guy, what's he doing with a Taser?"

"Tasers are supposed to stop people instantly and safely," said Maron.

"That was his rationale," Victoria agreed. "He told Casey and me that he didn't want a gun around that the boys might play with."

"So he keeps a Taser in an unlocked file drawer that the kids *do* find, take to school, and get caught playing with?" Jessica laughed. "If a Taser is so safe, why is it illegal in the commonwealth?"

The five women who'd gone in search of Jerry Sparks two days earlier glanced at one another.

"Girls," said Fran, watching them, "we have work to do. Don't even think about hunting down Mr. Watts. Suppose you'd found Jerry Sparks? What would you have done?"

Cherry giggled. "Someone already did it for us."

"Stop it!" said Fran. "You're not implying that you plan to harm Mr. Watts, are you? That's horrible."

"Sorry." Cherry put a hand up to her mouth.

Victoria watched the women closely. "Fran is right. LeRoy may have a simple explanation for his behavior."

"Yeah," said Jessica. "He gets off by talking dirty on the phone."

"When we stopped by the shop looking for Jerry Sparks," said Cherry, "he did act kind of odd."

"He's in the library a lot," said Jessica. "He knows most of us, at least by sight."

Cherry stood up. "Girls? Action!"

Victoria looked at the other girls.

"No, no!" cried Fran, getting to her feet. "LeRoy Watts is a good, kind man. We don't have time for this!"

But the five women had packed up their knitting and had flown out the door before anyone could stop them.

"They have no sense of responsibility," said Fran.

Maureen arrived at work early on Thursday after two days with her visiting daughter, son-in-law, and two grandchildren. She loved her grandchildren, but it was a relief to get back to work.

Usually, she was there before Mr. Watts, but this morning his van was parked out back and the door was unlocked.

"Morning, Mr. Watts!" she called out. "I'm back. What a lovely day." She raised the shades in the front windows. "Let in some of this glorious light. No need to waste electricity like this." She headed toward her desk. "Mr. Watts . . ."

He was slumped behind his desk. For an instant, she assumed he'd had a heart attack, all that stress he'd been under. Then she saw the blood. She stepped over to her desk and called 911, gave the address, and said the EMTs could park the ambulance behind the shop. She turned to see what she could do to help LeRoy, knelt down next to him, and felt his wrist, put her hand up to his neck. Nothing. She could do nothing.

She picked up the phone again, thinking to call his wife, and put it down again. Her hands were shaking too much to press the numbers.

Then it hit her. She started to put her hands up to her mouth. She didn't want them near her face. Her stomach churned. She was not a screamer, nor was she a fainter. She braced herself against the wall, her palms against the faux paneling, and, without knowing she was doing it, slid down into a sitting position, which is where she was when the EMTs arrived moments later.

Maureen was only semiaware during the time the EMTs checked LeRoy for any sign of life and found none. They had called the State Police and Doc Jeffers, who was on duty again as medical examiner. After taking care of that, they tended to Maureen.

She shook her head. "I'm fine. No, I'm fine, really. Please. Go about your business. I'll be all right." But one of the EMTs escorted her to a chair, sat her down gently, brought a wet towel from the washroom and washed her face and hands, and gave her a glass of water, which Maureen took with her shaking hands.

Junior Norton, West Tisbury's police sergeant, heard the 911 call, recognized the name, and notified Casey, who arrived at the scene with Victoria.

"Direct hit on the carotid artery," Doc Jeffers stated. "Sharp, slender object, like a fid."

"Fid?" someone asked.

Maureen was too muzzy to care what they said.

"Common tool on the Island, sharp, tapered," said Doc Jeffers. "Jab it into his neck and it would do the job."

"Yeah, but what's a fid?" someone else asked.

"Doc's a sailor. It's what sailors use to separate strands of rope," a third person said. "Fid, marlinspike. Same difference."

"What's a marlinspike?"

"We've got work to do," said Doc Jeffers. "Get busy."

A crowd gathered at the foot of Circuit Avenue as an Oak Bluffs police officer directed traffic away from the two-block area around Watts Electrical Supply. The state police cordoned off the scene with yellow tape. Doc Jeffers finished examining the body and left.

"A fid?" Casey asked no one in particular. "I've never heard of it. Why would Doc Jeffers come up with that as a weapon? Where would anyone get something like that?" She turned to Victoria. "You know what a fid is?"

Victoria nodded but said nothing.

"You're from off-Island," said Sergeant Smalley, looking up from the body. "People who mess with boats know what a fid is. Right, Victoria?"

She nodded.

"Use it to separate rope strands when you're splicing," he continued.

"Splicing?" said Casey.

"Please!" said Smalley. "Ask Emily Cameron at the boatyard to show you."

Casey paced until Sergeant Smalley took a break. "The Watts family lives in West Tisbury, Sergeant," she said. "Want Victoria and me to break the news to his wife?"

He stood up and pulled off his latex gloves. "I'd appreciate it, Chief. Not a pleasant job."

"It's going to be a terrible shock to Sarah," Victoria said. "They're a close family. LeRoy always went out of his way to help anyone who needed help."

"Is there anything we should avoid when we speak to her?" Casey asked.

"I wouldn't mention the weapon. That was a guess on Doc Jeffers's part anyway. Could have been any kind of sharp, pointed instrument."

"Knitting needle?" asked Victoria.

Smalley scratched his head. "I guess. Phillips-head screwdriver, awl. Something like that. Even a sharp pencil or a ballpoint pen."

"Would it have taken much strength?" Victoria asked.

Smalley shook his head. "Nope. Just a lucky strike in the right place." He put a hand up to the side of his neck. "Right about here."

CHAPTER 22

"Let's go, Victoria," said Casey as they left the crime scene at Watts Electrical Supply. "Work to do."

Victoria resumed her place in the Bronco. Casey started the engine and hit the siren to clear the street of the onlookers who'd gathered in the middle of Circuit Avenue. Once they were clear of the crowd, they rode in silence until they were on Barnes Road.

Casey broke the silence. "Some idiot was probably high on drugs."

"Or angry."

"Damn," said Casey, who seldom swore. "I hate this part of the job, telling Sarah Watts that her whole life has changed, hers and the boys."

Victoria nodded. She kept her eyes averted from the road in front of them and caught glimpses of Lagoon Pond through the trees to her right. The world outside the police vehicle seemed so normal. A sailboat at anchor at the head of the Lagoon was reflected in the still water, a black-hulled ketch. She knew the owners of the boat.

They passed Featherstone on the left, an art center founded only a few years ago. Victoria had read her poetry there. They paused at the blinker, now a four-way stop sign, and Casey hit the siren before she crossed the Vineyard Haven–Edgartown Road.

"I keep thinking how nice it was of Watts to check the breaker box in the station house," said Casey. "Only a couple of days ago. He did some work for you, too, didn't he, Victoria?"

Victoria nodded. "He stopped by Monday to fix . . ." Victoria didn't finish.

"What were you about to say?" Casey asked.

"I suddenly remembered that he left his tool chest in the upstairs room when he was repairing that outlet."

"I guess we should return it to his widow."

Victoria thought about the widow. "When we were in the principal's office, Sarah was furious with her husband for keeping the Taser where the twins could find it. Anger is a dreadful burden to carry now there can be no apology or forgiveness."

"Yeah," said Casey. "Stupid of him. Of course, when the kids found it, they'd want to show it off at school, even if they knew they weren't supposed to. They're nine-year-olds, after all."

Victoria was quiet again. How was she going to break the news to Sarah? Something like "We have some bad news for you, Sarah, you'd better sit down"? Sarah probably would be alerted to bad news simply by seeing two representatives of the police force at her door. She'd suppose it had to do with her boys and the Taser again, not her husband's death, Victoria thought.

Dead snags of red pine killed years ago by a rare fungus lined the road. This part of the state forest was ghostlike, with its silvery skeletons of trees. She felt a wash of relief when they'd turned onto the Edgartown–West Tisbury Road, passed the state forest boundary, and dipped down into the swale that marked the beginning of her property. They drove past her house, shaded by tall old maples in a haze of pale green blossom.

"I'll stop at the police station to let Junior Norton know what's going on," said Casey. "I didn't want to say anything over the radio."

Victoria suspected Casey was delaying the inevitable meeting with LeRoy's widow. *Widow* was such a final-sounding word. Not wife any longer, but widow, a single parent with two young boys.

Casey pulled into the parking area in front of the police station and left the engine running. "Won't take me a minute, Victoria." And then she was back in the driver's seat. "A cop's worst nightmare." She leaned forward, both hands on the steering wheel. "Telling a wife her husband's been murdered. Well, here goes."

She backed out onto the Edgartown Road and turned onto Old County Road. Just past the school, she left the paved road for the gravel lane and the Watts house.

Sarah apparently saw the police car turn into her drive, because she met them at the door, dish towel in hand. "Morning, Mrs. Trumbull, Casey."

Victoria noticed the ugly purple swelling on Sarah's face. "That's a nasty bruise. How did that happen?"

"Do you have time for a cup of tea?" asked Sarah. "The kettle's on."

"We'd appreciate that," said Casey.

They followed Sarah into her kitchen. The table was littered with papers, tape, scissors, and crayons. "A project the boys have to do." She shoved the papers off to one side. "Punishment for taking that Taser to school. I can't imagine what LeRoy was thinking, keeping it where the kids could find it." She touched her face absently and winced. "The boys are supposed to write a five-page paper explaining how Tasers work and why people shouldn't own them." She kept talking as she poured boiling water into a blue-and-white china teapot, swished it around, and dumped it into the sink. She talked as she measured tea into the pot and filled it with boiling water. "Their teacher wants them to make a display of weaponry from the days of the caveman to the present." She took down three mugs from a shelf above the counter. "I don't know what that's supposed to teach them."

Victoria sat at the table, waiting for a pause in Sarah's seamless monologue. It was as though Sarah didn't want to hear whatever it was they had come to tell her.

"She's a great teacher. I suppose the punishment fits the crime, but I'm not sure—"

Victoria interrupted. "Sarah, I'm afraid we have bad news for you. You might want to sit down."

Casey stood by the dining room door, letting Victoria deal with this.

"Oh?" said Sarah, and sat down. "Not the boys again?"

"Your boys are fine," said Victoria. "They're wonderful children." And she told Sarah, straight out, that her husband was dead, murdered.

"Oh!" Sarah put her hand to her throat. "That can't be." She stood. "LeRoy, dead?"

Victoria said nothing.

"What happened?"

"I'll pour tea for you, Mrs. Watts," said Casey.

Sarah slumped back into her chair, put her elbows on the table, and rested her forehead on her hands. Her hair fell over her fingers. "We had an argument a couple of nights ago. . . ."

"The bruise?" asked Victoria.

Sarah nodded. "He's never hit me before. Never. He stalked out and hasn't come home since. And now . . ."

"Yes," said Victoria softly.

Casey set the tea down in front of her. Sarah turned the mug around and around.

"How was he killed?" she asked.

Casey took a breath. "He was stabbed, Mrs. Watts."

"When did it happen?"

"We don't know yet. Yesterday or the day before, most likely."

Sarah stared into her mug. "Tuesday or Wednesday," she murmured.

Victoria thought about the symptoms of shock. Denial, disbelief, anger. Sometimes it took awhile for the grief to emerge. Often, shock was delayed, she knew. Someone should stay with Sarah for the next several days. Even tough New Englanders can break.

"Who found him?" Sarah looked up.

"His office manager," said Casey.

"Poor Maureen." Sarah reached into her pocket, brought out a tissue, and dabbed at her eyes.

Casey cleared her throat. "If you'd like me to, I'll pick up your boys at school. Victoria can stay with you until I return."

"Certainly," said Victoria.

"I'm okay," said Sarah. "I don't need a baby-sitter." She sat up straight and pushed her hair away from her face. "Thanks for fetching the boys. They need to be home."

"Do you want me to tell them about their father, Mrs. Watts, or would you prefer to?"

"I just don't know," said Sarah. "I don't know what to do. I guess I'd better tell them." She stood up again and wandered into the living room. "No, I'd rather you told them." She wandered back into the kitchen. "Where did I put my knitting?" She paced, turning in tight circles.

Victoria lifted the flowered oilcloth that covered the table. "It's under here, next to your chair." She pushed the basket with its partially finished sweater toward Sarah with her foot. Familiar tasks could be comforting.

Casey stepped out quietly, shutting the door behind her as she left. Victoria heard the Bronco start up and a burst of static on the police radio.

Sarah picked up her knitting and started a new row.

"I'll call your sister."

"I'm all right, Mrs. Trumbull. Really I am."

But Victoria looked up Jackie's phone number and called anyway, and Jackie promised to hurry right over.

"Mrs. Trumbull, I don't want my sister over here." Sarah

155

pulled a length of yarn out of her knitting bag and switched needles to start a new row.

"The sweater is a lovely color," said Victoria, hoping to keep Sarah's mind off her husband's death. "Do the different-size needles result in a special effect?"

Sarah looked down at the needles, one sturdy polished steel, one more flimsy plastic. "I misplaced the other steel one," she said. "I must have dropped it somewhere."

Within fifteen minutes, footsteps pounded up the kitchen steps, and Jackie burst through the door, a tall, well-built blonde. She flung her arms around Sarah. "Sweetie, I can't believe he's—" She stopped. "Your face! What did he do to you?"

Sarah shook her head.

Jackie looked at her sister closely. "If he hit me, even once, I'd have killed him, too."

CHAPTER 23

Victoria tried to think of a tactful way to tell Sarah the State Police would be coming to question her, decided there was no tactful way at all, blurted it out, and finished up, "I'm sorry you have to go through questioning at a time like this."

"I know it's necessary," said Sarah, and yanked another length of yarn out of the basket. "I watch the cop shows." She stopped knitting long enough to blot her nose. "I suppose I'm a prime suspect. The spouse always is." She leaned back to look at Jackie, who was standing close to her, gently rubbing her shoulders. "Would you stop doing that? You're driving me crazy."

Jackie said nothing, but stopped massaging her sister's shoulders and turned away.

Within the hour, the police Bronco returned to the Watts house. The siren wailed once and died down. The twins tumbled out of the backseat and followed Casey into the kitchen. "The boys wanted to use the siren," said Casey.

"Just once," Zeke said.

Sarah put her arms around both boys, hugging them close to her, burrowing her face in their tousled hair.

Victoria looked away.

Sarah glanced up from her boys. "We'll be all right."

Jackie walked Victoria to the door. "Thanks for being here for Sarah, Mrs. Trumbull. I hope you didn't think I meant it about, you know, her killing him. She wouldn't, you know. I was upset."

"Of course. Call me if Sarah needs anything."

Casey parked under the maple tree at the end of Victoria's drive. "I could use another cup of tea," said Victoria. "That wasn't a pleasant chore."

"Tea sounds good to me, too."

They climbed the steps and went through the entry into the kitchen. Victoria felt her age. Her sore toe throbbed. Her throat felt dry. Everything ached. McCavity appeared from some hideaway and rubbed up against her legs.

"What do you suppose caused LeRoy to strike his wife like that? I've never imagined him as a violent man."

"You never know what goes on behind closed doors in a marriage," said Casey.

"Sarah wasn't pleased to have me summon her sister," said Victoria when they were seated at the cookroom table with their tea. "I thought she needed to have someone with her, a family member." Victoria glanced up at the baskets hanging from the rafters overhead, then out the window, its frame festooned with loopy vines of philodendron.

"Sarah's probably in shock," said Casey, stirring sugar into her tea. "That's why she didn't react the way you'd expect. Sometime tonight the shock will wear off and she'll wake up to what's happened to her. I'm glad Jackie was able to get there so soon."

McCavity, sitting beside Victoria's chair, looked up expectantly. Victoria patted her lap, and he leaped up, kneaded his claws into her gray corduroys, yawned hugely, and dozed off.

"The police have to question her right away," said Casey. "Tough on a grieving spouse, but the first few hours are critical." She took a sip of her tea, then added another spoonful of sugar and stirred it. "They have to rule out spouses and family."

"I'm sure they'll be sensitive," said Victoria, stroking McCavity.

"When we were still at the shop, Sergeant Smalley called Howland Atherton and asked him to go through LeRoy Watts's computer to see if he'd had any threats or problems with anyone."

"I wouldn't think anyone would make a threat that could be so easily traced," said Victoria.

Casey shrugged. "Everything's got to be looked at. Once he checks with the State Police, Howland's going to call me either at the station or here."

They'd finished their tea when Howland called. Victoria handed the phone to Casey, who listened for a short time, nodded, and hung up.

"What is it?" asked Victoria.

"You know those videos on Jerry Sparks's computer?"

"Yes?" said Victoria.

"When the State Police asked Howland to check LeRoy Watts's computer, he found the same videos that were on Jerry Sparks's computer, only LeRoy's had even more shower scenes and more recent ones. Howland's on his way over."

"In other words—" Victoria started.

"Yeah. LeRoy Watts was the video guy."

Victoria sat back in her chair. "How strange. There must be some mistake. He was such a fine man."

Casey shrugged. "You never know."

Ten minutes later, Howland dropped into an empty chair at the cookroom table. Victoria offered him tea.

"Thanks," said Howland. He tore open a packet of sweetener and stirred the contents into his tea. "Looks like Watts was the creative talent behind the videos. Jerry Sparks copied them off of Watts's computer."

The phone rang, and Victoria answered again.

"I've been trying to reach you for the past half hour, Mother,"

Amelia said with a touch of irritation in her voice. "I'm in Woods Hole and hoped you could ask Elizabeth to pick me up in Vineyard Haven."

"What ferry will you be on?"

"The one-fifteen. I'm on it now."

"I'll be there," said Victoria.

"I don't want you driving, Mother."

"Don't worry," said Victoria, and hung up. She could feel heat rising in her face.

"Who was that?" asked Howland with concern.

"My daughter. She's on the ferry now and wants to be picked up. Would you mind giving me a ride?"

"I can take you," said Casey.

"Thank you, but you don't understand my daughter," said Victoria. "I'd rather not arrive at the dock in a police vehicle."

Casey laughed. "Call me when you can, Victoria. We have more to talk about."

"Had you heard about the Watts twins' problem at school?" Victoria asked as they headed into Vineyard Haven to meet the ferry.

"I understand they were reprimanded for taking their father's Taser to school."

"The preliminary coroner's report suggested Tasering as one possible cause for Jerry Sparks's death."

"Under certain circumstances, a Taser can kill. If the trigger is pulled repeatedly, it continues to send pulses of current into a victim. If he's in poor physical condition, that can kill him." They came to the end of Old County Road and Howland turned right onto State Road. "We may never know how he died. He'd been in that shed awhile."

"Then we still have the question of the phone breather," said Victoria. "Surely LeRoy wasn't both a phone stalker and a voyeur?"

"Could be." Howland paused while he passed a slowly moving

red Volvo station wagon. The driver, a young woman in her twenties, was talking on a cell phone.

"That should be illegal," said Victoria, referring to the phone.

"They've got to stay in touch," Howland said. "Back to Watts. Something drove him, something in his past, or in his genetic makeup. I don't know that anyone has worked out the puzzle of why stalkers stalk. He probably saw himself as playing a harmless game."

"With a camera?"

"Extending his phone call game to high tech," said Howland. "He was an electrician, after all."

Victoria was quiet for a few moments. "I've always been intrigued by his name. Watts. So appropriate for an electrician."

"I once knew a dentist named Dodrill," said Howland. "And an oceanographer named C. Weed. And Sparks, of course, worked for Watts."

"Both dead now," Victoria said.

They'd passed the Snake Hollow road when Howland spoke again. "Sergeant Smalley asked me to identify the women in the videos. I'd like you to view them, if you would. See if you recognise any of them."

Victoria frowned.

"I'm afraid it's necessary."

"As you know, Howland, I don't have a television set."

"I have my laptop with me," said Howland.

They pulled up to the curb at the Steamship Authority terminal just as the ferry was docking. Amelia was one of the first passengers to disembark, a tall, elegant woman in her early sixties, an older version of Elizabeth, slender, wearing an understated jacket and slacks.

She opened her arms to Victoria. "Darling! How good to see you." She held her mother at arm's length. "You look wonderful."

"You, too, Amelia."

"You're not still driving, are you?"

Victoria felt her face flush again. Her daughter knew how to irritate her within the first seconds of greeting her. "My friend Howland Atherton is chauffeuring us today," she said, trying for a light touch. "He's waiting by the terminal building. How was the flight from Denver?"

"The weather was lovely most of the way. We ran into clouds over the Appalachians. Have you been keeping busy, Mother? You really do look great, by the way."

"Thank you. Yes, we've been busy." Victoria held back, with some satisfaction, the fact that she'd just come from a murder scene.

Amelia lifted her suitcase from the baggage cart, set it on the ground, and pulled up the handle. "I don't believe I've ever met your friend. You say his name is Howland? Someone you met at the senior center?"

Victoria wished for Howland to appear, and at that very moment he did, striding toward her, looking young and vigorous and handsome, with his wavy silver hair, a nose almost as fine as her own, although not as large, and an early tan, testifying to his outdoor life.

"This must be Amelia," he said in his grand deep voice with a touch of Boston's Beacon Hill. "Here, let me take that."

Victoria noted with pleasure Amelia's look of astonishment as she relinquished her suitcase. "You're my mother's friend?"

"Friend, colleague, and cohort," said Howland. "We're involved in a murder case at the moment."

"Murder?" said Amelia in a small voice.

"We found the body just this morning."

"*You* found . . ." Amelia turned to Victoria. "Mother, you didn't tell me . . ."

"Here's the car," said Victoria. "I'll sit up front."

CHAPTER 24

Howland followed Amelia upstairs with her suitcase, and Victoria came slowly after them.

"Amelia," she called up. "I'm putting you in the West Room. I'm having some work done in your usual room."

Amelia paused at the top of the stairs and looked down at her mother. "Really? What sort of work?"

"Minor electrical work," said Victoria. "I'll get clean sheets."

"I can find them, Mother. Please, don't bother."

"I'd rather," Victoria said. As she headed for the linen closet, she heard her daughter say to Howland, "I worry about her. She's not as young as she thinks she is."

"I wouldn't worry about Victoria if I were you," said Howland. "It's fruitless."

Victoria emerged from the linen closet with an armload of lavender-scented sheets and pillowcases.

Amelia hurried to take them from her. "Thanks so much, Mother. You should have let me do that." She looked around at the paintings and photos on the wall. "I've always loved this room."

Afternoon sunlight poured through the west window, bathing the old furniture in a mellow gold that hid the scuff marks of generations of children. In one corner of the room was a crib piled with old patchwork quilts. Sailors had made the crib for Victoria's two aunts, born during a five-year whaling voyage. Victoria's grandmother had gone to sea with her husband, the captain, rather than stay home with her formidable mother-in-law.

"What sort of electrical work are you having done in my room?"

"Repairing an electrical outlet."

Howland snorted. "Actually, Amelia, the electrician repairing your mother's outlet was the murder victim."

Amelia abruptly dropped the linens on her bed. "Mother!"

Victoria suddenly remembered the tool chest LeRoy Watts had left. "Excuse me. I have to attend to something."

Amelia glanced at Howland, who avoided her eyes.

Victoria strode across the hall to the East Chamber. When LeRoy Watts had left his tools behind on Monday, she'd wondered why he would leave something so necessary for his work. Now, she was thinking, perhaps he'd hidden something in it, perhaps a clue to the videos he'd been taking. She heard Amelia talking softly to Howland, and suspected the conversation had to do with her. Was Amelia trying to enlist an ally? Or was she, Victoria, simply becoming paranoid?

The toolbox was under the window, at right angles to the wall. It was a large chest, about the size of a filing cabinet drawer. Now that she saw it, she could understand why LeRoy decided to leave it here rather than toting the heavy chest back and forth. She tried to move it herself, but it was much too heavy.

"Need a hand, Victoria?" Howland came into the room, followed closely by Amelia.

"What is it, Mother?"

"LeRoy Watts's tool chest. I'd like to look inside."

"But Mother . . ."

"Absolutely right, Victoria," said Howland. "It's not locked, is it?"

Victoria eased herself to her knees, twisted the latch that held the lid down, and lifted the top. The box smelled of WD-40.

Inside, the tools were neatly nested, pliers and wrenches and screwdrivers, all clean with a sheen of oil. At one end of the chest was a cigarette pack–size plastic box with thin wires wrapped around it.

"Aha!" said Howland.

Victoria took a napkin out of her pocket and lifted the plastic box out of the tool chest. "Is this what I think it is?"

"A spent Taser cartridge," said Howland. "Nice going, Victoria. Shall I call the State Police, or do you want to?"

Victoria held onto the arms of the rocking chair by the window to get to her feet again, and winced as her sore toe bumped against her shoe.

"Mother . . . are you all right?"

Victoria ignored her daughter. "I'd better go through channels and call Casey first. She can contact Sergeant Smalley."

Amelia glanced from Howland to her mother. "What is going on?"

Casey arrived ten minutes later, and Sergeant Smalley followed shortly after. Smalley snapped on latex gloves, took charge of the tool chest, and carried it away.

The remaining four went downstairs.

"I hope you're not overdoing things, Mother." Amelia reached out and patted Victoria's hand.

Casey laughed. "During the past week, your mother was barely getting warmed up. Video stalkings, obscene phone calls, stolen Tasers, and two murders."

Howland added a few details, and Casey added a few more on top of his.

Amelia kept looking from Howland to the police chief, avoiding her mother's bland expression. Occasionally she interrupted, saying, "But . . ." or "Really . . ." or "I can't believe . . ." or, one time with a glance at Victoria, "Oh, Mother!"

After that, Howland set up his laptop on the cookroom table and Amelia went to the cupboard where Victoria kept her spirits. Without asking, she poured hefty drinks for everyone—Howland, Casey, Victoria, and herself. She delivered the drinks on a black tray decorated with a painted still life of onions.

With a look at Howland's laptop, she lifted her own glass of Scotch off the tray and said, "If you don't really need me, I believe I'll go upstairs and read." With that, she left.

Howland, Casey, and Victoria huddled around the laptop, drinks untouched.

"We need to identify as many of the women as possible," Howland said as he started up the computer.

"I'm not sure I understand why we're doing this," said Victoria.

"We'll have to contact the women and find out who worked on their bathroom electrical systems. Was it LeRoy Watts or Jerry Sparks or possibly someone else."

He inserted the small metal thumb drive into the laptop. The thumb drive, smaller than a child-size domino, seemed much too small to hold any information at all, let alone movies with sound. Movies should come in metal canisters, reels of film that seemed substantial enough to mean something.

Howland continued to explain. "We also need to find out where the cameras were located and if any are still in place."

Victoria nodded away her mental image of a humming movie projector and settled back in her chair. "I'll do what I can."

The pictures popped up on the laptop screen. Sounds of water running. A voice, singing.

"I don't know her," said Victoria.

"Nor I," said Casey.

"I'll fast-forward," said Howland.

Water running. A voice called out, "Honey, I forgot the soap. Would you bring me a fresh bar?"

"Why, that's Jessica Gordon, one of the knitters," said Victoria. "I thought she lived alone."

"Her boyfriend lived with her up until a couple of weeks ago," said Casey.

"Fast-forward," said Howland.

Water running. A young girl was shampooing her hair.

"Good heavens!" said Victoria. "That's Jim Weiss's daughter, Lily. He's another one of the mathematical knitters."

Howland pushed the pause button. Casey looked closely. "It's Lily all right. She's barely sixteen."

"This is ugly," said Victoria.

On and on and on, through a dozen short videos. Victoria didn't know all of the women, but she knew most.

"I've seen enough," said Casey.

"We're almost at the end."

Casey made notes. "I'll contact the people we've identified, have them notify me if they find a camera. We'll also send an announcement to the *Enquirer*."

"I'll write up something for my column. Not all the victims are from West Tisbury, but quite a few people from other towns read my column." Victoria smoothed her hair.

CHAPTER 25

When the phone rang the next morning, Amelia was still asleep. Her daughter, Victoria supposed, was on West Coast time. She pushed her typewriter aside and answered. The caller was Myrna, her lawyer friend.

"Five women are here in my office, Victoria, apparently at your instigation."

"From the knitting group, I assume."

Myrna laughed. "Well, they're all knitting up a storm at this very moment."

"I'm glad they've gone to you."

"I'm not sure how glad you're going to be when you hear what they have to say. You need to be in on the discussion. Can you get here in the next half hour or so?"

Victoria checked her watch. "Yes, certainly. What's the trouble?"

"I'd rather not talk on the phone. Would you like me to call a cab?"

"No, thank you." Victoria thought of the blue dump truck. "I've got transportation." After she hung up, she called Bill O'Malley's cell-phone number. "Do you think you could give me a ride?"

"Sure thing, Mrs. T. Where do you want to go and how soon?"

"Myrna Luce's again. As soon as possible."

"Problems?"

"I don't know," said Victoria.

"Be there in ten minutes."

Victoria shrugged into her coat and was searching for her baseball cap when Amelia came downstairs, hair combed, her clothing tidy. Was she actually wearing makeup? On the Vineyard? At nine o'clock in the morning? At times, her daughter seemed to have been spawned by a different set of parents.

Amelia reached out her arms and hugged her mother. "Good morning, darling. You look as though you're ready to go out."

"Good morning," said Victoria. "The coffee's on, and you know where the cereal is."

Amelia strode into the kitchen, carrying herself regally, like a Trumbull, Victoria thought. Amelia turned when she reached the coffeemaker and smiled, a sunny smile that seemed to brighten the morning. "Where are you off to?"

"Vineyard Haven." For some reason, Victoria didn't want to be more specific.

"Is Howland Atherton giving you a ride?"

"Not this morning." Victoria found her hat under the table, where McCavity must have knocked it.

"Oh?"

"Another friend is giving me a ride."

Amelia poured herself a cup of coffee and took a sip. "You make the most superb coffee." She held up her mug and smiled again.

"I shouldn't be too long," Victoria said.

"You don't need to be so mysterious about your ride," Amelia said. "Another handsome gentleman friend?"

"The toaster is in the cabinet under the kitchen counter," said Victoria. "And there's beach plum jam in the icebox."

"Darling, you're too much!" Amelia found the bread and the jam, and plugged in the toaster. Victoria, in the meantime, was settling her hat at a becoming angle.

"I love your chapeau, Mother. It looks cute on you," said Amelia.

Her badge of authority. Her identity as a deputy police officer. Cute?

Victoria gave her daughter an airy wave and marched out to the west step to wait for O'Malley. She would love to see her daughter's expression when the dump truck pulled up. Victoria could see Amelia's reflection in the outside entry window. She could even make out her daughter's concerned expression as she waited to see who would pick up her mother. Victoria heard the rumble of O'Malley's truck, and could make out the dumbfounded look on Amelia's reflected face as the truck braked and O'Malley emerged—young, handsome, vigorous, with longish curly black hair. His broad shoulders strained against his T-shirt. He hiked up his jeans and tightened his belt, then set down the milk-crate step for Victoria, and grinned broadly at her as she approached. He helped her up into the high seat.

Once seated, Victoria turned to Amelia, still standing by the window, mouth partly open, and lifted her hand in a regal wave.

"That was quick," said Victoria as she settled her blue coat under her.

"I was at the airport," he said. "Who was that?"

"My daughter Amelia. Elizabeth's mother. She's come to cart me off to an assisted-living facility."

"What?" O'Malley looked at her in horror.

"I'm exaggerating. My daughter is one of those 'caring' people."

"Ah. I understand." O'Malley stopped at the end of the drive and looked both ways before turning onto the Edgartown Road. "What's with Myrna?"

"I have no idea. She didn't want to tell me over the phone."

On the way to Vineyard Haven, the oak trees were haloed with a faint pink haze that softened their winter-stark branches.

"We always called new oak leaves 'mouse ears,'" said Victoria. "When oaks leaf out, it's time to plant corn. Oaks are always the last to recognize spring has come."

She turned, about to say more, when O'Malley said, "How does your granddaughter like her job?"

"She's busy. The harbor is getting ready for summer."

"I took my boat around there the other day. Must have missed her."

"Elizabeth has odd hours," said Victoria, and suddenly realized, of course. It was spring. Sap was flowing. She glanced over at O'Malley. Such a nice man, right around Elizabeth's age. Taller than her granddaughter, and in possession of a magnificent new dump truck. "Why don't you come for supper tomorrow evening?"

"Great," he said. "What time?"

His answer was so prompt, Victoria wondered why she hadn't thought of him weeks earlier. "Elizabeth's mathematical knitting group meets until seven every evening," she said. "Do you mind a late supper? Seven-thirty or so?"

"Perfect. I usually eat around eight. Mathematical knitting?"

"They're knitting Möbius-strip kelp and Klein-bottle sea anemones for a coral-reef quilt."

O'Malley scratched his head and laughed. "I don't need to worry about a topic of conversation. What can I bring?"

They discussed the logistics of supper until O'Malley turned off the main road and onto the lane where Myrna had her office.

"Give me a call when you're ready to be picked up," he said. "I've got business to attend to in Oak Bluffs, but it'll take me only a few minutes to get here."

He set out the milk crate again and helped Victoria climb down from the passenger seat.

"Thank you," said Victoria, touching the visor of her baseball cap.

"Pleasure's all mine," he said.

Myrna flung the door open. "Come in." She ushered Victoria into the office.

The five women knitters were sitting in a semicircle around Myrna's desk—Jessica, Maron, Cherry, Alyssa, and Roberta.

"Hi, Mrs. Trumbull," said Maron.

"Thanks for coming," said Jessica.

"Glad you could get here," said Roberta.

"We took your advice," said Cherry.

"My advice?" Victoria settled herself into the chair Myrna held for her.

"To talk with Ms. Luce. We decided we needed legal help."

Victoria removed her hat, placed it on Myrna's desk, and waited.

The women looked at one another, then at Myrna.

"These women are convinced LeRoy Watts was the phone stalker," Myrna said, waving a beringed hand at the five. "And, as you know, they set off to teach him a lesson."

"I was there when they left to do so," said Victoria.

"We didn't find Mr. Watts," said Cherry, who apparently spoke for the five. "We went to his shop, but it was closed and the shades were drawn. We didn't want to go to his home, so we returned to the library, where we'd parked."

"However," Myrna went on, "each of the five decided, independently, according to them, to confront Mr. Watts. And now he's dead."

"Are you saying one of you killed him?" Victoria leaned forward.

Jessica set her knitting in her lap. "Yes. One of us did." She pointed to herself. "I could be the killer, but I'm not saying, one way or the other."

"None of us is talking," said Maron. "I knew Mr. Watts from the time I was a little kid." She set her knitting aside and took a tissue out of her pocket and blew her nose. "He betrayed me. Us. All of us." She wadded up the tissue in one hand and went back to her knitting.

"Sorry about all this knitting, but we're working on deadline," explained Jessica.

"Yes, yes, I know," said Victoria.

"All of us trusted him," said Cherry. "He went to my church, for heaven's sake." She jabbed a needle into her woolen coral.

Roberta sat forward on the edge of her chair. "It took awhile for me to believe Mr. Watts could be such a . . . such a . . ." she stopped. "I mean, he was involved in Scouts and sports, all kinds of community activity." She looked down at her work. "Darn, I dropped a stitch." The knitters waited until she'd retrieved it. "Everybody thought what a nice man he was. And here . . ."

"It's the betrayal," said Alyssa, smoothing her Möbius-strip kelp. "We all feel the same. We know for sure that one of us killed him. One of us stabbed him in the neck with a knitting needle."

"We're convinced whoever did it didn't mean to kill him," said Maron. "It wasn't an intentional murder. She was probably just trying to make a point."

The other four nodded in agreement.

"A knitting needle isn't exactly a dangerous weapon," said someone.

Jessica said, "We came to Myrna's to ask her to defend us as a group. We don't know which one of us did the deed, and we agreed that none of us would confess. We refuse to even try to identify the actual killer among us."

"Not one of us is sorry he's dead, although, of course, we didn't set out to kill him," said Roberta, continuing to knit while she looked around at the other women, who nodded. "I mean, we didn't want to actually kill him, but we wouldn't have minded if someone else did. So someone did, and it's one of us."

"That's right," said Maron, brushing bits of her disintegrated tissue off her multicolored brain coral onto the floor. "We're, like,

174

equally guilty. I mean, if you want someone dead and you hire a killer, you're guilty, right?"

Victoria listened attentively, then turned to Myrna. "What do you think about this?"

"I called you, Victoria, because I can't defend them. It's both unethical and illegal." Myrna shrugged, setting the beads in her dreadlocks in motion. "I can give them legal advice, but that's it. As far as I'm concerned, they're all innocent."

"We're all guilty," said Roberta. "One for all, all for one. No question about it."

Myrna held up a hand, its line of gold rings glittering with precious stones. She laughed and shook her head. "No, no. You're innocent until proven guilty, and I can't defend you."

Victoria turned to the women. "Do I understand that not one of you knows which one did the deed?"

Knitting needles clicked.

"That's right."

"Yes."

"We're sticking together."

"Have you considered," said Victoria, "that it's most likely that none of you is the killer?"

"Of course," said Jessica. "We discussed the murder in general terms, so as not to point to one person. Every one of us had motive. None of us can account for every minute of our time from the evening we tried to talk to him until Maureen found his body, so we guess every one of us had opportunity,"

"And every one of us had the means." Alyssa held up one of her steel needles.

Victoria turned to Myrna. "Speaking of advice, what do you think I can do for them?"

"I believe," said Myrna, "they'd like you to be a character witness, if this should go to court."

Five heads nodded.

"I can recommend five lawyers," said Myrna.

"This won't go to court," said Victoria, getting to her feet. "May I use your phone?"

"Of course," said Myrna. "Dial nine first."

Except for the sounds of needles, the group was silent while Victoria called Bill O'Malley and asked for a ride home. When she hung up, they looked up quizzically.

"You just got here," said Jessica.

"You haven't even listened to us," said Roberta.

"Will you . . . ?" asked Alyssa, holding her kelp under her chin, a brown-and-green beard.

"I've got to get busy," Victoria said. "I intend to find the killer. And it's not one of you."

CHAPTER 26

"That was short and sweet," said Bill O'Malley when he picked Victoria up at Myrna's law office.

"Five silly young women," Victoria said as she adjusted her blue coat under her and fastened her seat belt. And she told him how each of the five was claiming to be the murderer of LeRoy Watts, the stalker. Bill listened attentively.

Before he pulled into Victoria's drive, he stopped the truck. "Shall we give your daughter a thrill?"

"I'm not sure Amelia can deal with whatever you have in mind, but go ahead."

He grinned, shifted into reverse, and backed into the drive, the insistent *beep, beep, beep* alerting everyone in the neighborhood, especially Amelia.

She appeared at the door looking concerned, a mixing spoon in her hand, a dish towel around her waist.

Victoria immediately felt bad. "I really shouldn't tease her. She means well."

"It's time she learned you have a life of your own." O'Malley backed up to the west door, shifted into neutral, pulled on the brake, and the backup alarm shut off.

Amelia put her hand to her throat.

O'Malley set out the milk-crate step for Victoria and offered her his arm, which she took and stepped down.

"Mother?" said Amelia.

Victoria released his arm. "Amelia, this is my friend Bill O'Malley."

"Howdy, ma'am." O'Malley, the Stanford graduate, was suddenly a good ole boy. He nudged the visor of his cap with a knuckle.

"Mother?" Amelia said again. Then she turned to O'Malley and said formally, "How do you do." She glanced at her mother, then back at O'Malley. "Would you care to come in for a cup of tea?"

"Thank you, ma'am, but I got to be goin'." O'Malley set the milk crate behind the passenger seat, slammed the door, went around to the driver's side, shifted into gear, and the dump truck lumbered away from the house.

"Where on earth did you find *him*?" Amelia asked.

"He's a longtime friend of mine."

"A dump truck driver?"

"A dump truck *owner*," replied Victoria. "He gives me a ride whenever I need one."

"Oh, Mother! But where—?"

"Let's have tea. Something smells good."

"Gingerbread," said Amelia. "I know how much you like it. But Mother . . . ?"

Victoria tossed her blue coat over the back of the captain's chair by the door, went in to her usual spot at the cookroom table, and sat down.

Amelia carried two plates, two napkins, a knife, and the pan of fragrant gingerbread into the cookroom and cut into it. "How was your morning?" she asked, handing a plate to her mother. "You were so mysterious when you left."

Victoria felt a pang of guilt. She really must try to understand Amelia's concern and deal with it like an adult. "I wasn't sure myself what I was getting into when I left," she said. "Myrna Luce, my lawyer friend, asked me to come to her office because . . ." And then Victoria realized the story was too complicated to explain simply. "She told me it had something to do with the murder."

"Mother, must you really . . ." Amelia didn't finish. She sat down in the chair, at right angles to Victoria. "I'm sorry. I'm afraid I'm being my usual busybody. I'll try to control myself. Tell me about the work you're doing."

So Victoria did. She explained about the mathematical knitters and the global-warming quilt, about the breathing phone calls, the mysterious death of Jerry Sparks, the death of LeRoy Watts, and the five women who claimed to have killed him.

Amelia listened. She sipped her tea and nibbled her gingerbread, and when Victoria finished, she put her hand over her mother's. "I love you, you know?"

And Victoria did know.

Victoria mashed up the last crumbs of her gingerbread with her fork tines, licked the fork clean, finished the rest of her tea, and pushed her plate and mug to one side.

"Thank you, Amelia. That hit the spot."

Of one thing, Victoria was sure. None of the five women she'd met with at the lawyer's office was capable of killing LeRoy Watts, even though each one of the five insisted on confessing to the murder. Since Myrna refused to represent them, either singly or as a group, Victoria felt it incumbent upon herself to clear the five of blame—in other words, to identify the murderer.

"Would you care for more tea, Mother?"

"No, thank you."

Victoria knew the State Police were working to solve the murder of LeRoy Watts, but they had to wait for autopsy and forensic results, which might take weeks. They were also hamstrung by regulations and restrictions and bureaucracy. Even Casey, the town's chief of police, had to move slowly through the tangle of rules, regulations, and people's rights.

Amelia stood and gathered up the plates. "Your expression, I remember it from childhood. You're determined to solve the murders, aren't you?"

"I'm determined to help the authorities," Victoria said with a smile. She fished an envelope out of the wastepaper basket, looked in the marmalade jar by the telephone for a pen that still had ink, and began her list.

"Your asparagus is up," Amelia said. "My neighbor in San Francisco, Alvida Jones, gave me a delicious recipe for asparagus soup. Would you like that for supper?"

"Perfect," said Victoria, thinking about her list of suspects rather than supper.

Amelia went out to the asparagus bed, and a short time later returned with a basket of the tender spears and busied herself in the kitchen.

First, Victoria wrote on her list, she'd need to talk with the person who knew LeRoy Watts best, and that was Sarah, his wife. She needed to visit the widow again to see how she was faring, and do that right away.

She'd have to talk to Sarah's sister Jackie again. Sarah's and Jackie's feelings toward each other seemed to go beyond normal sibling rivalry into something quite nasty. Had Jackie trifled with her brother-in-law?

She added Jim Weiss to the list. She couldn't begin to imagine how he must feel. His wife dead and his only daughter, sixteen years old, so humiliated. How difficult it was to be sixteen.

Then there were the several women she'd recognized in the shower videos. Someone needed to talk with them, and she would be the logical, least intimidating choice to do the interviews. She'd want to know how the women had reacted to that violation of their privacy.

Of course she'd talk to the five knitters who'd received the phone calls. All of them, Victoria, too, had assumed Jerry Sparks was the culprit until they'd found his body. Victoria shuddered at the remembered stench.

Going back to the death of Jerry Sparks. He was Emily Cameron's first love, her first real man friend. She had every reason to believe LeRoy Watts had killed him. How would she have reacted? Victoria underlined her name on her list of people to interview.

There was Jerry's landlady. Victoria had no reason to suspect Mrs. Rudge of murder, but she might provide some small clue, some inkling of what might have happened to Jerry.

She added to the bottom of her list, "How can we prove that Jerry Sparks was killed with LeRoy Watts's Taser? Marks on his body? His clothing?"

Amelia came back from the kitchen, where she'd loaded the dishwasher. "How's the list coming along?"

Victoria pushed her chair back and reached for the telephone. "I've got enough to get me started."

Victoria dialed the police station, got a busy signal, and hung up. "Casey and I need to make another condolence call on the widow."

"The poor woman," said Amelia. "I can't imagine what it must be like for your husband to be murdered, then find out he was spying on half the young women in town, and have two nine-year-olds to raise." She wiped the tile counter with a damp cloth and hung it on the towel rack. "Think of how it must feel, trying to keep their daddy's memory alive without letting them know what a louse he was."

"I don't envy her," said Victoria. She got to her feet. "I haven't been able to get through to Casey. It's a lovely morning, so I think I'll walk to the police station. Will you be all right while I'm gone?"

"I'll be fine. Elizabeth left her car for me to use, and I thought I'd go into Edgartown to shop." Amelia gathered up her purse and shrugged into her traveling jacket. "Let me give you a ride to the station house."

"No, thanks. I can use the exercise."

"Are you sure? It's quite a long ways."

"I enjoy the walk."

After Amelia left, Victoria went to the basket of stale bread she kept next to the stove for the ducks that gathered around the station house. She emptied the bread into a paper bag, slipped on her blue coat, gathered up her cloth bag and lilac-wood walking stick, and hiked to the police station.

"It's only a quarter of a mile," she said out loud for no one at all to hear.

For weeks, whenever Victoria walked to the station, she'd watched the coming of spring. It had been unusually cool and long drawn out. First, the patch of old-fashioned double daffodils poked their pointed green shoots through the earth, produced fat buds, then burst into sunny bloom. The daffodils had escaped from Mabel Johnson's garden years ago and established themselves by the side of the road. The flowers had faded, and now Victoria breathed in the scent of full-blown spring. Lilacs, apple blossoms, and new leaves. She walked briskly, keeping in mind someone had told her not long ago that she walked like a ten-year-old. Occasionally she'd stop to catch her breath, using, to herself, the excuse that she wanted to smell the new-mown grass, wafted to her great nose by a wandering breeze.

At the parking area in front of the police station, Victoria emptied stale bread out of her paper bag onto the grass. Ducks fluttered up from the Mill Pond as she shook out the last few crumbs, folded up the paper bag, and put it back into her cloth bag. Then she climbed the steps to the police station.

Casey looked up from her computer. "Morning, Victoria. What's up?"

Victoria unbuttoned her coat and seated herself in the wooden armchair in front of Casey's desk. "Since we last talked, has there been any progress on the LeRoy Watts murder case?"

Casey turned away from the computer to face her deputy. "It's too soon. Do you have any thoughts?"

"Earlier today, Myrna Luce asked me to meet at her law office with the five women from the knitters' group who'd formed a posse to go after Jerry Sparks."

"Hoping to teach him a lesson. Yeah." Casey picked up the beach-stone paperweight that held down her papers. She ran her hand over the sea-smoothed surface of the stone.

"But Jerry Sparks wasn't the breather."

"Nor did he make the shower-scene videos." Casey straightened her papers and put the stone back on top. "I can't believe all the paperwork we have to fill out for every little complaint. Kids throwing green apples at cars. Paperwork. Junior Norton told me his father used to take the kids out behind the police station and smack them one, and that took care of it. I can't even yell at the kids."

Victoria nodded sympathetically. "Each of the five women insists she killed LeRoy."

"*What?*"

Victoria nodded.

"Where did you hear that?"

"They'd asked Myrna to represent them as a group."

"That's not legal."

"That's what Myrna said. She told them she'd be glad to give them advice, but because of ethical—and legal—considerations, she couldn't represent them."

"So then Myrna called you." Casey smiled.

"Yes. Since I'd already spoken to Myrna before the five showed up at her office, she called me."

Casey picked up the stone again and flipped it from one hand to the other.

"I don't believe for an instant any one of them killed him." Victoria stood up.

"Doesn't seem likely, I must say. Have you checked their alibis?"

"I will. But I'd like to talk to LeRoy's widow again."

"The State Police have already questioned her."

"We're her neighbors. We ought to stop by and see how she is, ask if she needs anything, find out if her sister is still with her."

Casey sighed, dropped the stone on top of her papers again, and stood up. "I need a break from the phone and this pesky paperwork, and it's too nice a day to be indoors. Let's go."

CHAPTER 27

Sarah answered their knock, holding her knitting up to her face, not quite covering the bruise on her cheek, which had turned from purple to a yellowish green. The swelling was gone. "Good morning, Mrs. Trumbull. Casey. Come in."

"How are you?" asked Victoria.

Sarah wobbled her free hand, palm down. "So-so. Can I give you a cup of coffee? I've made a fresh pot."

"It smells good," said Victoria, feeling already full of tea and gingerbread. She unbuttoned her coat and she and Casey followed Sarah into the kitchen. They sat at the table. Sarah laid down her knitting and brought out mugs.

"Sugar? Cream?"

"Black," said Victoria.

"Cream and sugar," said Casey.

Sarah poured, then set the pot back on the coffeemaker. She sat down and picked up her knitting again.

"I see you found the other needle," said Victoria.

"What?" Sarah looked up and then down at her work. "Oh, yes." She flushed slightly. "It had fallen between the couch cushions."

"Does it make a difference in your stitches to use different-size needles?"

"Not too much." Sarah held up the sweater. Three or four rows seemed slightly looser than the rest, but only with a close look. "After I wash the sweater the first time, it won't show at all."

Casey stirred sugar and then more sugar into her coffee. "We stopped by to see if there's anything we can do for you, Mrs. Watts. Is your sister still here?"

"I told her to leave. She was making things worse."

"Sisters know how to do that," said Victoria. "What was her problem?"

Sarah worked one stitch after another before answering. "I don't know how to say this."

Victoria waited.

Sarah pressed her lips together tightly.

Victoria waited another moment, then said, "If you'd rather not . . ."

Sarah continued to look down at her work. "Roy installed a video camera in her shower."

Victoria watched her closely. "Oh?"

"He did some electrical work for her a couple of months ago."

"How did she discover the camera?"

Sarah sighed before she answered. "Jackie's new boyfriend found it, or so she said. She thought at first he'd installed it as a joke."

"But he didn't," said Victoria.

"No, he didn't install it. Roy did."

"You're sure?" asked Victoria.

"The minute Jackie showed me the camera, I knew it was Roy. When I think how long we were married . . ."

Victoria and Casey glanced at each other.

"Jackie never liked Roy," Sarah said. "I know I shouldn't rat on my sister, but I can't help feeling . . ."

"Feeling what?" Victoria asked.

"Well, it wouldn't surprise me a bit if she'd killed him. She was always flirting with him, trying to make me jealous. One of her favorite tricks." Sarah concentrated on her work. "She's spoiled. Has to have her way. That video Roy took of her taking a shower was the last straw. He refused to pay any attention to her, but all the time he was secretly ogling her in her shower."

Casey shifted position and the equipment on her tool belt rattled.

"I trusted Roy. I was so sure of him. He was always a decent guy. Only lately . . ." She jabbed a needle into the next stitch.

"Had he been acting different lately?"

Sarah twisted yarn around a needle, hooked it with the other needle, and slipped the stitch off. "Some woman's been calling him. If I answer, she hangs up."

"Someone from his past?" asked Victoria.

"I didn't think so. Now I wonder."

"Has she ever threatened him?" asked Casey.

"She never says anything. Sometimes she mumbles his name. I've never really heard her voice except for the first time, when she asked for him."

"How long ago did she start calling him?"

Sarah thought for a while. "It may have been a year ago. Just one call when she asked for him, and I didn't think anything of it." She knit three or four stitches before going on. "A couple of months later, she called again, just said 'Roy?' when I answered, and hung up. I recognized the voice, distinctive, tinny-sounding, as if she was disguising it. Lately, she'd been calling a couple of times a week."

"That must have been aggravating," said Victoria.

"It was. But Roy said it wouldn't do any good to report it to the telephone company or the police." She laughed bitterly. "I guess he knew, didn't he?"

"It's ironic that he was being stalked," Victoria agreed, then changed the subject, trying to lighten things up a bit. "I'd always liked having a man named Watts as my electrician."

"That was his idea, Mrs. Trumbull. His family name was something long and unpronounceable. When he was in college he

187

decided he'd go into business for himself, and changed it to a name customers would recognize that would look good on his trucks."

Casey asked, "How did your sister happen to tell you about the camera?"

"Before Roy . . . A couple of days ago . . . Well, the day the boys got into trouble for taking that Taser to school, Jackie came over and tossed this video camera onto the table. I knew right away what it was." Sarah knit fiercely. "Emily Cameron had come by on Sunday, the day before."

Victoria leaned forward and set her elbows on the table. "Emily was Jerry Sparks's girlfriend."

"Jerry had disappeared. Emily hadn't seen him for several days and she was worried. She baby-sat for us occasionally."

"When I saw her at the boatyard a week ago, she was excited about her boyfriend." Victoria sat back again. "She and Jerry were to celebrate their three weeks of being together that day."

"The day she came here, she thought Jerry had left her. He'd left a couple of DVDs in her apartment—for safekeeping, he said— and told her to hold onto them for him. The DVDs had Roy's name on them, so she brought them to me. I had a feeling she was clearing his stuff out of her apartment."

"We saw the videos," said Victoria.

"I suppose now the entire Island knows about my husband and his little hobby." Sarah looked up from her knitting, her eyes magnified by unshed tears. "How could he have done this to me? To me and my boys?"

"Well, what do you think, Victoria?" Casey asked when they were on their way back to the police station. "LeRoy Watts wasn't LeRoy Watts after all, and his widow is not exactly prostrate with grief."

"The reality of her husband's death hasn't hit her yet. Right now, she's angry that he's left her in a mess with two boys to raise."

"I notice she said 'my boys.' Cutting LeRoy out of the family already." Casey parked in front of the station house and they went around to the side and up the steps. Junior Norton was at his desk, filling out paperwork.

"Afternoon, Mrs. Trumbull. You got a call from your daughter." He handed her a pink message slip.

"Did she say what she wanted?"

Junior leaned his chair back on two legs and folded his arms. "She said she was worried about you."

Casey laughed. "How long is Amelia going to be here?"

"Too long, I'm afraid," sniffed Victoria.

"Have you thought about involving her in some community activity? The library or the arboretum?"

"I don't want her to settle here permanently."

"She has a job out west, doesn't she? California?" asked Junior.

"She's a consultant," said Victoria. "She's a retired petroleum geologist and can work anywhere as long as she has her computer and her cell phone."

Junior set his chair down. "She still married?"

"Divorced," said Victoria.

"What about—"

"If you're about to suggest we find a romantic interest for her," Victoria said, "don't. She's off men at the moment. She recently broke up with her longtime live-in gentleman friend."

"Bill O'Malley, your truck driver friend, is about her age, isn't he?" asked Junior.

"He must be twenty years younger, and I believe he's interested in Elizabeth. In fact, he's coming to dinner tomorrow night."

Junior shook his head. "He's too old for Elizabeth."

The phone rang. Junior picked it up. "West Tisbury Police, Sergeant Norton speaking." He listened, looked up at Victoria, and grinned. "Yes, ma'am, she just came in." He put his hand over the mouthpiece and handed the phone to Victoria. "Your daughter."

Victoria frowned. "Hello!"

"Mother, where have you been? I've had lunch waiting for you for hours. I've been worried about you!"

Victoria felt her face flush. "Amelia," she interrupted, "I'm busy. I'm dealing with two murders. I'll be home when I get there. Go ahead and eat your lunch. Don't wait for me," and she handed the telephone back to Junior, who hung it up with a grin.

Casey and her sergeant watched Victoria with amused expressions, which didn't help Victoria's growing irritation. She settled back in her chair, arms tightly folded, her mouth a firm line.

"O'Malley's not married," said Junior, fanning the flames.

"Amelia doesn't understand why I associate with a dump truck driver."

"Did you tell her he's not exactly poor?"

"Bill O'Malley didn't help, with his good ole boy impersonation."

"He's interested," said Junior. "Likes a challenge. How many wives has he had? Three or four at least."

"I don't have time for this," said Victoria, standing up. "The chief and I need to interview the women who appeared on the videos." She turned to Casey, her face still flushed. "Are you ready?"

"We need lunch," said Casey. "I don't suppose you want to stop by your house?"

Victoria didn't answer, but strode to the door, opened it, and marched down the steps.

Casey called back to Junior. "We'll pick up some chowder at Fella's, the place next to the post office."

"Have fun," said Junior.

"I raised my children to be independent," said Victoria when they were in the Bronco, heading toward North Tisbury. "I raised them to respect one another's privacy. I can't understand why . . ." She stopped talking and rolled down the window. "Chowder sounds good. I *am* hungry."

CHAPTER 28

Casey bought two carryout containers of chowder at Fella's and gave one to Victoria, who was sitting on a bench, protected by the overhanging roof.

Victoria hadn't realized how hungry she was. She finished her chowder before Casey, who set her cup aside and went back for seconds for her deputy.

Victoria blotted her mouth with a paper napkin. "Thank you. I'll be in a much better mood now to talk to Amelia."

"Ah," said Casey. "Are you going to confront her?"

"I'm going to win her over." Victoria sprinkled oyster crackers over her second helping of chowder and dug in.

Casey glanced up. "How, may I ask?"

"I'll invite her to come with me to interview the women who were in the shower videos."

"But . . ."

"That way, you needn't be involved in any official way until I report back to you."

"You're assuming Amelia will then realize her mother isn't ready to be put out to pasture."

"Something like that." Victoria had finished her second cup of chowder while Casey was scraping out the last spoonful of her first. "Don't you want seconds? I've been quite greedy."

"I'm fine, Victoria." Casey stood, collected the cups, and tossed them into the trash barrel next to the bench. "I'll stop by the station and get that list of women and their addresses." She looked at her watch. "Most of them probably aren't home now, but you'll find one or two."

"I'll keep trying," said Victoria.

Amelia had awakened from her nap when her mother came home. She stretched her arms and yawned. "That's such a comfortable bed. It has a better mattress than mine at home. Would you like a cup of tea?"

"No, thank you. Casey and I had lunch."

"That's nice. I'm so glad our police chief is female. I imagine West Tisbury is a quiet town, not too difficult to police."

Victoria's jaw tensed. No matter what she said in defense, she would insult either the town or its police chief. She changed the subject. "I have a few interviews to carry out this afternoon. Would you care to come along? You can drive. You might be interested in the work we do."

"I'd love to. Let me freshen up. I'll be ready in a minute."

Victoria spent the time studying her list and making new notes.

"What sort of interviews are you doing, Mother?" Amelia asked when she emerged from the bathroom.

"We believe LeRoy Watts was spying on young women, taking videos of them in their showers."

Amelia hugged herself. "How horribly intrusive."

"I want to find out when they discovered the cameras and their reactions, learn more about the women and offer support."

"What kind of monster was he? You said he was the electrician working on your blown outlet?"

"He wasn't a monster. He was a polite man, a college graduate, active in church, active in the community, with a nice family. Twin boys and an attractive wife. It's distressing to everyone who knew him or worked with him."

"Are you sure he was the one who took the videos?"

Victoria paused before she answered. "Everything seems to indicate he was guilty. We may learn more as we talk to the women." Victoria got up from the table, found her cloth bag and her lilac-wood stick, and headed for the door.

The first person they found at home was Jim Weiss. He came to the door, the latest copy of the *Island Enquirer* in hand, glasses pushed up on top of his head. He was wearing jeans and a sweatshirt and his feet were bare.

"Afternoon, Victoria. What brings you here?"

"This is Amelia, my daughter, Jim. She's visiting from California."

Jim reached out his hand. "Glad we have nice weather for you. How long are you here for?"

"I'm not sure," said Amelia. "At least a week."

After the civilities were over, Victoria said, "Our reason for calling on you is semiofficial."

"Come in, won't you?" Jim stood aside and ushered them into the living room. "Please, have a seat. Can I get you something to drink? Coffee? Tea?"

Amelia smiled. "No, thanks."

Victoria got right to the point. "I understand your daughter was one of the victims of the video voyeur—"

She didn't finish. Jim practically exploded. "That freak. My daughter's only a kid." He slammed a fist into the palm of his hand. "She's just turned sixteen. It's as though she's been date-raped, didn't have a clue."

"Who found the camera?" Victoria asked. "Did you?"

"Lily's girlfriend found the camera. I had no idea there was one hidden in the downstairs shower. Lily's the only one who uses that one."

"Where was it, in the exhaust vent?"

"Yes. Lily's girlfriend had come for an overnight. She noticed it, told Lily. Lily told me the next morning, and I went to the police at once."

Amelia was sitting quietly in an armchair over to one side. Victoria took notes. "Do you have any idea when the camera might have been installed?"

"I have a good idea. The heater in the downstairs bathroom wasn't functioning properly, so I called LeRoy Watts. This was about three months ago. I have the bills and can give you the exact date." Jim started to get up.

"That's not necessary," said Victoria. "It may be later. You know, of course, that LeRoy Watts was killed."

"So I'd heard." Jim sat back down.

"His office manager found his body yesterday."

Jim got up again and started to pace. "He was not only filming women—girls, really—in their showers; he was phoning them. Five women in my knitters' group." He stopped pacing and faced Victoria. "You know all about that. Casper Martin and I were feeling as though we were suspects." He sat down again and leaned forward, elbows on his knees. "I hope you don't need to talk to Lily. I'm not sure what that would accomplish. Just upset her still more."

"I don't think so," said Victoria. "I know it's difficult for her."

"She's mortified."

"As we all are." Victoria stood.

He dropped his head into his hands. "The kids in school found out about it."

"Her girlfriend, I suppose. The one who found the camera," said Victoria.

"Now they're teasing her about her future as a porn star. They think it's funny. They think teasing her will lighten things up."

"How cruel!"

Jim turned away so Victoria couldn't see his face. "That's kids for you," he said.

CHAPTER 29

"I don't blame Mr. Weiss for being so upset," Amelia said when they were in the car after talking to Jim Weiss. "Some lecher spying on his daughter? I can't imagine how I'd feel if some man were spying on Elizabeth. And his daughter's only sixteen."

"A sophomore in high school."

"Elizabeth is old enough to take care of herself, but I might have been tempted to do violence to whoever did that to her." She looked away from the road briefly. "Mr. Watts was stabbed in the throat with a knitting needle, wasn't he? And Jim Weiss is one of the knitters?"

"The weapon that killed LeRoy wasn't necessarily a knitting needle. He was stabbed right about here." Victoria ran her fingers down the side of her neck.

"But that would have done the job, right?"

"It was my thought that a knitting needle could be the weapon. Doc Jeffers, the medical examiner, said the weapon was a sharp, pointed implement, like an awl or screwdriver, or fid, or even a pencil or ballpoint pen."

The afternoon had turned a misty gray. In the glacial swales, mist had thickened into dense fog that rose fender-high, an opaque cloud that flowed like batter toward the sea to their right. Wisps of fog drifted through the branches of the oaks and spangled the new grass.

"The knitters' group Mr. Weiss belongs to isn't exactly an old ladies'—" Amelia stopped abruptly.

Victoria ignored the implied slur. "The group hopes to finish the quilt by mid-June. All of them carry around at least one set of knitting needles. . . ." She stopped, thinking again of LeRoy's widow with her mismatched needles.

"What is it? What were you about to say?"

"Nothing," Victoria replied.

Amelia tightened her grip on the wheel. "Whether one's daughter is sixteen or thirty, it's equally upsetting."

"Of course."

Slightly ahead of them to the left was a large patch of showy pink flowers. Victoria was absorbed in her thoughts and didn't notice them.

Amelia slowed the car and stopped. "Lady slippers, Mother. Just look! I remember how every May around this time you pointed them out to us."

Victoria sat up. She welcomed the first sight of the Vineyard's rare, showy orchids. The Island had as many species of orchids as Hawaii, but they tended to be tiny and inconspicuous. These were neither. About a dozen plants clustered together, standing almost a foot high. The flowers had light pink pouchlike lower petals with dark pink veining, overhung by dark magenta upper petals.

Victoria turned to her daughter and smiled. "Every May my mother pointed them out to me, too. Old County Road was nothing but rutted sand then."

"Would you like to get out?"

"Perhaps tomorrow. I want to interview as many women as we can today, then get home to write up my notes. Before I forget them," she added, then felt ashamed of herself, hoping Amelia hadn't noticed the wicked little dig.

Amelia checked behind her and pulled away from the side of the road, and they drove in companionable silence.

Victoria said, "I recall distinctly how I felt as a teenager.

I trusted adults, and no adult ever betrayed that trust. At sixteen, I felt awkward and unsure of myself. I was painfully modest. In part, that was the times, but I don't believe teenagers have changed much."

"I don't believe they have, either." Amelia slowed to a crawl to pass a horse and rider. The rider, a helmeted young girl, lifted her hand in thanks. Victoria waved back.

"What's our next stop?"

Victoria consulted the list Casey had drawn up for her and sighed. "This is not going to be pleasant." She gave Amelia directions to the home of one of the victims.

That afternoon, they spoke to three women and heard their identical reactions when they'd found out about the videos. Shock. Embarrassment. Violation. Anger. Disgust.

On the way home, Victoria was silent.

Amelia said, "Thank you for letting me come with you. You're quite a remarkable woman."

Victoria continued to gaze out the window.

"You were sensitive," said Amelia, eyes back on the road. "You always were sensitive to our feelings when we were growing up."

Victoria smiled faintly.

"You must feel drained. Let's light the fire and have a good strong drink."

"That sounds good." Victoria looked at her watch. "Elizabeth should be home by now."

Elizabeth had lighted the fire and it danced welcome warmth and light into the parlor.

Victoria held her glass up. Firelight flickered through the ruby red drink. "I invited Bill O'Malley for dinner tomorrow night, Elizabeth. He'd asked about you."

"He brought his boat into the harbor to show me," said Elizabeth. "Only I was off duty and didn't see him."

"The dump truck person," said Amelia. "So he has a boat, too?"

"A boat and an airplane," said Victoria.

"I'll cook," Elizabeth offered. "The striped bass are running, and I bet I can get Janet to give us one."

"Boston baked beans tomorrow." Victoria eased herself out of her chair. "I'll put the beans to soak."

"Beans go nicely with fish," said Elizabeth.

"What do I wear to dinner with this man?" asked Amelia.

"Clean jeans, Mom," replied Elizabeth.

The following morning, a day of drizzling rain, Victoria boiled the beans she'd soaked all night, then spooned them into her bean pot with an onion, molasses, and salt pork and put them in a slow oven to cook all day.

Then she and Amelia set out again.

"Who's next on our list?" Amelia asked before she started the car.

Victoria looked down at the paper. Too many names. What a swath LeRoy Watts had cut. How many lives he'd hurt. "We should probably talk next to Jackie, LeRoy's sister-in-law. She and Sarah don't get along. After LeRoy was killed, I made the mistake of asking Jackie to stay with her sister. A poor choice on my part." She looked up. "You'll want to head toward Up-Island Cronig's."

Jackie lived in a small house in Island Farms. She came to the door with a towel wrapped like a turban around her head. She was almost as tall as Victoria and had a perfect peaches and cream complexion.

"I just stepped out of the shower. I looked for hidden cameras first." Jackie made a wry face. "What can I do for you, Mrs. Trumbull?"

"May we come in? This is my daughter Amelia. I wanted to talk to you about LeRoy Watts's murder."

Jackie offered her hand to Amelia. "Come in. I don't know what I can tell you. LeRoy was an asshole—excuse me, Mrs. Trumbull." She led the way to a small, neat living room with an L-shaped couch facing a gigantic TV screen with a game show playing. Jackie turned off the sound. Victoria was transfixed by the characters, who were emoting soundlessly with great enthusiasm. "Keeps me company," Jackie said. "Have a seat. Don't mind me if I comb out my hair."

Amelia glanced at her mother, who nodded. Victoria had been strict about the impropriety of fussing with one's hair outside the privacy of the bedroom or bath.

"I hadn't realized he'd changed his name to Watts," Victoria said.

"Oh, sure. He thought that was terribly smart. He'd changed it before I knew him, so I never heard his real name," said Jackie, unwrapping the damp towel from her head.

"I was hoping to get your reactions to the murder. Do you have any thoughts?"

"Damn right I do. I know for sure who killed him." Jackie shot up. "Excuse me. I have to get my comb from the bathroom."

She returned, running a large pink comb through her tangled damp hair. She picked out loose hairs from the comb and tossed them into the wastepaper basket.

Amelia smiled.

Victoria frowned.

"You asked if I had any thoughts about who killed him. Don't hold me to it. The obvious killer is my dear sweet sister, his wife. Widow. What I said in the first place."

"But you denied what you said."

"Look at it logically," Jackie went on. "She's married to God's gift to the Island, and all of a sudden—wham!—the guy's done worse than sleeping around. Drooling over chickies in their showers, Island chickies he knows, calling women and breathing at them. Slavering. You know? Totally disgusting. The entire Island is snickering behind her back. 'Wasn't she giving out at home?' You know, that kind of stuff. Blaming her for the way he acted."

"Really?" said Victoria.

"I know my sister." Jackie combed her hair over her face, then swept it to one side. "You know the way this Island is, Mrs. Trumbull. We love weird stuff like this."

"But why would she kill her husband?" Amelia put in. "Sorry, Mother. I should keep quiet."

"Quite all right," said Victoria.

"I know my sister," Jackie repeated. "She's wound so tight, butter wouldn't melt in her mouth."

Amelia coughed politely.

"You think she snapped?" asked Victoria.

"Of course she snapped. She sees that video that Emily Cameron got from her boyfriend. She could hardly believe her dear gentle Roy would do such a thing. Then her twins get caught playing with Roy's Taser at school. Coulda killed someone. The same day, Roy is handed a court date for owning the Taser and thinks he might go to jail. The last straw is he hits her. Did you see the bruise?"

Victoria nodded.

Jackie combed, shook out her hair, and combed again. "He had the hots for me. For years." Jackie smiled. "I told Sarah he was hitting on me, and my dumb sister thought I was making it all up. That it was the other way around. She accused *me* of hitting on *him*."

Victoria waited to see if Jackie had anything else to say, but she continued to fix her hair. "Can you think of anything to add? That you'd like to tell me?"

"It's so obvious, Mrs. Trumbull. I mean, who else could it be?" Jackie stood up. "Excuse me a sec. I'm going to the bathroom to get my nail polish. Paint my toenails."

Victoria got up. "This has been . . ." she paused, searching for the right word. "I appreciate your taking the time. May I come back if I have more questions?"

"Sure, Mrs. Trumbull. Anytime. It'll be hard to pin it on her, but believe you me, she's guilty as sin."

Victoria got up, and so did Amelia.

"Thank you." Victoria glanced at Jackie's hands, one holding the comb with a few more loose hairs, the other holding the damp towel, and didn't offer to shake.

CHAPTER 30

"Is she serious?" Amelia asked when they were on the road again. "Accusing her own sister of murdering her husband? The father of her boys?"

The rain had let up briefly while they'd talked to Jackie, but was now coming down in a steady drizzle. The windshield wipers slatted back and forth, flicking water from one side to the other.

"There's a bit of animosity between the two sisters," Victoria replied. "I'm not sure we can take what she said seriously."

"Where would you like to go next?"

Victoria referred to her list. "I need to talk to Emily Cameron again. The boatyard is open on Saturdays now, getting ready for the season."

"Is she one of the women who was stalked?"

"No," replied Victoria. "Her boyfriend was Jerry Sparks, the one who was killed." She looked at her watch. "I'll invite her to lunch."

"To the boatyard, then," said Amelia, turning onto State Road from Island Farms.

On the hillside to their right, young lambs rollicked together, oblivious of the rain, and not too far away from their grazing mothers. On their left, they passed a grove of beeches, Victoria's favorite tree. One of her favorites, that is. New brilliant green leaves seemed even brighter against the gray sky, a touch of sunshine when the sun wasn't around. New leaves had shoved aside the dry golden leaves of winter that now lay on the ground in a golden tumble. Rugged oaks had put out their delicate pink mouse-ear leaves, the sign Island farmers went by to plant their corn and squash.

They passed through Five Corners without having to wait for traffic coming off the ferry and turned in at the boatyard.

Emily was at her desk behind the partition. Her eyes and nose were red and swollen. Her bangs hung limply over the tops of her glasses. When she noticed Victoria and Amelia, she stopped turning over the pages that lay on her desk, looked up, and sighed.

"Hi, Mrs. Trumbull."

Victoria introduced her daughter.

"Can you take a break, Emily?" Victoria asked. "We'd like to treat you to lunch at the ArtCliff, if you're free. And talk to you about Jerry."

Emily sighed again and looked at her watch. "I guess so. I didn't even take a break this morning. I'm not getting much done just sitting here."

"A lunch break will do you good," said Victoria.

Emily shut down her computer, pushed her bangs out of her eyes, and stood up. "I always bring my lunch with me."

"Save it for tomorrow," said Victoria. She led the way back to the car, holding down the brim of her fuzzy gray hat against the rain,.

"Actually, the ArtCliff is within walking distance," said Victoria once Emily had seated herself in the back, "but we might as well ride in comfort."

Dottie, the waitress, seated them in a booth. "Hi, Mrs. Trumbull. Haven't seen you for ages. And Amelia! I would've recognized you anywhere. How long's it been?"

"A couple of years, I'm afraid," said Amelia.

"And Emily. Sorry to hear about Jerry. You guys were pretty close."

"Yeah. Thanks." Emily stared down at her lap.

"What do you recommend?" Victoria asked.

"Quahaug chowder." Dottie pronounced it *chow'-duh,* the way most Islanders did. And she pronounced *quahaug* as it should be pronounced, *quo-hog.*

Victoria pushed aside her menu. "A bowl, please."

"Same for me," said Amelia.

"How about you, Emily?" Dottie held her pencil at the ready.

"I'm not hungry."

"A cup, then," said Dottie, writing. "Salads, anyone?"

"No, thank you," said Victoria.

"Not I," said Amelia.

All three ordered coffee. Dottie stuck her pencil into her hairdo and headed to the kitchen. She was back with three heavy white mugs of coffee and a pitcher of cream before they'd shucked off their damp coats.

After Dottie left, Victoria reached her gnarled hands across the table. "Would you like to talk about Jerry?"

Emily lifted her hands from her lap as though they belonged to someone else and took Victoria's in her own. She glanced up. "You're the only person who's asked me about him."

"I'm so sorry."

"I thought he'd left me. I was getting rid of all his things. And now . . ."

"I understand," said Victoria. "What was he like, your Jerry?"

"He was kind. He was gentle. He told me he liked my looks. No one had, like, ever told me that."

"You do have nice looks, Emily."

She glanced away, still holding Victoria's hands. "He made me feel special. I knew he had a problem with drugs, but he was trying to get clean."

"I know that's hard to do."

Dottie reappeared with two bowls and a cup lined up on her

arm. Victoria withdrew her hands, and Dottie set everything down. "Can I get you anything else?"

"No, thank you," said Victoria. "That looks just right."

Dottie left, and Victoria asked, "Did he talk to you about his work with Mr. Watts?"

"Not much. He liked Mr. Watts okay, you know?"

"Jerry did some work for me. I was pleased with what he did." Emily smiled thinly.

"Had he told you he'd been fired?"

Emily shook her head.

"What about the day you were supposed to go to the movies at the library?"

Emily set down her spoon. She hadn't touched the chowder. "That morning, he was, you know, totally sober. He said he was going to talk to Mr. Watts that afternoon about his job and then we'd meet at the library to see the movie." She wadded up her napkin and tossed it onto the table. "Later that day, I saw him again near Cumberland Farms, and I could tell he was on something, acting, you know, really weird."

"Did he see you?"

Emily shook her head.

"That's the last time you saw him?"

Emily nodded. She picked up the wadded-up napkin and dabbed at her eyes. "Mr. Watts killed him. I know he did. I'm glad he's dead. He killed my Jerry."

Victoria waited until Emily calmed down. Amelia had finished her chowder, while Victoria had eaten only a couple of spoonfuls.

"Do you have any idea who might have killed Mr. Watts?" she asked, looking closely at the distraught young woman.

Emily hiccuped. "I know who killed him, and I don't blame her one bit."

"Her?"

"Mrs. Watts's sister, Jackie. She hated Mr. Watts. He was always hitting on her, and you could tell she hated him."

"Had you seen her near his shop?"

"I never went near his shop. I used to baby-sit for the Wattses, and she'd come by sometimes and tell me to stay away from Mr. Watts." Emily looked at her watch again. "I gotta get back to work. I can't eat anything. I'm sorry. Thanks for inviting me to lunch." Her words were hurried. "I gotta run."

Amelia got up. "I'll drive you back to work, Emily. You can wait here, Mother, where it's nice and dry. Finish your soup. I'll take care of the bill."

"Not soup," said Victoria. "Chowder."

CHAPTER 31

The knitters met that evening, even though it was Saturday and the library was closed. The coral-reef quilt was laid out on the table, where they could all see it. Bright blue-and-yellow fish trembled on hidden wires above pink and purple anemones. Pale tentacles of anemones reached toward the fish. Brown kelp lay in deckle-edged ribbons. Brain coral, starfish, and woolly conch shells covered the purled sea floor.

Fran stopped knitting. She reached up and turned the page of the library's wall calendar to June. "We don't have much time," she said. "Can we finish in just over two weeks?"

"Of course we can," said Jessica. "We've completed the flora and fauna, and all we have to do is bind the edges of the quilt."

"And pack it for shipping," said Casper.

Fran dropped May back on top of June and picked up her knitting. "It's a shame about finding that body. That delayed us a full afternoon."

"I honestly don't think the deceased feels any disrespect," said Casper, looking over the top of his glasses at Fran.

"That hardly delayed us at all," said Maron. "I mean, how often do you find a body? Seems to me that takes precedence over a knitted coral."

"I didn't mean any disrespect."

"We don't have any more than a week's work to do." Jessica held up the anemone she was working on. "This is my third and final one."

"It's going to take time to figure out how to stabilize the coral reef for shipping," said Jim. "Can we tack it to a sheet of plywood?"

"The rules specify a quilt," said Fran. "I think we've bent that rule a bit. As Mrs. Trumbull said, it would not be comfortable to sleep under."

"Speaking of Mrs. Trumbull, has anyone heard any new developments?" Jessica turned to Elizabeth. "What does your grandmother have to say?"

"Victoria talked to me yesterday," Jim said before Elizabeth had a chance to reply. "She's interviewing everyone with any knowledge or interest in either Jerry Sparks or LeRoy Watts."

"Both of them?" asked Jessica.

"She says the deaths are connected," said Elizabeth.

"When Victoria spoke to me, she was circumspect," said Jim. "She didn't comment on her suspicions, and she was also sensitive." He looked up from his knitting at Fran.

"Your daughter," said Jessica.

"My daughter. Yes, Lily, my sixteen-year-old daughter. A kid. She was all excited about the Junior Prom, the way a kid should be. Nice boy, a junior, invited her. A pretty new dress." He stared down at the lump of knitting in his lap. "Then everybody in school learned about the shower video. Kids started teasing her. She told the boy she wouldn't go to the prom. Poor kid." Jim jabbed his needle into his coral. The needle went through the coral and hit the palm of his hand. "Ouch! Damnation!" He tugged a handkerchief out of his pocket and held it against his hand.

"You didn't bloody your coral, did you?" asked Fran with concern.

"My coral be damned!" Jim stood up, dropped his coral on his seat, and stalked out of the room.

"I'm afraid I said the wrong thing," said Fran.

"I'm sure he'd have reacted the same way no matter what you said," said Roberta.

Fran glanced at her watch.

Maron changed the subject. "I know our quilt isn't really a quilt. But it's for a good cause. It's not as if we're trying to win the Olympics or anything."

Fran tilted her head to view their reef from a new angle. "It's wonderful," she said. "Simply wonderful. If this were the Olympics, we'd win a gold."

Jim returned, smoothing a Band-Aid onto his palm. "Sorry. I overreacted."

"No apology needed," said Fran. "I'm being obsessive."

"I can't imagine that any other group is knitting a three-dimensional quilt." Maron pointed her knitting needle at it. "Since we're hoping to draw attention to global warming through our quilt, I think we will."

"Point well taken," said Casper with a smirk.

"You're really not funny, you know?" said Maron.

"We'll need two people to work on the binding," said Fran. "What about you, Alyssa, and you, Elizabeth?"

"Sure."

"Of course. Show us what to do."

"And Jim, would you and Casper pack the quilt for shipping?"

Jim scratched his head with his needle. "Bubble wrap, I suppose. Roll the quilt up around a core of bubble wrap."

"Whatever you think will protect it," said Fran.

Elizabeth stood. "I've got to leave early. My mother's visiting, and my grandmother has invited some guy to dinner. She's trying to matchmake."

"Has your grandmother commented any further on the situation?" asked Fran.

"Only that she believes that LeRoy Watts killed Jerry Sparks with his Taser, whether he intended to or not."

"The police have been awfully quiet," said Jessica.

Elizabeth packed up her knitting. "Gram told me they're waiting for results from the autopsies and the forensics people. I don't think the police have much to report at this time."

"We'll want a report back on her matchmaking attempt," said Casper.

Bill O'Malley arrived promptly at seven, clean jeans, clean plaid shirt. "Do I smell Saturday-night baked beans?"

"Of course," said Victoria.

"My favorite meal." He handed Victoria a large bouquet of lilacs in a gallon plastic jug with the top sliced off. "Coals to Newcastle."

"One can never have too many lilacs in the house." Victoria arranged them in her grandmother's ceramic cachepot and set it under the stairs, where the lilacs would perfume the front hall.

Elizabeth's fisherman friend, Janet Messineo, had given her four large striped bass filets, and Elizabeth baked them with mayonnaise and fresh dill, served with Victoria's Boston baked beans and lettuce from the garden.

Conversation started out formally between Amelia and Bill O'Malley—where they lived, what they did. After the first refill of their wineglasses, talk morphed into a discussion of books the four had read. After a second refill, conversation veered to local politics and issues.

Amelia was the first to talk murder. She sipped her third glass of wine as she spoke. "Can you believe," she said to O'Malley, ignoring Victoria, "here's my mother, in her nineties, involving herself in something so sordid as murder?" Amelia set her glass down.

Victoria set her own glass down firmly. Elizabeth looked first at her grandmother, then at her mother with even more concern.

O'Malley said, "You don't understand Victoria."

"What do you mean? She's my mother." Amelia ran her finger around the rim of her glass, making it sing.

O'Malley indicated Victoria with a nod. "Mrs. T., you're not hard of hearing, are you?"

"Certainly not." Victoria's cheeks had bright spots.

Elizabeth still had a small piece of bass on her plate. She looked down and moved it around with her fork.

O'Malley set his knife on his plate and turned to Amelia, who was sitting on his right. "Since your mother hears all right, don't you think it would be nice to include her in the conversation?"

Amelia flushed. Elizabeth looked up. Victoria smiled and looked down.

"Also, since we're talking about your mother, don't you think she's capable of making her own decisions about her life?"

Amelia stopped running her finger around the rim of her glass. Her hands were shaking. She folded them out of sight in her lap. It took her a moment before she sputtered, "Who do you think you are!"

"A friend of Victoria's, that's who I am."

Victoria coughed politely. Elizabeth glanced at her. O'Malley and Amelia continued their two-way conversation.

"What right have you to—" Amelia stopped and tossed her napkin onto the table.

"You haven't seen your mother for a couple of years. Now you've dropped into her life with what seems to be a preformed image of how a ninety-two-year-old should behave. Well, that's ageism, stereotyping, prejudice, and intolerance, all rolled into one. I suspect you weren't brought up to be as intolerant as you sound." O'Malley picked up his fork and dug into the remains of his fish. "This meal is too good for us to squabble." He looked up with a grin. "Want to meet at dawn with drawn rapiers? Victoria and Elizabeth can be our seconds."

Victoria said, "This fish is wonderful, Elizabeth. Cooked to perfection."

O'Malley scraped his plate. "You don't happen to have seconds of those beans, do you?"

"We do." Elizabeth got up and went into the kitchen.

By the time she returned, Amelia's face had regained its normal color and she was sipping the last of her wine. "Everything's delicious, darlings, but I'll pass on the seconds, thank you."

Conversation veered away from the sensitive to the banal—the weather, the coming season, the garden.

"The touch-me-not I planted from wild seed may bloom this year," said Victoria. "Did you know it's an antidote for poison ivy?"

CHAPTER 32

After supper, Elizabeth lighted the parlor fire. The fragrant smell of after-dinner coffee mingled with the homely smell of wood smoke. Victoria sat in her mouse-colored wing chair and O'Malley lowered himself onto the stiff couch. Conversation veered again to something more substantial than weather.

"Amelia and I interviewed Sarah's sister Jackie this morning," Victoria said.

"I was only an observer," said Amelia.

"What did Jackie say for herself?" asked O'Malley.

"She blamed LeRoy Watts's murder on her sister."

The fire snapped and a live spark flew onto the rug. Elizabeth brushed it back into the fire with the hearth broom and returned to her seat.

"Have you talked to Sarah?" asked O'Malley.

"Sarah accused Jackie of the murder." Victoria sipped her coffee, half-closing her eyes against the steam, and set her mug on the coffee table. "After we talked to Jackie, we met with Emily Cameron. Jerry Sparks was her boyfriend. It was his body we found in the book shed."

"Have you come to any conclusions?"

"I'm more baffled than ever," said Victoria.

The rain continued all day Sunday. It drummed on the cookroom roof, a soothing, cozy sound. In the morning, after braving the weather to pick up the Sunday *New York Times* at Alley's

Store, the three women worked together on the crossword puzzle.

"How on earth is anyone supposed to know the definition," Victoria muttered, "for some British melodic death metal group? Ten letters starting with *N*."

"Any letters in between?" asked Elizabeth.

Victoria was filling in the blanks. She studied the cross words. "The third letter might be a *v*. The last letter is probably an *e*. I suppose 'death metal' is considered music? What happened to Beethoven?"

"Death metal is the Shostokovich of the future," said Amelia.

"I doubt it," said Victoria.

"Neverborne," said Elizabeth.

"Oh, for heaven's sake." Victoria firmly inked in the word.

Monday morning was what Victoria called a "typical Vineyard day," bright, sunny, and dry. She awoke early and went downstairs. Elizabeth had left a note on the kitchen table. "Short day today. Back around 2."

Victoria stood at the top of the stone steps and breathed in the scent of the new day. Wind and rain had knocked blossoms off the maple trees during the night, and the ground was carpeted with bright chartreuse flowers that sparkled in the morning sunshine.

She went back to the kitchen and measured grounds into the coffeemaker. Soon the aroma of fresh coffee brought Amelia downstairs. "Morning, darling! A glorious day. What are your plans, more murder investigation?"

"Not this morning." Victoria collected cereal boxes from the closet under the stairs and set them on the counter. "The State Police and forensics team are sifting through evidence. Casey is compiling a list of people she'd like me to talk to." She lifted down two bowls from the cabinet above the counter.

"Shouldn't the police be the ones to do the questioning?"

"I won't be interviewing anyone in my police capacity," Victoria said. "I'll be talking to a few persons of interest, unofficially." She removed the half-and-half from the refrigerator and set it on the counter. "The State Police and Casey believe I'll be able to get certain types of information better than a uniformed officer, who, no matter how sensitive, can be perceived as threatening." She reached down two mugs. "I plan to work in the garden this morning."

After breakfast, Amelia joined her mother, and they worked companionably, pulling weeds from the rain-softened earth, occasionally talking, mostly quiet. The air smelled of fresh green growth. A catbird mewed from the cedar tree. Four polka-dotted guinea fowl strutted past them, the hen calling out a tiresome "Go back! Go back! Go back! Go back!" until Victoria hurled a clump of grass at her and the hen scurried off. Redwing blackbirds called. The honeybees from Neil Flynn's hives hummed in the wisteria.

Amelia talked about her work, her travels, and the condominium she'd bought, which had a view of the Golden Gate Bridge. "I hope you'll visit me this winter," she said, looking sideways at her mother. Victoria listened with an occasional question. The morning passed pleasantly. Amelia carted the heap of pulled weeds to the compost heap while Victoria thinned the lettuce. Rain had spurred its growth.

That afternoon, Elizabeth and Amelia washed the tender lettuce Victoria had thinned. Victoria was in the cookroom, working on her weekly column.

"Would you like to come to the knitters' group this afternoon, Mom?" asked Elizabeth. "We're meeting every afternoon at four and," she pushed up her sleeve to check her watch, "it's three-fifteen now."

"I'd love to go, darling. Where shall I put the roots I'm snipping off? Does your grandmother still have a compost bucket?"

Victoria looked up from her typewriter. "The compost bucket is under the sink."

"Righto." Amelia opened the door under the sink, swept a small heap of lettuce roots into her hand, and dropped them into the bucket. "Why on earth did you decide to form a mathematical knitting group, darling? That seems awfully esoteric."

"It's great fun, actually," said Elizabeth. "A retired math professor started the group. She's taken complicated equations for different shapes like Möbius strips and Klein bottles and projective planes and changed the equations into knitting instructions that we nonmath types can follow. I think you'll like her. She's about your age."

"I look forward to meeting her," said Amelia. "Math was one of my favorite subjects in college. I almost majored in it. What's her name?"

Elizabeth lifted the freshly washed lettuce out of the sink and dropped it into the salad spinner. "Fran Bacon. She taught at Northeastern."

"Really! Fran Bacon?" asked Amelia. "I wonder if she's the same Fran Bacon I went to college with?"

"I think she graduated from the University of Massachusetts, too."

"I didn't know Fran Bacon well, but it seems to me she did major in math."

Elizabeth ripped a paper towel from the roll above the sink and dried her hands. "Want to join us, Gram?"

"No, thanks. I need to finish my column. I'll have supper ready when you come home."

"You've had an awfully full day, Mother," said Amelia. "You needn't go to all that trouble. I'll pick up some takeout in Vineyard Haven."

"Thank you, but I'd prefer to make supper."

Amelia sighed. "I'm trying to be helpful, Mother."

"Enjoy the meeting," said Victoria with a regal wave.

Elizabeth gathered together her knitting. "We're off, Gram. See you a little after seven."

CHAPTER 33

"Your grandmother is certainly testy these days," Amelia said as they were on their way to the library. "I'm glad to have some time with you, Elizabeth. You've been so busy, between work and the knitting project."

"Ummm," Elizabeth murmured.

"I want to talk to you about your grandmother."

At that, Elizabeth looked up from the road. "What about Gram?"

"She's not as young as she thinks she is. I know she's busy with her important work, but there comes a time . . ."

"Ummm."

"You're so involved with her, you don't realize how much you're missing out on. You're really not able to lead the kind of life you . . ." Amelia looked over at Elizabeth and stopped before she finished the sentence.

Elizabeth had tightened her grip on the steering wheel. "I'm leading exactly the kind of life I want to lead, Mom. And Gram isn't keeping me from doing anything."

"I like to hear you defending her, darling."

"I'm not defending her. She may be ninety-two, but her mind is better than yours and mine put together."

"Really, now, darling."

The two said no more until they reached the library.

"We can continue the discussion on our way home," Amelia said.

"There's nothing to discuss," said Elizabeth. "If you think Gram is holding me back in some way, you're wrong. She's taking care of me, not the other way around."

"Well. We'll discuss it later."

Daughter and granddaughter strode into the library, looking much like Victoria, tall, heads high, jaws set in identical firm lines.

"Hi, Elizabeth," someone called out. "This must be your mother."

Elizabeth nodded, still annoyed by the exchange in her car. "My mother. Amelia."

"Welcome!"

"Nice to have you here, Amelia."

Elizabeth glanced around the group. "Where's Fran?"

"Here she comes now," said Jim.

"Fran," Elizabeth said, "this is my mother, Amelia."

"For heaven's sake!" said Fran. "Amelia Trumbull. Of course!" She dropped the package of yarn she was carrying on the table and held out both hands. "With Elizabeth Trumbull in the group, I ought to have put two and two together. How are you? It's been a long time. Sit down and let's talk while I work, if you don't mind."

"I understand. A deadline coming up," said Amelia, sitting next to Fran. "I had no idea you'd settled on the Vineyard. I thought your family had a place in Maine?"

"A student of mine invited me to visit and, well, I fell in love."

Amelia smiled. "With the student or with the Island?"

Fran flushed. "One doesn't fraternize with one's students."

"I'm sorry." Amelia put her hand on top of Fran's. "That was tasteless. Tell me about the quilt."

The color slowly faded back to normal in Fran's face. "The quilt needs only a few minor adjustments before we ship if off for the exhibit." She moved a pink anemone closer to a green ribbon of kelp, shifted a small blue-and-yellow fish on a wire nearer a red coral.

"How are you going to ship this creation?" Amelia asked, fingering the hem. "It seems so fragile."

"Jim and Casper are in charge of packing and shipping." Fran nodded at the two men. "That was an interesting comment you just made. That's precisely the point we hope to make."

"You mean about the fragility of the quilt?"

"The fragility of coral reefs," said Fran.

"It's wonderful," said Amelia, studying the colorful display. "Just wonderful."

On the way home, Amelia reminisced about Fran Bacon, recalling times they'd had together that she hadn't thought about in years.

"She was dedicated to her studies. I don't think she ever dated in college," Amelia said. "She was always in the mathematics lab. Do you know if she married?"

"I have no idea. I never thought about it."

Elizabeth slowed as they passed the Mill Pond, and they both looked toward the head of the pond, where the swans nested. While they watched, a swan sailed out of the rushes and dipped its head underwater to nibble the sprouting marsh grass.

"I wonder how many generations of swans have lived in the pond since I left," said Amelia. "I remember when the town introduced the first pair to control the weeds."

"I always thought the swans had been there forever."

"It seems that way," Amelia said. "Does Fran use a title? Mrs. or Miss or Dr.?"

"I've only known her as Fran Bacon."

"She's kept her maiden name, then," said Amelia. "I did, too, of course. And you chose to be a Trumbull instead of taking either Daddy's name or your husband's. I must say, it always seemed terribly unfair for the male side of the family to carry the name through the generations."

They turned in at Victoria's drive, and Elizabeth parked under the maple tree, mightily relieved they'd never had that threatened talk.

"What an interesting afternoon at the knitting group," Amelia said. The three women were having drinks in front of the fire. "Fran Bacon of the knitters is the same Fran Bacon I went to college with. The coral-reef quilt is absolutely amazing. You wouldn't think you could knit something like a coral using a mathematical equation and have it actually look so real."

"The knitters are remarkable," said Victoria.

"Fran is the one who's amazing," Elizabeth said. "She's absolutely obsessed with the quilt competition. She started the mathematical knitting group, found out about the competition, designed the quilt, and converted equations into knitting instructions. I mean, it's like magic."

"I never did find out whether she ever married," said Amelia, holding up her glass the same way Victoria did. The fire snapped and a shower of sparks flew up the chimney. McCavity leaped to his feet, then flopped down again and cleaned himself.

Amelia set her glass down. "She had an odd reaction when I made a little joke about some small thing."

"I noticed that, too," Elizabeth said. "Fran told Mom she came to the Island at the invitation of a student and fell in love. Mom teased her—"

"I didn't really tease, her, just a light comment."

"All Mom said was, 'in love with the student or the Island?'"

"That seems innocuous enough," said Victoria.

"You would think so. But Fran got all bent out of shape. She practically snapped at Mom, saying professors don't fraternize with students, or something like that."

"They do, of course, even though that's totally unethical," said Amelia. "I wonder what set her off?"

"She undoubtedly feels under great pressure to have the quilt finished and sent off," said Victoria.

Elizabeth got up and put another log on the fire. "That's true. Fran's been snappish for the past week or so." She returned to her seat. "It'll be a relief to have the quilt shipped off, even though it's been fun. But Fran had the responsibility of showing us how to knit these weird shapes and making us stick to our deadline. She deserves a medal."

"It's a work of art," said Amelia. "It should run away with whatever the top prize is. I'll get refills on our drinks." Amelia gathered up the glasses and headed for the kitchen.

Victoria's thoughts had drifted from Fran Bacon and the deadline to the people she wanted to talk to in the morning. She said, "Elizabeth, Fran had a student who was stalked, didn't she?"

"More than one."

"I'd like to talk with her. She may have insight into why LeRoy Watts, with all the positive things going on in his life, would become a stalker. Nothing I've read sheds much light."

"Is that likely to help identify the killer?" asked Elizabeth.

"I don't know," said Victoria. "I really don't know."

Chapter 34

Tuesday morning was bright, sunny, and dry, another typical Vineyard day. Spiderwebs were spread on the grass like freshly washed sheets. Dewdrops caught in the webs cast rainbows into the air.

Victoria, Amelia, and Elizabeth were finishing their breakfast in the cookroom. Victoria brushed toast crumbs into her hand and dropped them on her plate.

"I'd like to talk to Fran Bacon today," she said. "Do you know what time she's likely to be at the library, Elizabeth?"

"From about noon on," Elizabeth said. "She's making last-minute adjustments to the quilt before Casper and Jim pack it for shipping. Can I take your plate, Mom?"

"Yes, thanks." Amelia handed the empty dishes to Elizabeth, who carried them into the kitchen.

"Fran has to make sure everything's exactly right," Elizabeth explained when she returned to the cookroom. "More coffee, either of you?" She held up the coffeepot.

"Please," said Victoria. "Fran certainly runs a tight ship."

"Typical of the Fran I remembered," said Amelia. "That discipline of hers has paid off in that quilt."

"Before I meet with Fran this afternoon, I'd like to talk to Emily Cameron again," said Victoria. "She didn't have much to say when we had lunch with her on Saturday. I assume she'll be at the boatyard today."

"You can use my car if you want," said Elizabeth.

"Thank you," said Victoria. "We can give you a lift to the harbor, since it's on our way."

Elizabeth gathered up her black uniform sweater and smoothed her khaki shorts, Amelia went into the bathroom to repair her face, and Victoria headed out to the car.

After they dropped off Elizabeth at the harbor, Amelia and Victoria continued on to the boatyard, driving the longer, more scenic way around East Chop.

"It's early," said Amelia. "Shall we park at the lighthouse? We can have a nice chat."

Victoria hesitated. She didn't really want a heart-to-heart talk with her daughter. But she thought of the magnificent view from the lighthouse of Nantucket Sound and the distant mainland and nodded.

They parked at the top of the hill, walked to the benches at the edge of the cliff, and sat down. Below them on the sound, one lone sailboat heeled over in the brisk southwest breeze. The mainland seemed close this morning, so close they could make out individual buildings.

"I'm trying to fit the pieces of this puzzle together," Amelia said after they'd admired the view for a while. "The body you found in the library book shed was Emily's boyfriend, wasn't it?"

"Yes." This wasn't a conversation Victoria wanted, but it was preferable to the conversation she'd expected—namely, Amelia deciding to be overly daughterly.

The wind sighed in the pines at the cliff's edge, moved on to twist the leaves of wild cherry, then ruffled Amelia's neat hair. She brushed it away from her face.

"You think LeRoy Watts killed the boyfriend?"

"Yes, I do."

Amelia frowned. "I don't understand."

Victoria shaded her eyes with a hand and gazed out at the sailboat. It was early in the season to be out on the water. "Certain things we know to be facts." She turned to Amelia. "LeRoy Watts owned a Taser. He'd fired Jerry Sparks because of his problem with drugs. According to Emily, Jerry headed to Watts Electrical to ask for his job back. Emily and Jerry planned to go to the movies that evening. I suppose she called Jerry's cell phone to confirm their date and got no answer."

"Jerry Sparks was dead by then?"

"I'm sure he was."

"I still don't understand."

A dandelion had grown beside the bench where they sat. Victoria plucked one of the fluffy seed heads and held the stem so the breeze could scatter the seeds on their filmy parachutes.

"We hadn't found Jerry Sparks's body yet when I asked LeRoy Watts to repair the outlet in the East Chamber. LeRoy said he needed to spend more time on the repairs, and left his tool chest there, intending to finish the work later. At the time, I had a feeling he'd left the chest for some reason other than simple convenience."

A gust whisked away the last of the dandelion seeds and Victoria dropped the stem and its buttonlike head onto the ground. "We found LeRoy's body the day you arrived."

"I know. That was quite a shock."

"You were there, of course, when I looked inside his tool chest and found the spent Taser cartridge."

"I'm surprised you recognized it. I barely know what a Taser is. I wouldn't know a Taser cartridge if I saw one."

The sailboat tacked. Victoria watched the boat change direction, the sails luff, then fill again. A fishing vessel, outriggers lifted high out of the water, passed on its way to the Georges Bank fishing grounds. A stream of seagulls followed, dipping into the trailing wake. The two women watched until the boat was out of sight.

Victoria took an envelope and pen out of her cloth bag. "The cartridges have two long, slender wires with tiny darts at the ends, like this." She drew a sketch. "When someone shoots a Taser, the darts hook into the victim's clothing or skin. A strong current flows through the wires and stops the individual instantly. Usually, a Taser does no harm. But under some circumstances, it can kill."

"A victim such as a drug user, I suppose."

"Habitual drug user, someone in poor health, or if the shooter pulls the trigger repeatedly. Jerry Sparks, the boyfriend, was both a drug user and in poor health."

"It's going to be almost impossible to find proof, isn't it?"

"I believe we have the proof we need. The forensics team examined a fiber caught in one of the barbs," said Victoria, tucking her envelope and pen back into her cloth bag. "The fiber was the same material as the fiber of Jerry Sparks's jacket. Casey called yesterday while you were at the knitting group to tell me." She set her bag back on the ground beside them. "There was a tiny tear in Jerry's jacket. The torn ends of the fiber in the barb matched the torn ends in the tear."

"Amazing," said Amelia.

"Yes."

The ferry from Oak Bluffs passed below them on its way to Woods Hole. They watched.

"You heard what Emily said Saturday," Victoria continued after a while. "She's believed from the beginning that LeRoy Watts killed her Jerry."

"Emily certainly had a strong motive to kill LeRoy."

"At least a half dozen people had motives. That's the problem, and that's why I want to talk to Fran Bacon this afternoon. According to Elizabeth, she's had considerable experience with the problem of stalking."

"Oh?" Amelia sat forward abruptly.

"What is it?" asked Victoria.

Amelia shook her head. "I don't know. Something you said

about Fran reminded me of something, but I can't put my finger on it."

"It will come to you."

"Two o'clock in the morning, probably. Go on. You were saying about Fran?"

"She was a student advisor on ways to deal with stalkers."

"I wish I could recall—"

"Don't try."

"Emily wasn't a stalking victim of LeRoy's, was she?"

"No." Victoria shook her head. "Several individuals had reason to be upset with LeRoy. Jim Weiss was understandably angry at his daughter's humiliation. The knitters and the phone calls. Emily's boyfriend killed. Sarah betrayed. Her sister Jackie furious at her brother-in-law's deception." Victoria got up from the bench. "I know there are motives I haven't thought of." She walked, stiffly at first, toward the car, Amelia beside her.

"You needn't feel so responsible for solving this, Mother. It's the job of the police."

"Let's talk to Emily," said Victoria.

"You want Emily Cameron, Mrs. Trumbull?" asked one of the boatyard workers. "I think she's in the shed, splicing dock lines. You can go on in."

"Thank you," said Victoria.

She and Amelia crossed the road to the large metal shed and entered through a side door. Somewhere in the shed, a radio blasted out raucous music. After the bright sunlight, Victoria's eyes needed a moment to adjust to the dimness of the shed. She paused just inside the door. The music hurt her ears.

Emily was seated on a stool, with her back to Victoria and Amelia. A length of white rope was coiled on the workbench in front of her. She was weaving individual strands into the rope to form a loop, using a sharp, tapered tool to part the rope. She apparently hadn't heard them enter the shed. She was working in time to the music. Jab the tool into the rope, thrust the strand into the opening, twist the rope, jab the tool into the rope again, thrust the strand into the opening, again and again.

"Emily?" Victoria touched her shoulder gently, trying not to startle her.

Emily swiveled around on her stool. "Who . . . ? Oh, Mrs. Trumbull. Hi. I didn't hear you come in."

"I'm sorry to disturb you. Is this a bad time to talk to you?"

"No, ma'am." Emily reached over to the radio on the workbench and turned down the volume "Splicing is just like knitting. I can do it in my sleep."

"Do you feel able to talk to me now?"

Emily sighed. "I guess."

"You remember my daughter Amelia."

Emily peered up at Amelia through her thick glasses. "Hi." She brushed hair out of her eyes with her shoulder, still holding the splicing tool in one hand, the looped rope in the other. "Sorry I can't shake hands."

"Quite all right," said Amelia. "I see you're busy."

"Want to sit down, Mrs. Trumbull?" Emily kept working. "Pull up another stool."

"I'll get it, Mother." Amelia found two stools and set them down beside Emily.

"I wanted to stop by to see how you're doing," Victoria said when she'd settled herself.

Emily laid her work down in her lap. "That's so nice of you." She pulled a tissue out of her pocket and dabbed at her eyes. "It's just awful. I was so angry with Jerry, and all the time . . ." She stopped. "All the time, he was lying in the shed. For days. All alone."

"You had no way of knowing," Victoria said, and waited for Emily to pick up her work again. "Did you ever find out why LeRoy Watts fired your Jerry?"

Emily looked up sharply. "That man! I know he killed Jerry."
She jabbed the tool into the rope. "Jerry was going to see him
about getting his job back. When I called Jerry's cell phone, there
was no answer. He always had his cell with him, always." Jab,
thrust, twist. "So I called the shop. Jerry was supposed to be there.
Maureen answered. I could hear her ask Mr. Watts if Jerry Sparks
had come by, and I could hear Mr. Watts answer. He sounded
funny."

"In what way?"

Emily shifted the rope in her lap, thrust the tool into it, twisted
it, jabbed the strand into the hole, pulled it through, twisted,
thrust the tool into the rope again, jabbed the strand into the
hole. . . . "Maureen asked him if he'd seen Jerry Sparks. Mr. Watts
said, 'He's not here now' or something like that in a real weird
voice. Real high and quavery. You know how he has a real deep
voice? Had, I guess." She looked up again. "I don't know . . . that
doesn't sound like a big deal now, but at the time it didn't sound
right, you know what I mean?"

Victoria nodded. "Did you have a chance to talk to Mr. Watts
before he was killed?"

Emily looked down. "I didn't want to, Mrs. Trumbull."

Both Victoria and Emily were quiet for a while. The music
played softly in the background. Victoria could discern a vague
melody that hadn't been obvious before at high volume. Amelia
sat quietly, arms folded, legs crossed. Emily didn't seem to be
aware of her. She continued to work on the rope.

Emily broke the silence. "I baby-sat for the Watts twins when
they were little. I liked Mrs. Watts a lot. Mr. Watts was always
polite. I had a lot of respect for him, you know? All the stuff he
did for the Little League and the church and everything."

"And the library," Victoria said.

"When Jerry went missing . . ." Emily stopped.

"Go on," Victoria said.

"Before Jerry went missing, he left some DVDs in my apartment, kind of hid them in the bookcase, you know?"

Victoria nodded.

"Well, when he went missing, I found them again, and they had Mr. Watts's name on them, so I took them to Mrs. Watts. I was mad at Jerry and wanted to get rid of them."

"I see. I believe I know what was on the DVDs."

Amelia shifted on her stool, recrossed her legs, and cleared her throat.

"Yeah," said Emily. "Jerry was going to show those videos to the police. I knew he was." She jabbed the tool into the rope. "That's why Mr. Watts killed him."

CHAPTER 35

They shut the door behind them and Emily's music swelled back to a superloud blast.

"She's destroying her hearing," said Amelia.

"I suppose they don't want to hear our advice; they're unable to listen to reason." Victoria smiled at her unintentional small joke.

They crossed the road again and returned to the parked car. "Well!" said Amelia once they'd buckled themselves in. "No doubt about it. We know now who killed LeRoy Watts."

Victoria shook her head. "Not Emily."

"That tool of hers is lethal-looking. A fid, right?"

"Yes," said Victoria. "A good weapon."

"She certainly had a motive. I don't know when I've seen such an angry person." Amelia backed out carefully into the road and they headed up-Island.

"She didn't kill him," Victoria said with assurance.

"I can picture that girl jabbing her fid into LeRoy's neck."

"Emily's not the killer." Victoria shook her head. "Shall we stop at the Black Dog and get a cup of coffee?"

"It's almost lunchtime. I'll treat," said Amelia.

They ordered lobster rolls and iced tea, and when the waitress brought their orders, heaping plates of food that would serve a small family, they decided to split one lobster roll and take the rest home.

"I'm so delighted with the touch-me-not I planted," said Victoria after she'd decided to attack her half of the lobster roll with a knife and fork. "The plants are already about five inches high."

"I saw them," said Amelia. "Such a fun plant. Do you remember when we were just little kids how I used to love going down to the brook and popping those fat seedpods."

"So did I," said Victoria. "And so did my mother. I still do. Just the slightest touch."

"Stalkers and touch-me-not," said Amelia. "Seems appropriate, somehow." She held her half of the lobster roll in both hands and nibbled at it from the side. "Delicious. Not something we get in California."

"Have you thought any more about Fran? The days you were in college together?" asked Victoria. "Sometimes a memory will come to you quite unexpectedly."

"I didn't know her well in college, and, of course, I haven't seen her for over forty years."

"What do you remember?"

"Well, she was what the kids would call a nerd today. Very bright, obsessive, highly focused. I'm not surprised she decided to teach math."

"She hasn't lived on the Vineyard for long," said Victoria. "Four or five years."

Amelia shrugged. "I wouldn't know."

"Did you live in the same dormitory?"

Amelia thought. "Come to think of it, yes, we did. She was on the third floor; I was on the second. But everyone in the dorm shared common rooms and the kitchen. Actually, I saw quite a bit of her."

"What was her social life like?"

"I was so busy with my own, I had no idea what hers was like." Amelia laughed. "When I think about it, I don't believe she had much of any life. She was dedicated to her studies and didn't have time."

"I wonder about the student who encouraged her to come to the Vineyard," Victoria said.

"Anything to do with a student of hers came long after I knew her." Amelia dipped a french fry into a pool of ketchup she'd dribbled on her plate. "Oh my!" She dropped the fry onto her plate.

"What is it?"

"I just remembered what it was I was trying to recall when we were at the lighthouse. She had a crush on a physics professor."

"That's not uncommon," said Victoria. "I can remember my feelings about a teacher—"

"No, no." Amelia held up her hand as though she was stopping traffic. "At the lighthouse, you said Fran might be able to give you some insight into stalking."

Victoria set her fork down beside the remains of her lobster roll and turned her full attention to Amelia.

"It wasn't like the high school crushes we all had on some teacher we admired, Mother. Fran followed this physics professor of hers around, wrote him notes, and called him at home. She told his wife he was in love with her, Fran. She said he was going to leave the wife and marry her. It caused a big flap at the time. I'd forgotten all about it until now."

"What happened?"

"The professor was at least thirty years older than Fran, one of those stereotypical absentminded professors. He didn't have a clue, as I recall. We used to joke about how his wife probably taught him everything . . . well, everything." Fran picked up the fry again and bit off the ketchup coated end.

"And?"

"I think the dean called Fran in and gave her a talking-to. We students never really found out for sure, although we tried."

"What about the professor?"

"He kept on going as though nothing had happened. As far as he was concerned, nothing did. But to Fran, I guess, it was a huge embarrassment. She dropped the physics course and switched to math."

"I suppose that's what the school demanded."

"Probably. One grows out of that sort of adolescent behavior."

"I wonder," said Victoria. She picked up her fork again and finished the last shreds of lobster.

Amelia said, "Since she knew stalking from the standpoint of the stalker, Fran probably was an effective advisor. She's very bright."

The waitress brought the check and turned to Victoria. "Was everything all right, Mrs. Trumbull?"

"Delicious," said Victoria.

"Would you like a doggie bag?"

"Please," said Amelia, giving the waitress her credit card.

Victoria picked up her cloth bag while they waited for the waitress to return. "Her reaction to your gentle teasing was interesting."

"Odd at least," said Amelia. "Fran said she'd visited the Island and fallen in love, and all I said was, 'With the student or the Island?' at which point she got quite upset."

"Humorless, to say the least," said Victoria.

"That's Fran for you."

As they passed the police station, Victoria said, "I need to see Casey. Why don't you go on to the library and Casey will drive me there in an hour or so. That will give you time to talk with Fran."

Amelia pulled into the oyster-shell parking area and Victoria got out.

"I can come back for you, Mother."

"Casey will give me a ride, thanks. I'll see you in a bit." Victoria brushed aside the ducks and climbed the steps that led into the police station.

Casey looked up from her computer. "How are the interviews going, Victoria?"

Victoria sat in her usual chair by Casey's desk. "We may need to look at the situation differently."

"What do you mean?"

"Can you find any background information on Fran Bacon?"

"The knitter?"

"Amelia went to college with her, and she apparently got into trouble for stalking one of her professors."

"Sure. Let me back out of this program, and I'll look her up. Where did she go to school?"

"University of Massachusetts."

"There's a problem with confidentiality of records, but I think I can get around that for police business. That's what you're talking about, isn't it?"

"Yes." Victoria had brought her lilac-wood stick with her, and leaned it against her chair. "I told my daughter I'd meet her at the library in about an hour."

"That should do it," said Casey, tapping keys and humming to herself.

After a few minutes, she said, "Aha!"

Victoria looked up. Then when she saw Casey was still concentrating, she gazed out the window at the Mill Pond, where the swans were feeding.

"Okay!" Casey said after what seemed like a long time. She stood up.

"What have you found?"

"Fran Bacon, a sophomore at the time, was reprimanded for harassing her physics professor, a Dr. Breznikowski, writing letters to his wife claiming she was having relations with her husband, calling the wife, following the prof around, yadadda do. The professor and his wife had a young son they called Lee, eight years old. They didn't want publicity that would touch the kid."

"Any criminal charges filed?"

"The professor refused to file a complaint, and his wife did, too, and the whole thing was dropped." Casey looked up. "Am I following your line of reasoning? Let's look more closely at Fran?"

"Did you know that LeRoy Watts was a student of hers at Northeastern?"

"Small world," said Casey.

Victoria nodded. "Will you give me a ride up to the library?"

Casey stood up and fastened on her belt with its multitude of tools. "Let's go."

Chapter 36

Casey parked in the filtered shade of a maple that overhung the library's parking lot. The lot was empty except for the librarian's recumbent tricycle, the assistant librarian's Jeep, and Elizabeth's convertible.

"What time is it, Victoria?"

Victoria lifted the sleeve of her turtleneck. "Almost three o'clock."

"Elizabeth's car is here. I don't know what Fran drives."

"They probably went to get a snack."

"Alley's is just across the road." Casey slid out of the Bronco. "I'll go in and ask Lucinda where they are. Wait here, Victoria."

But Victoria eased herself out of the high passenger seat and followed Casey into the library.

Lucinda Chandler was at the computer behind the checkout counter. She looked up and smiled. "Hi, Chief. Mrs. Trumbull."

Casey glanced around the library. The bank of computers in the center of the main room was deserted. So was the reading room. Even the children's section was empty. "Seems awfully quiet today."

"It's the lull between the lunch crowd and kids getting out of school," said Lucinda. "Come three-thirty, four, we'll be busy." She looked out the window. "Here's the first wave."

The front door slammed open and three adolescent girls burst in, giggling about something.

"Shhhh!" The redhead held a finger to her lips.

"Hi, Ms. Chandler."

"Afternoon, girls." Lucinda turned to Casey. "Excuse me, Chief. My clients." Then to the girls. "What's tonight's assignment?"

"Lucinda . . ." said Casey, adjusting her utility belt.

"We're supposed to write a five-hundred-word essay on bees," said the redhead.

Lucinda held up a finger. "Be right with you, Chief. Won't be a minute." To the girls she said, "We have lots of books on bees," and she came out from behind the counter.

Victoria looked at her watch. Casey folded her arms. Victoria coughed politely.

"One second more," said Lucinda. To the girls she said again, "There's an article on bees in the latest copy of *Junior Scholastic*. You know where to find the magazines? I want to talk to the chief."

"Sure." The three trooped into the reading room.

"Sorry," said Lucinda, turning back to Victoria and Casey. "Are you here for the knitters' group? Fran should be back in a half hour or so, in time for their meeting."

"Lucinda . . ." Casey began.

"They've finished the quilt," Lucinda said. "What do you think of it?"

"Lovely," said Victoria. "But we need to know where Amelia and Fran went."

"Fran wanted to show Amelia something. I wasn't paying much attention."

Casey paced away from the counter, then back again.

"How long ago did they leave?" Victoria asked.

"About fifteen minutes ago, maybe quarter to three?"

"What did Fran want to show Amelia?"

"I really wasn't paying attention."

Casey stopped in front of the counter. "Maybe a building or a garden or a beach, something like that?"

Lucinda leaned back against the counter and held her chin in one hand. "Let me think."

Casey said, so only Victoria heard, "Quickly!"

"Amelia hasn't been here for two years," said Victoria. "Might Fran have wanted to show her something that's occurred during that time?"

"I heard them talk about plants, and Fran mentioned a new planting at the Polly Hill Arboretum. They left shortly after that. They'll be back in time for the knitting group, I guarantee. You know how obsessive Fran is about that quilt. She was even carrying her knitting with her." Lucinda laughed. "Has to polish the last stitch on a brain coral or whatever."

"Does that seem likely, that they went to the arboretum?" asked Victoria.

"Ummmm, yes. They were talking about plants."

"Thanks," said Casey. "Let's go, Victoria."

"Ask Amelia to call me if she returns with Fran while we're gone, would you please?" Victoria gave her Casey's cell-phone number.

As they left the library, Victoria said, "I'm being overly concerned about this, I'm afraid."

"Probably. Fran has no reason to hassle Amelia." Casey shrugged. "But your instincts are uncanny, Victoria, so let's go."

They were at the Bronco when Victoria said, "Amelia knew about Fran and the physics professor. Fran wouldn't have forgotten that."

"Fran's wound kind of tight," agreed Casey.

Victoria climbed into the high passenger seat, and Casey walked around to the driver's side and got in.

"That physics professor bit was in the dim past," said Casey, starting the engine. "Fran was, what, eighteen or nineteen? Not something Amelia is likely to remind Fran of in casual conversation."

"Fran moved here because of a student of hers."

Casey backed out of the parking space and headed out. "What does that have to do with anything?"

"Fran was a math professor. One of her extracurricular tasks was to counsel students on dealing with stalkers."

"Yeah?"

Casey pulled out of the parking lot and turned onto State Road.

"You knew, didn't you, that LeRoy Watts got his engineering degree from Northeastern?"

"Sure."

"Fran taught mathematics at Northeastern."

"Was he a student of hers?"

"Yes."

"Whew!" said Casey. "A stalker being stalked by a stalker, is that what you're saying?"

"Something like that," said Victoria. "The lecturer we heard at the law enforcement meeting a couple of weeks ago said stalkers often turn violent if they're thwarted."

"We'll be at the arboretum in a couple of minutes," Casey said. She cornered Dead Man's Curve, cutting over the center line. Victoria held onto her seat bottom with both hands. They passed Whiting's hay field in a blur.

"The arboretum is fifty acres," said Victoria. "A large area to cover."

"They'll be there. We'll find them," said Casey.

Victoria sat back again. "It's probably nothing. We're worrying about nothing. They're taking a break from that quilt before the meeting to let Amelia see the arboretum."

Casey's hands were high on the steering wheel.

Victoria said, "If we see them, we can say—"

"We won't need to explain a thing, Victoria. It's perfectly natural for us to drop by the arboretum and join them." She signaled a left turn and pulled into the arboretum's parking area.

As they drove around the oval area, they counted nine cars and a tour bus parked in the dozen shaded spaces, each space designed for three or four cars.

"Any idea what Fran drives?" asked Casey.

"None whatsoever."

"We can stop by the visitors' center and ask if Amelia and Fran are here." Casey got out of the Bronco, and the two walked the short distance to the visitors' center.

A dozen people milled around the center, checking the books and gifts, studying the displays. The volunteer at the desk, her name tag identifying her simply as ANN, looked over the top of her glasses. Her hair was a halo of curls, a tangled mixure of auburn and silver. A pair of reading glasses hung from a cord around her neck.

"Hello, Mrs. Trumbull. May I help you?"

"Has Amelia stopped by with Fran Bacon?"

Ann shook her head. "You know, I've been so busy, I haven't noticed." She brushed curls away from her forehead. "They may not have stopped at the center." She lifted her glasses up and perched them on her nose, then scrabbled around in a desk drawer and brought out a visitors' guide. "Would you like a map? They may have gone on one of the walks without stopping here. They don't need to, you know."

"Thanks," said Casey. "A map would help."

"It's been a lovely day," said Ann, handing the map over. "They're predicting rain this afternoon. Good for our gardens."

"Do you know where Fran might want to take Amelia to show her a new planting?" asked Victoria. "Something within the past two years, perhaps?"

"I don't know about specific new plantings," said Ann. "We're constantly adding specimens to the arboretum." She thought a moment, tugged off her glasses, then put them back on. "I'll show you some of the lovely spots."

245

Casey handed the map over and Ann opened it up. "The azaleas are spectacular right now." She removed the cap from a yellow marker pen and circled the azalea plantings. "And the rhododendrons are in bud. Some may already be in bloom." She handed the map to Victoria, who passed it on to Casey. "You know where the West Field is?"

"Yes," said Victoria. "Thank you. If Amelia shows up, would you mind calling Casey on her cell phone?"

"I'd be glad to. I think I have your number, Chief, don't I?"

"Let me write it out for you," said Casey, and did.

"Thanks ever so much," said Ann, taking off her glasses. "Have a nice walk. I hope you meet up with them."

"So do we," said Casey, and Victoria noticed that behind Casey's back, her fingers on both hands were crossed.

CHAPTER 37

"Does this make sense?" asked Casey, studying the map once they were outside. "Let's think before we go racing off in all directions. Fifty acres is a huge area."

"Perhaps we should split up." Victoria pointed out the paths on the map. "You go this way and I'll go the other."

"We stick together. You know the arboretum and I don't. Is there an open area where we can look over the place?"

Victoria thought a bit. "There are two meadows, the North Field and the West Field. The West Field is somewhat more remote." Casey held out the map so Victoria could show her the area. "There are dense plantings on three sides, so we can't see much from there."

"Dense plantings," mused Casey. "What about the North Field?"

"It's bounded on three sides by buildings and the road."

"Then we'll strike out for the West Field, stop there and give you a chance to rest. . . ." She glanced at Victoria. "I meant," Casey continued, "we can stop to reconnoiter, decide where to go from there."

On their way to the closer North Field, they passed through a picnic grove where trees and dense underbrush could have hidden two people, but it seemed unlikely that Amelia and Fran would stop so close to the visitors' center and the rest rooms. The field was an easy stroll from the center. However, they strode briskly and Victoria was glad when they finally halted in the middle of the grassy area so Casey could catch her breath.

For most of the day, the wind had blown from the southwest, a warm, sweet-scented spring air, bright and dry. Now the sky had clouded over. As they stood in the center of the field, Victoria felt a slight bite in the air, as though winter hadn't departed entirely. The walk had warmed her and the breeze was welcome.

Ahead of them and to their right, azaleas bloomed in masses of red, pink, and white, with a few clusters of orange and yellow. Tall rhododendrons, not yet in bloom, towered over the azaleas, their dense foliage forming a screen behind the azaleas.

To their left, a couple with two small children strolled toward the cow barn. A group of senior citizens, who'd apparently come on the tour bus, chattered.

The still air was full of birdcalls, cardinals, wrens, chickadees, tohees staking out their territory.

"It's getting chilly," said Casey. "Are you warm enough, Victoria?"

Victoria swept her arm in an arc that included half of the pasture. "We need to search behind the rhododendrons. Most of the visitors are heading toward the dogwood allée and the arbor."

"I'm not familiar with this place," Casey said again. "What's behind the trees?"

"A screened-in area where Polly Hill grew special plants that needed protection from deer and rabbits."

"Where visitors are likely to stroll?"

"I would think so, yes."

"We're looking for a place that's not too public. With people around, Amelia won't get in trouble. How about over there?" Casey pointed to their right.

"That's off the beaten path."

"A good place to start," said Casey.

A gust of wind ruffled Victoria's hair. "The wind's backed around to the northeast. I smell rain in the air."

"We'd better hurry," said Casey. She folded the map to show

the west side of the pasture. "Any thoughts on which end to approach from?"

"This is a good place for us to split up. I think we should. I'll start from the north end, you from the south, and we can close in. We won't be far apart and can call out if we need help."

"I don't like it, Victoria. Cops work in pairs."

But Victoria was already heading off to their right, walking briskly toward the stone wall that fenced in the field. She waved at the opposite end of the wall. "You need to hurry," she called over her shoulder. "The rain isn't far off and neither of us has foul-weather gear."

"Victoria, wait!"

"If we don't find them here, we'll have to look elsewhere." Victoria strode off, flicking the tall meadow grasses with her lilac-wood stick.

Casey stood for a moment, then shrugged and headed for the far end. Victoria's instincts were good, at least, almost always. She doubted they'd find Amelia and Fran this easily, and even if they did, she doubted the women would be doing anything other than appreciating flowers.

Even she could smell rain in the air. Not like Victoria, whose nose could sense smells on the slightest movement of air. Victoria was right. They'd better hurry. A lot of ground to cover and not pleasant when you're soaking wet.

Her cell phone rang. Before she looked at it, she thought it must be Lucinda at the library, calling to say Amelia and Fran had returned. But the call was from Junior Norton, who said results were in on the Watts autopsy.

"Later, Junior. Can't talk right now." Casey closed the phone. She was at the edge of the field, where the map showed the stone wall making a right-angle turn. The rhododendrons towered above her, fifteen feet tall or taller, their leathery leaves a dense wall. She pushed through them to a sort of deer path that followed the stone wall, and headed to the right, the direction from which Victoria would come.

Victoria, too, had slipped behind the screen of rhododendrons. Here, the stone wall extended quite a distance to the west before turning south, then halfway down the field, it turned east before turning south again, forming an extension of several acres where the rhododendrons grew thickly.

She stopped to rest, leaning heavily on her stick, when she was out of sight of Casey. She didn't want to sit down, only to have to go to the trouble of getting up again. Somewhat rested, she continued along the path. The rhododendron screen blocked out sound from the outside world. She could no longer hear cars on State Road or the voices of the sightseers or children calling to one another. If she weren't so concerned about Amelia, she would treasure this place of silence. She moved slowly, trying to respect that silence. She took twenty steps, then rested.

She had almost reached her second twenty-step rest stop when she heard voices. She stopped. Was she entirely sure she'd heard voices? The sound was indistinct and might have been birds chatting or even wind in the treetops. She wanted desperately to hear Amelia and Fran.

The wind had started to move the leaves above her, making human sounds. She could feel the rain approaching. She moved ten steps and stopped. The voices had stopped, too. Perhaps they were in her imagination after all.

She moved another ten steps, and heard the voices again. People, not the voices of leaves moving in the rain-wind.

Another ten steps. She was no longer tired.

And another ten.

Women were talking, low, musical voices, like Amelia's and Fran's. She could see nothing ahead of her except the deer path.

The branches over the path were low, and in places she had to crouch. She moved one step at a time, stopping to listen each time until she could make out words. She tried to peer through the rhododendrons but could see only more leaves and fat buds. The blossoms would be out in another week or two, she thought briefly.

Then she realized where she was and what she was doing and knew that she was frightened for Amelia, the caring young daughter who'd grown up to be a caring woman. Retired. How quickly that had happened.

Victoria heard, "I've never been to this part of the arboretum. It's lovely." Amelia's voice, and Victoria's heart skipped. "What a perfect spot for this bench, protected from the world."

Victoria felt a rush of relief. Amelia was safe. She was about to call out, but stopped herself. Was Amelia really safe? Victoria told herself she was being overly protective, the very reason she'd been so critical of Amelia. Victoria leaned on her stick and waited.

"It is lovely here, isn't it. Quiet and private. I come here often, summer and winter, to think." Fran's voice. A friendly voice, soft and mellow. Victoria felt as though she were intruding, and again, almost called out.

"I'm so glad to meet up with you again," said Amelia. "What a surprise to find you here on the Vineyard, and my daughter working with you."

"I must admit, I was surprised to see you at the library," said Fran. "At first, I hadn't connected Elizabeth Trumbull and her grandmother with you, for some reason. When your daughter said you were visiting, well, things snapped into place."

"I've been away for too long, I'm afraid."

"Two years, your daughter told me. But I do understand why you came back."

Amelia responded. "Yes, of course. It was time for me to be with my mother and daughter. I thought my mother—"

Fran interrupted. "That's not really the reason, though, is it?"

"What?" Amelia sounded puzzled.

Fran's voice was clear. "You know precisely what I mean, Amelia."

CHAPTER 38

"I don't know what you're talking about," said Amelia.

"Professor Breznikowski. Does that ring a bell?"

Silence.

Victoria leaned on her stick to ease the strain on her leg muscles, which were beginning to cramp.

"Professor Breznikowski! You were there when the dean forced us to separate."

"Ahhhhh . . ." said Amelia.

"'Ahhhhh,'" mimicked Fran. "Comes back to you, doesn't it? Professor Breznikowski. He was in love with me."

Amelia cleared her throat. "I recall something about—"

Fran interrupted. "He was in *love* with me, did you know that? He was going to leave his wife and marry me."

"I didn't know that. It was a long time ago."

"Forty-three years," said Fran. "I haven't forgotten."

Victoria moved a few steps closer. She could see the edge of a small glade where the rhododendrons had been cleared away. She supposed Amelia and Fran were sitting on a bench within the clearing. She leaned on her stick and thought how nice it would be to sit. She was stiffening from standing still.

The conversation in the glade had become tense, and Victoria wasn't sure what she could or should do at this point. Where was Casey?

"Let's head back to the library," said Amelia. "Do you have the time? I forgot my watch. It must be close to four o'clock. You probably want to finish up the last few—"

"The quilt can wait. I know full well why you came back, Amelia. You were jealous."

"Jealous?" Amelia's voice was incredulous. "Of what?"

"You don't need to play dumb. Not 'of what,' Amelia. Of me. And my man."

"I don't understand, Fran." Amelia's voice had become unnaturally calm.

"You're too intelligent to fake it like this, Amelia. You know perfectly well what I'm talking about. You even made that nasty comment when we met in the library."

"What comment?"

"Don't be coy, Amelia."

Victoria felt a drop of rain on her face. Where was Casey? That utter calmness in Amelia's voice meant she'd realized Fran was unbalanced. Did she realize her danger?

"Ahhhh," said Amelia. "Your student. When I asked if you'd fallen in love with your student . . ."

"That was uncalled for," said Fran.

"I apologize. I realize now how much he means to you, and I had no right to be so flippant. I'm sorry, Fran."

"Meant to me," said Fran.

"'Meant'?"

"He's dead. You know he's dead."

"I'm so sorry." Victoria heard a movement, as though Amelia was getting up. "It's raining. We need to go back to the library."

"Sit," said Fran. "We're not going to the library."

"Would you like to talk about him?" asked Amelia.

High up in the rhododendrons, the rain began to patter on the thick foliage. A few drops trickled through. Victoria moved closer to the edge of the glade, where there was more shelter and she'd be closer to Amelia.

"He was Professor Breznikowski's son," said Fran.

"I had no idea."

"Lee was eight years old at the time. The professor was going to marry me and we were going to move to West Virginia with Lee to start a new life, but you—"

"Fran, I had nothing to do with—"

"—you and others like you at school—"

"None of us students knew you and the professor . . . Well, nobody knew anything until after you switched your major to math."

"*I* didn't switch. The dean forced me."

"Whatever," said Amelia.

Victoria's leg muscles began to cramp.

"What about your man?" Amelia asked. "Does he live on the Vineyard?"

"I told you, he's dead."

"I'm sorry. When did he die?" Amelia asked, so softly Victoria wasn't sure she heard.

"I killed him." Fran's voice was flat.

"*You* killed him? Your student . . ." Amelia's voice trailed off. "Not LeRoy Watts? You killed LeRoy?"

"He wouldn't listen to me. He denied knowing you."

"But LeRoy Watts didn't know me, Fran. I didn't know him, either. I never met him."

Victoria felt a sick lurch in her stomach. Casey ought to be here by now.

"He was LeRoy Breznikowski," said Fran. "Not Watts."

"The professor's son . . ."

"Yes. The professor's son. Lee changed his name to Watts when he changed his major to electrical engineering. He thought that was clever."

"I see."

"They wouldn't let his father marry me. Lee was going to marry me instead."

"But he was already married, with two children, Fran."

"He was going to leave that wife of his for me."

"He was ten or eleven years younger than you."

"Age doesn't matter."

"But . . ." said Amelia, "but . . . why kill him?"

"To keep you away from him."

"Me?" Amelia sounded astonished. "I didn't even know the man. And you killed him before I got here!"

"I've known all along who you were. Your daughter told the knitting group you'd be visiting."

"How did you kill him?"

"Victoria Trumbull figured it out. Your mother."

"You killed him with a knitting needle? He was a big, strong, athletic man. How could you take him by surprise like that?"

"When I went to talk to him, I hadn't intended to kill him. I tried to reason with him, to insist that he leave his wife, but he wouldn't listen. He pretended he didn't know what I was talking about when I mentioned your name. I had my knitting with me, of course. I pointed a needle at him for emphasis, simply trying to get his attention." Fran's voice had become shrill. "He laughed and I lost my temper. I aimed at his neck and lunged at him. . . ."

Victoria tensed.

"I could see his blood throbbing through his carotid artery. I focused on that artery, and he never saw it coming."

Victoria heard a sudden rustle of clothing and she lurched into the glade, her cramped leg on fire, just as Fran shouted, "Like this!"

Victoria burst onto the scene, her lilac-wood stick held high in both gnarled hands.

Fran was lunging toward Amelia, a long steel knitting needle aimed at her neck.

Amelia was shrinking back on the bench, both hands held against her throat, staring in frozen horror at Fran.

Victoria uttered a horrendous, prolonged, primal shriek and slammed her stick down on Fran's hand with a hideous crack.

Fran screamed and dropped the needle. Amelia leaped up and twisted Fran's arm behind her back.

"Casey!" Victoria's voice was a mere whisper. "Casey!"

Running footsteps pounded on the deer path.

"Casey?" Victoria could only form the word. No sound came out.

"Victoria!" Casey arrived, out of breath, gun drawn.

Casey called Junior Norton on her cell phone. Then Elizabeth at the library. Elizabeth's car was parked in the library's parking area, where Amelia had left it. She retrieved her keys from under the seat and drove, somewhat too fast, to the arboretum, where she found her grandmother sitting placidly on a stone wall under the shelter of the arboretum's gift shop roof, her hands folded on top of the lilac-wood stick Elizabeth had made for her. Amelia hovered in the background like an unsure hummingbird.

Fran Bacon was gone. Junior Norton and Casey had driven her to the County of Dukes County jail, where they filled out reams of paperwork and left her.

"Mother," said Amelia later that evening when they had dropped into their respective seats in the parlor, "what can I say?"

Victoria, her throat raw from that shriek, whispered, "Mothers take care of their young."

Elizabeth carried drinks into the parlor. Victoria's and Amelia's were suspiciously pale, indicating a high percentage of rum to cranberry juice.

Elizabeth lit the fire and sat on the floor at Victoria's feet.

"What made you suspect Fran, Gram?"

"Can't talk," Victoria whispered.

"I think," said Amelia, "it was when I told your grandmother about Fran stalking Professor Breznikowski, right, Mother?"

"Erotomania," Victoria whispered.

"What?" said Elizabeth.

"You said 'erotomania'?" said Amelia.

Victoria nodded and took a large gulp of her drink.

Amelia said, "It's when an otherwise-normal, usually intelligent person becomes obsessed with someone, is convinced that person loves her, and believes people are standing in the way of that love match, right?"

Victoria nodded.

"She'll do anything to get the obstacles out of her way. It's often a woman. Most other stalkers are men."

"Why kill the guy she believes loves her?"

"She thought I was going to steal her man away from her." Amelia looked down into her drink. "She had to kill him to prevent that. I was the cause of LeRoy Watts's death."

Victoria shook her head vigorously. "Nonsense," she whispered.

"We were wondering where Fran was," said Elizabeth. "Casper and Jim had packed up the quilt and we'd called FedEx to pick it up. We chilled a bottle of champagne to celebrate and were waiting for Fran so we could pop the cork. That's when Casey called and told me to get to the arboretum right away."

It took time for Victoria's voice to return to normal. During that time, Amelia waited on her, and Victoria welcomed the attention. Amelia soaked a facecloth in witch hazel for her mother to hold against her throat. She brewed cups of herbal tea laced with honey, offered scoops of soothing coffee ice cream, raspberry Jell-O. Victoria spent most of her time, when she wasn't writing her column, in the garden, and Amelia worked with her, quietly weeding close to her mother.

Casey dropped by every day. On the third day, Victoria's voice returned to normal, her deep, strong ordinary voice. She was out in the garden, weeding the touch-me-not that now had small flower buds. Casey knelt down beside her to help.

"What about LeRoy Watts, or Breznikowski, or whoever he was, Victoria? There are a lot of loose ends."

"Be careful of the poison ivy," said Victoria, pointing her weeder at a healthy patch next to the touch-me-not. "Fran was afflicted with erotomania, a strange disorder that can affect otherwise healthy people who function normally, except for that one obsession. You can pile the weeds there." Victoria pointed. "I'll cart them to the compost heap later."

"Go on with what you were saying," said Casey.

"In the case of erotomania, the obsession is usually directed at a single love object. Stalking can go on for years, as it did in Fran's case, and can suddenly shift. Her love object was Professor Breznikowski, who was oblivious to his student's obsession. When the university intercepted Fran, her attention switched to the son they called Lee. In her fantasies, he was her son."

"But he was only eight at the time," said Casey. "And she was, what, nineteen or so?"

"A big age gap when one is eight and the other is nineteen, but the gap closes. LeRoy enrolled in Northeastern, knowing nothing about Fran's obsession with his father." Victoria held the handles of her kneeler and got to her feet. "I'm going to pull that poison ivy vine out before you tangle with it. You're getting awfully close."

"But . . ."

"I'm not particularly suscetible to poison ivy." Victoria tugged the shiny three-leafed vine out by its roots and dropped it onto the compost pile.

"But . . ." said Casey again.

"I'll rub some touch-me-not on my hands, just in case."

"Back to LeRoy Watts and Fran," said Casey.

"From what I can gather, LeRoy intended to major in math and took a couple of courses with Fran—Dr. Bacon. Fran apparently had lost track of the Bresnikowskis. She, of course, recognized the name, LeRoy Breznikowski, and immediately targeted him."

"Where did the Watts name come in?"

"That was partly in response to her unwanted attention. He switched his major to electrical engineering and changed his name. He thought Watts would be a easy name for customers to remember for his intended electrical career."

Amelia came out to the garden with a pitcher of lemonade and poured cups for her mother and Casey. She'd heard some of the conversation. "His widow spoke about the phone calls he'd been getting. Were those from Fran?"

"I assume so," said Victoria, sipping her lemonade.

"What puzzles me, Mother, is the fact that LeRoy Watts was also a stalker. According to everyone I've talked to, he was a pleasant, normal-seeming man."

"I'm not sure anyone fully understands the psychology of stalking. Was the fact that he himself had been stalked by his professor a factor? Who knows."

"He stalked with a video camera as well as with phone calls. Isn't that unusual?"

"It's not uncommon for a stalker to use more than one approach. Look at the paparazzi, who aren't even considered deviates. They go to any length to capture a celebrity on film. Digital, now, I suppose."

Amelia said, "As an object of a stalker, couldn't he see what he was doing to others?"

"An obsession can be blinding," said Victoria.

At the end of the week, Howland Atherton drove Amelia to the ferry. Victoria rode in the front seat. Howland carried Amelia's suitcase to the baggage cart, and Victoria and her daughter parted at the gangplank.

"You'll let me know if you need help of any kind, won't you?" said Victoria to her daughter.

"Darling, I will," said her daughter.